The Angel Dictionary

The Angel Dictionary

A NOVEL

Therese England

ARCHWAY
PUBLISHING

Archway Publishing books may be ordered through booksellers or by contacting:

Archway Publishing
1663 Liberty Drive
Bloomington, IN 47403
www.archwaypublishing.com
1 (888) 242-5904

Scripture quotations taken from the King James Version of the Bible.

ISBN: 978-1-4808-8256-0 (sc)
ISBN: 978-1-4808-8255-3 (hc)
ISBN: 978-1-4808-8257-7 (e)

Library of Congress Control Number: 2019915796

Print information available on the last page.

Archway Publishing rev. date: 10/18/2019

To my sister, Marianne,
Patrick Foy, and my daughter, Kyna.
Also posthumously dedicated to Geoff S. Liss.

PROLOGUE

I am Beauty, and I am not a lower case noun. I am a Capital Noun. I am power and strength. I sometimes control the lives of those who possess me, both men and women.

I make those who seek me out do "things" in my name, and not always for the betterment of the world. Lustful things. Financially suspicious things. Illegal things. Sacrilegious things. Desperate things. All for their own self-aggrandizement.

Selfish things.

I once twisted the life of a young woman in Chicago in 1991 who possessed an unnaturally large portion of me, one might say unfairly so. She had used me to get what she wanted and paid a price. She used me like a bucket of well water to drink from, but one can't keep constantly pulling on the rope to bring up the bucket. A drop here, a drop there, all spent to conquer, entice, plunder, and pander. Eventually, everything in me becomes dry, used up.

Nevertheless, I was her tool, her bucket. She took me for granted so often that she forgot that I can be possessed by other competitors in her world—young women who went on using me in the same way she did, even for the same conquest.

This is her story, but it is not a story of my unforgettable feminine self within her. It is how she came to squander and waste me. No, not lose me completely, but maybe she came to understand that I am not a siren singing on a rock, and there are certainly no guarantees of what you gain by me.

I am merely a trait, like red hair or blue eyes, that people will remark about. I am fleeting, but not in the way power and wealth can be, and I am *not* the most important thing in life. There are intangible nouns that matter more—love, intelligence, charity, and empathy.

This young woman discovered that. She had, you see, a helper who opened her eyes and showed her my nemesis—the world's ugliest form— evil, and how she could deflect it. Because when I go, I go slowly, often painfully.

What follows is the tale of how she intrinsically maneuvered me, counting far too deeply on what I could achieve.

CHAPTER 1

October 20, 1991

If he could just slide off the hospital gurney, maybe he could get out. Sam Streitnum, forty-two, was unmarried, shiftless, and jobless. And if you were to ask anybody, he might be considered a "scumbag." He hated hospitals, especially their medicinal smells. More important, he couldn't risk staying here for any prolonged length of time.

It was a mistake to drive here. Maybe I'm not that bad, he thought. He stretched to push aside the white sheet to look in either direction for an escape.

Jesus, too many people. Blood oozed from him, dripping into obsidian pools on the floor. *Shit! Don't care how bad I'm hurt. Can't be here. Cops will investigate.* His mind raced ahead of any reasonable thoughts he had about his leaking legs. But as he squirmed, the pain reintroduced itself, and he flopped heedlessly back to a reclining position like some land-locked dying fish.

Then the ER doc bustled in, all business. Boredom and fatigue left his face as he stared questioningly at Sam's limbs. "How'd he get these, uh, lacerations? They look like whip marks, only worse," he asked the nurse behind him, not considering that Sam might have been able to answer him.

"Don't know. He wouldn't say when he came in," she replied, staring at the doctor wide-eyed.

"Doc, when can I get out?" Sam asked.

"You just got here," the doctor answered as he examined the landscape of Sam's legs, his gloved fingers nudging the four deep, horizontal slashes on both limbs. The bone-deep wounds had scalpel-sharp edges and were bleeding heavily now.

Two other nurses came from behind the white privacy sheets. *Christ, a quorum!* Sam thought. One of the nurses began to remove his flannel shirt, where he had stashed the drugs and dough in his upper pocket. "Leave it. I'm cold," he snarled.

"How did you get these?" The doc had moved toward Sam's head, at the same time muttering to the adjacent nurse for three milligrams of Dilaudid for pain.

"Some goddamned creature did it! Wasn't a dog. And no, I'm not drunk. I-I couldn't see very well. The thing was black and huge! All of a sudden, these thread things appeared, and they splayed out. I was hit and barely made it to the car. Like it was going to kill me! The thing was …"

Sam stopped when he saw that the doc looked pained by the story. Sam knew he was thinking there were hallucinogens inside him, but damn, he was clean.

The nurse again tried to remove his shirt, but Sam slapped her arm away.

"It also looks like there's a knife or even a bullet graze on your arm," the doctor remarked after seeing Sam's upper bicep.

"Naw, that's just from my … er … friend," Sam lied. "Just clean me up, and I'll be on my way. Ohhh, Jesus! Son of a bitch, it hurts."

"I'm afraid you can't leave with these serious wounds. They require care. If there has been a confrontation with firearms, we have to report it to the police—"

"No! No cops!" Sam interrupted. He sat up suddenly, eyes wide with fear. "Really, I just need some bandages and something for the pain, and I'll be good to go. Ugh, owww!"

"Surgery," the doctor said. "He needs stitches. He's lost too much blood."

Sam's head banged back on the gurney. It felt like a block of ice. His mind went over the last hour. That dark alley he shouldn't have visited. In Maywood, not his regular scene. What had he been thinking? He only needed a little more juice and crack, just enough to service the high school kids tonight. Hell, maybe he could've even gotten lucky with one of those girls from Niles High School.

As Sam closed his eyes and fainted and the clank of wheels beneath him pushed him into surgery, he didn't know that he was already dying. No more hospital smells now. But he could still smell the rankness of that creature.

CHAPTER 2

Chicago Loop, April 1991

It was a day so warm for April that Dina Kinnit, twenty-nine years old this August, longed to stuff it into her lunchbox and take it home, perhaps take it out on some gloomy winter day, a day indigenous to Chicago and whose mid-November arrival was as habitual as the mailman's. Then she could admire it later, like some brightly lit terrarium with its loamy smell that would sweep her back to this park bench where she now sat, and all the feelings of blueness would be drowned from sight.

She could feel the warm air on her skin, the unnatural heat traveling around her. The sun shone prism-like on the water bottle she held in her hand, turning it to a glassy crystalline shrine. *A shrine to what?* she wondered. Her perseverance to staying unattached, locking out romance for one reason or another.

She came from the Chicago suburbs in the '70s, succumbing in her twenties to the siren call of the big city, and that siren was Sandoval, Inc. Her father had died from an illness when she was a child. She didn't remember him much, yet in ways she couldn't account for, she did. Perhaps he was a black smudge in the corner of her eye. Perhaps it was a stranger walking on the street, who vanished when she turned to look. Dina knew she had been given a small quantity of foresight, so when the men she attracted scoffed at that, she buried this revelation, not relaying any further information. Didn't everyone know just when the phone would ring or that a specific letter would appear just that day? So every time she tested the waters by revealing her oddity to the many men infatuated with her, if they appeared skeptical, they were shown the exit ramp from her heart. With a smile and a shake of the head of that long, blonde-streaked, chestnut hair—which so many suitors had driven their hands into—they were summarily cast out, leaving forever the full lips and cat-shaped green eyes, features that would haunt their dreams for a long time. This ostracizing may have even brought a few converts to the religion of clairvoyance.

But some young men would grow savvy, possibly knowing the history of their kinsmen, but the lines to admire her continued to form—football players, basketball players, nerds, bad boys, ne'er-do-wells. "A line likened," Karen Eiderman, her best friend and coworker used to say, "to the exit at the end of the world."

For a while now, Dina decided she would no longer date within company walls. If a man approached her within the confines of work, he was turned away.

Karen used to ponder why her friend shied away from commitment. Dina had jaw-dropping good looks and a body and smile like a streetlamp lit on a snowy December evening. Even Dina's mother couldn't keep track of who she had left or kept at any moment. And when Dina visited home, Mrs. Kinnit, who was usually exasperated, almost always started the conversation with "Well, who is it now?"

Dina sighed and put the bottle on the bench beside her. Did the secret to her apathy really lie in longing to preserve a forced romantic mystery about herself and not relinquish it to just anybody so that, in the end, she would be stuck, regrettably, with some man whose personal light chased hers away? And his new shininess? Would it be worn so thin to her that, with everything put together, the special qualities that originally enticed her wouldn't last?

She'd taken a cab to Lincoln Park to bask like a sunbather and eat her lunch in a quiet spot. She studied the massive building a few blocks to the south that had housed her office for the last five years—Sandoval, truly a firm on the fast track to becoming one of the city's software giants. Dina had a confident nature. Business had never overtaken her so much that she clung to reputation and dollars, rolling them around in her life like the street people she occasionally saw who rolled away their lives in shopping carts.

Work sometimes seemed to be a place where her coworkers, like wasps working on a paper nest, scurried between cubicles with the latest gossip about the untouchable queen. Her. And because she was extremely good looking, she got the brunt of their inquisitions and overheard stupefying chastisements not worthy of her attention.

"Why is she not engaged by now?"

"I heard she took up with Andy. You hear that?"

"Who'd she dump last week?"

When Dina was home from senior year at college, Mrs. Kinnit put forth a question. They were in the kitchen, Dina sipping a soda, standing near the window and looking out at the new snow. "So, why isn't anyone good enough? Sometimes you give up on them in a spate of two weeks." Mrs. Kinnit loved saying "spate" of this, "spate" of that. She inherited an anachronistic penchant for older terms from her Irish mother, including, "prit near" instead of "pretty near."

Dina smiled. Still gazing at the snow, she replied, "Mom, I'll find the right one. Maybe I'll even use Grandma Roberta's gift and channel her psychic ability." She giggled, but Mrs. Kinnit misunderstood the laugh.

"Pshaw! I never got any such ability. And trying out men like flavors of ice cream—"

Dina interrupted, "No, no, Mom. It's not my fault that they fall for a pretty face. I enjoy guys while I'm with them, but they're all just temporary, stepping stones to the *right* one. Besides, too many judge me, doubt my ability." She straightened her shoulders, feigning affront.

"God help you when you really fall, Dina. You do take after your grandmother in looks and determination. My mother, I am told, had prit near the whole male population of the town after her. She lived downstate, you remember. Only moved up here after my dad got a better job. But before Grandpa, she went through men like a combine through corn."Dina laughed at the comparison to her grandmother and reached over and patted her mother's back. "Yeah, well what's wrong with waiting? Maybe *I* want to be the inspector in the meat market."

Her daughter looked defiant, but the older woman only smiled. "So, with your history and your grandmother's so-called gift, you should be able to see him pretty damn soon."

Dina sat down at the table and cast a serious look toward the window, ignoring her mother's jab at her clairvoyance. "It *is* enigmatic," she began, choosing her words carefully. "One, almost all women depend on their looks sometimes, as I guess I have. We count on the fact that our looks will always be there and ugliness will remain far away."

"Life's more than beauty and keeping up one's appearances," Mrs. Kinnit interrupted, turning from the counter.

"I know. It sounds self-centered when I say it. It's a flimsy excuse at best. But I can't help my looks. And I'd never admit this to anyone but you, Mom. Honestly, I *do* put a lot of weight in my ability to attract, and as strange as it may sound, it is attractiveness that keeps me going. It's nice to wake up to see my face in the mirror and count on what it will attain for me that day. The favors. The stares. The perks."

"I think you rate it *too* highly." Her mother was angry. "And *some* things not highly enough."

Her mother didn't understand. "*You* were very pretty yourself in your twenties," Dina groveled. "It's just that women, beautiful women, don't want to talk about this … *invisible power*. Those who really look inside a person will be too smart to walk away. They'll recognize my depth and my gift. Anyway, looks have been a barrier too! People are quick to label and judge and … and …"

She didn't know how to finish her argument.

Her mother sighed. "The world is wide. Just be careful. Remember how the mighty have fallen. You could too."

"There you go with those aphorisms, Mom." Dina laughed, breaking the sober tone the conversation had taken.

"It's just a hunch, or maybe I have got the gift. "Mrs. Kinnit smirked, looked down at the kitchen floor. "So just stop and think, when you are finally ready to plunge full tilt into a romance you suddenly find you cannot live without, make sure you're not standing on a cliff. Money goes. Looks go. Sadly, even love goes. Sometimes, I wish I had seen you hurt more—God forgive me for saying it about my own child—if only for the empathy, the character it would have built in you. Seen far too many hearts that you broke."

Dina smiled a look far too careworn for her age and kissed her mother. "I promise to remember your advice."

Another breeze, more aggressive this time, blew across Dina's face up from Lake Michigan, going westward, way beyond Rush Street. Its coldness seemed to be a wake-up call. Should she really be doing less serial dating? Karen seemed to think so, but then, Karen was bombastic, larger than life, and a born rule-breaker.

Dina continued to scold herself inwardly. No more sparkling for a time, accepting gifts, compliments, and proposals from men as she had throughout her twenties, only to have these heartfelt scenarios and the feelings entangled with them blow away.

Suddenly there was that small voice of warning.

It's what anyone fears! I reject so I don't get rejected first!

The awful truth hit her forcefully, and she breathed heavily. *Okay,* she calmed herself, *that isn't it.* Most men couldn't figure out that returning affection bespoke the need for them to encompass *all* parts of a woman. *Even those who were witness to my clairvoyant side.*

Dina's long hair rippled in the wind, and she smoothed it down care-fully as if it were fragile. While others looked for their internal sustenance in good health, fortune, family, and cleverness in opportunity, she had gazed into the deep pool of her mirror and carried on. She did not con-sider herself conceited, and she would have none of people like that. Her loveliness existed both inward and outward, a Prozac in a scary world where the media made it easy to unabashedly raze one's visage to the foun-dation and rebuild it anew with drugs, concoctions, and plastic surgery. Nonetheless, she was not naïve to the power her particular allure held.

For today, at least, Dina had convinced herself to give romance, maybe, another chance? Then, why did this personal jargon feel not only redundant but foreboding?

CHAPTER 3

Clarence Trenter (a.k.a., Big Sandy) staked out Sandoval's corridor, where a wiry little man tugged on the grey aluminum mail cart as if it were a mule train. He smiled ruefully and ducked back to hide in the short hall that led to the bathrooms. Randy Clentow held the mail cart steady as he now turned left into an alcove, tossing each individual's mail on their desk with a "thunk," the gesture afterward followed (sometimes) by a listless "thanks."

Randy was scrawny and bereft of any trace of handsomeness, a sexless nerd who was often joked about, luckily not to his face. He seemed to have perpetual stubble and spoke listlessly, in a nasally monotone.

Every so often, he poked his crazy, curly head toward the various letters, lingering, inspecting, and finally grasping hold of one, checking once again to see if the name was correct.

"Randy, haven't you figured out who's who and in what order by now?"

Andy, an employee in software development, smirked and punched Wyatt, the coworker to this right.

"Just getting it straight," he drawled, his bent stoop resembling an elderly man who might drool at any moment. Dina's office was next, but the door was closed so he slid her mail underneath. Next, he was out again in the long corridor, lethargically dragging the clattering aluminum rectangle. The hall was particularly long, and Randy took his time marching onward, soldier-like, his ribs seemingly sucked out to his flannel shirt. He resembled his own mailroom, disheveled, seedy, and vacant.

The next stop was Big Sandy's office, but he had awhile to go, fifteen yards or so, never seeing Big Sandy huddled in the corner watching. Randy trudged on with the swaying cart, wheels a bit unbalanced, until he arrived at Sandy's door, where he punched the mail under the closed door and swerved the cart back in the opposite direction to start back down the hall. He wasn't paying attention to his footing as he leaned backward, one hand now fidgeting with the letters as though he might have missed someone.

Suddenly a foot came out, kicking his knee, and Randy tumbled backward, hitting both his temple and arm on the sharp corner, causing the cart to upend in a heap of envelopes polka-dotting the carpet. He rubbed his throbbing head, scrutinizing the avalanche of letters, and looked up questionably. Big Sandy moved into view now, ignoring that Randy's bleeding temple.

"What d'ya do that for?" Randy whined while rising up on his knees, throwing the big man a deadly look as he helplessly tried to re-sort the mail.

Big Sandy straightened up, his lip curled with an attitude of both superciliousness and belligerence. "Because you forgot to *knock* on my door when you had something to give me, you little scab."

He gave Randy a swift, light kick to the shoulder, sending him sprawling again, then sauntered away from the mess. Farther down the hall, not even one employee's head was raised at the sudden noise, as they had all chalked it up to Randy's usual buffoonery.

To Clarence Trenter, a six-year employee at Sandoval, the memory of his former years was well beyond overbearing. Evil had made a home in his personality, decency only a word to him. He could not kill what ate him alive, so he simply absorbed it.

Cruelly he went about his mischief at Sandoval, didactically announcing his uncensored opinion of all his coworkers and their love affairs, intentionally flirting with and once actually stealing another guy's girl, although the equation was never solved as to how a man as vile as Sandy could've gotten any date at all.

Since college, the Texan who hailed from the city he was nicknamed after had never really rested well. Plotting and calculating were extracurricular activities for him. At college, his fellow dorm mates would find him awake, scribbling and writing at 4:30 a.m. or even fussing around his room, his hulking frame dominating the small living space. By his sophomore year, his reputation had been sealed. No one elected to bunk with the quirky monster, his freshman roommate deserting him by October first.

It wasn't Sandy's size; a smaller man could've easily put him in his place for all of Sandy's lack of muscle tone and fighting skill. He skewered victims in their weakest links. Perhaps a broken heart, an absentee father, a zinging of otherwise healthy confidences that were thrown into a withered pile.

And indifference couldn't work against Sandy. Finding and recognizing dirt, he blew apart egos with hurtful, telling words, even while attempts were made to brush aside his taunts like pestiferous gnats. Sandy could crawl into peaceful daydreams bearing both guilt and shame.

Yet he remained at Sandoval because he was good at his job. Too good. He was fat, and he knew his face was unattractive, his clothes out of date and often sloppy. If employees teased him about his weight—well, no one did after one try.

There was a time once where the opposition thought they had him: his exuberant attraction to Dina. She, of course, would reject and repeatedly refuse him, even though it was more in a spirit of pity than revulsion. Now the staff could chide him with this tidbit. *Now* he had to fall like a big tree! Employees waited, plying him with a not-so-subtle dig: How was your date with her? Like hounds circling a fox, they were still unable to catch him. Sandy's emotional radar registered barely a blip, and he sat at his computer day after day sporting a knowing grimace and the equanimity of a monk.

At length, hecklers gave up remaining discouraged; they could not unearth the detritus of his past, which could have been leveled as possible retribution for his nastiness. It was rumored that Sandy had ostensibly broken off with his relatives long ago, and since he held these mysterious clues tucked tightly away, they had nothing with which to goad him. It was very bad to bruise Big Sandy. They knew he could and would wait.

Away from the office, Sandy brooded in the confines of his apartment. No girl anywhere ever captured his enthusiasm like Dina had. Conversely, he would pep-talk himself over and over that he was not smitten. The downplay of feeling suddenly made everyone at the office notice; his nonchalance, however, didn't make them believe that this conclusion of affection would ever lead to any kind of revenge for the lady. He seemed to quietly give up on Dina. She was nothing but a toy he had once wanted, and Sandy had no use for toys or competitive games. That is, until Frank appeared.

CHAPTER 4

"Franco ... er ... Frank Ciarelli comes to us from Rimstead International, and we are lucky to have him."

Bradley Hendricks, one of the main company heads and Dina's boss, was always poor at introductions. The gentleman beside him blinked at the weak greeting. He smiled and nodded almost sympathetically. Both men had entered Dina's office without knocking, interrupting her work. Hendricks moved toward Dina, bumping her hip without apologizing. He was grinning broadly as if *he* were the one demanding the congratulations.

The soft-spoken brown-eyed man extended his hand. His eyes pulled Dina's gaze from her work. Disturbed in more ways than she had felt in a long time, she rattled the papers before her, dropping one under the desk in confusion. She had pulled down her reading glasses, expecting to be met with some aloof fifty-ish man with graying hair. Instead, she saw the twinkling somehow deceptive quality of Frank's eyes more clearly now, which spoke of sexual damage, despite his immaculate designer apparel. His look into her eyes smarted, as if the sun were throwing off a glare, and she felt herself pulled into its vacuum. Frank coughed quickly then to break the heat of their gazes.

"I'm Dina Kinnit," she said in a small, wobbly voice.

"She ... er ... Dina will be working on the Boyko account, which you will supervise ... er coordinate," Hendricks said.

Supervise? Dina heard this despite the fluttery glow in her stomach after meeting Frank. She took this word in and saw warning crossbones flagging her ability. Why a newcomer?

As if he heard her thoughts, Frank downplayed the exaggeration. "I will enjoy working beside … I mean with you."

He smiled again, his voice almost holding the lilt of a lovemaking murmur, for Dina's beauty had not escaped him. Frank almost seemed to be cross-referencing it in his mind. His last little wave to her as he was turning to go seemed a connection of a wholly different sort, which only they two could decipher.

"Well, we better get going; we've got a few more intros today for the new hire before lunchbreak." Hendricks was foolishly rubbing his hands together, a petty, stupid gesture, Dina thought. She wished he would go away on his own so she and Frank could talk. Hendricks lumbered out, and Frank followed, striding like a Lipizzaner stallion.

Dina watched them go, hearing Hendricks' voice booming again, then trailing off, oblivious to the quiet work around him, as if he were a circus ringleader instead of one of the top men of a multimillion-dollar software company. How could such a man get by this far in the corporate world, let alone be part owner of this company? Dina shook her head, amazed as always at Hendrick's buffoonish behavior.

And Frank? A Boyko supervisor? Her thoughts jolted back. And his eyes? She pondered a little on the announcement, but she was so caught up in Frank's attractiveness that the title did not bother her for long. Frank stood over six feet tall, with brown eyes and brownish-black hair, with a face chiseled for movie stardom. His kind of looks did not merely gambol out in front of a female audience; they strutted out like some cut, high-paid supermodel. Where did they get him? Did he have experience? He looked as if he had turned the corner into the wrong office; this wasn't the Calvin Klein office for male models!

Surely his looks helped him land this job; she knew he would be well paid. Hendricks wasn't that stupid. Would Frank be like some beguiling and beautiful movie one would enjoy watching, feeling a part in yet expect something from? But Dina was already being swept away by the seductive and dangerous pull of his magnetism. She smiled inwardly, but her hands knotted nervously, and she grasped them protectively around her knees as if to ward off a real or imagined sexual advance. She slumped forward now, still hearing Hendricks' loud patter: "Did I mention our state-of-the-art lunchroom? This way, Frank."

Dina squeezed her eyes shut. Never had she met such a man. She felt exhilarated but at the same time like a cheap lush in a well-worn '50s novel. His eyes! Eyes of bedrooms, not of boardrooms. A shudder raked her. What was she doing? How could she work with … *him?*

She didn't know how long she remained gazing in thought, eyes riveted to the wall. A noise startled her, and Karen moved into her office.

"So, I see you are as smitten as half the office—the female half, that is."

Her voice was strident; the redhead twirled a button on her blazer, then rested a finger on it, squeezing it contemplatively as she studied her friend.

"W-What?" Dina swiveled her chair around to face Karen, her face ashen.

"Whoa! The bee bit you, I see. That look on your face could short your computer. 'Course, we all know he'll want *you* first. Miss Good-Looking. Better looking than anyone I know. Just be sure you play fair and share. And remember your ol' friend Karen when he becomes your leftovers. Hey! I know that look of yours. Don't try to cover it up. Like a damned forest ranger spotting a forest fire. You're holding the match, Smokey Bear. Guilty! It's something like that, right? And what happened to your old promise of not dating within Sandoval?"

"Okay, Karen, stop."

Dina hated when her friend referred to her as if she were some cartoon-like figure. Karen's manner was funny and welcome, but today it was just too suggestive and abusive. Dina wanted just her to leave. Like a

smitten high school girl, she wanted simply to daydream about the vision
that had just swept into her office minutes earlier.

"I'm not interested in Frank. So my promise stands," she lied.

"No?" the arch smile, Karen's best tool, came out. "Well, pretty soon,
if not, let's say … by four o'clock today? Hey, honey, don't trust a man who
can give Brad Pitt a run for his money. Did you see him in the *Thelma &
Louise* movie? Frank has that same Mt. Rushmore jawline? Of course you
did. And the enveloping brown eyes? No question! Wake up and smell
the smoking gun, Dina."

"Yeah, and what have you been smoking today?" Dina snickered back.
Frank hadn't spoken even twenty words to her, but the electricity across
the room for those few seconds had short-wired her. She just wanted to
be ravished by him, the sooner the better.

Karen prattled on, but Dina was beyond listening, her mind imagining the special days, and especially nights, that Frank might invent for
her. A calendar's worth of witticisms would be plied on him, making him
laugh. Then she would strike and make him totally hers. It was her well-
honed, dangerous plan. She was adept, she knew, not once imagining any
slight rejection.

Dina stood up now, almost dizzy with thought, but Karen never
stopped chattering.

"I want to get some water. Is it lunchtime yet?" Her abrupt sidelong
glance finally silenced her friend as she brushed past Karen, weary of the
scolding. Karen couldn't resist the last jab. "Well, I see he's got that effect
on you already!"

At the water cooler, Dina felt calmer, gripping the Styrofoam cup,
flexing and un-flexing her fingers against its surface. She felt hot, as if
she couldn't quench her thirst fast enough. Did Frank remind her of
someone? An old boyfriend? She questioned her histories, the ashes of
old flames in a sooty pile that she no longer cared to rekindle or remember, but there seemed to be no one like Frank. She hesitated several more
minutes just to be sure Karen would tire of waiting for her and leave her

office. Hendricks and Frank were probably well down the hall by now, headed in the direction of the tacky lime-colored lunchroom. Leave it to Hendricks to be proud of that! State-of-the-art? More like state of mental chaos to even think of hunger in that sulfur-colored room!

Dina sighed and looked up at the wintry sky out an adjacent window. It had already started to snow, even though it was mid-April. Chicago waited for spring for so long, it seemed!

Two giggly women now approached the cooler. They were extremely young, carrying folders and wearing almost identical navy blue suits. Interns from college. Dina sniffed disdainfully to herself as she overheard their conversation.

"Seth says we'll go to Christie's on Saturday night. Won't that be exquisite?"

"Great! You'll love it. Hey, Did Hendricks bring that new hunk by your workstation yet?"

Dina somehow could not bear overhearing other women gossip about Frank, especially juveniles with enough sexuality mapped into their DNA to blow open the lockers of a hundred college football hunks. She darted quickly away, full of muffled fury, taking the long way to her office to stall in case Karen was still there.

While other women thought of men and wondered, perhaps, what their children might look like, Dina felt herself measuring all of Frank's characteristics and physical assets against her own. Because even if she got him—well, how could that not be?—what about her original promise to herself? About dating within the company? History. But careful. Confidence! If some other woman were to intervene …

Dina volleyed the caution back and forth. That's how it would be—it *had* to be! *I can't be hurt, can I? I'm committed to … yet I do feel something more for him, in my heart and bones.* And what if he didn't?

Deep down, the fire of her foresight, the telling gift that warned her of possible tragedy, was ignored.

CHAPTER 5

An assembly of men in white shirts, like a staggered picket fence, grouped around a table to the far left of the lunchroom. As they finished their meal, babbling loudly and gruffly, one clear voice ascended the herd. Its owner now stood at the head of the table, like a preacher at his pulpit. Adroitly, the voice sledge-hammered down, cracking through their conversations, which centered mostly on sports. Officious and brash, its timbre maneuvered the talk away from the recent Cubs game and onto the female track.

"So, you think you found an inroad by now where you can make a dent in the company of Dina? Yeah, that Dina, she's all male-friendly." Big Sandy's eyes rolled in exaggeration, grinning as he sought out takers to his sermon, primarily honing in on Frank. "Oh yeah, she's all lip and no tongue, if ya know what I mean."

The speaker ended his remark with an ugly sneer, the kind of look that, when combined with words, immediately made Frank wary. He had met Big Sandy earlier, at the big man's office, and he had been polite and businesslike, smiling at Hendricks and shaking hands. But now he was away from the work environment with a testosterone-infused audience who he could whip to attention.

A few men in the group laughed appreciatively and knowingly, embarrassed as they noted there were still two elderly women left in the lunchroom who had heard the lewd comments. Sandy, however, knew these two women, and their observations didn't matter. They would never be talking to or meeting with Dina. Their departments were too far away. He knew everything about everybody.

He had been five years at Sandoval and an occasional dabbler in the "sexual petty cash reserve," as the men put it. Blond, statuesque, and born into money (and posturing about it), he swaggered and bragged his way through the workday, stretching his bravado from the water cooler to the boardroom, mostly making adjacent and unwitting eavesdroppers miserable. Hendricks loved him, although he was a modern-day Eddie Haskell.

Frank decided that this was a man not worth knowing. He had no need for sexual advice from such a smarmy, two-faced source. Almost every man on his floor had had a run-in with Sandy, he'd heard. Frank had sized him up quickly and decided not to remain in Sandy's crosshairs.

"Well, I just got here, man." Frank shoved his coffee cup down and looked Sandy coolly in the eye. "I met Dina. She seems okay."

"Yeeeah."

Big Sandy drew the word out. If any word could sound lascivious, he could make it so.

Frank changed the subject. "I will say, I hope the lunchroom cafeteria food improves." He launched his tray across the table, the food half-eaten. The men laughed again, a polite audience trying to be chivalrous in their approval of Frank's comeback.

Sandy cut off their laughter, unwilling to back down. "Hey, you've been here almost a week. That's enough, right, man?" He was surrounded by bored coughs and uncomfortable looks. "Shall we bet?"

"No!" Frank's intense liquid brown eyes sought to drown out Sandy's buffoonery. The men's interest perked up.

"No? To me, Big Sandy?" he said, puffing out his chest.

"*Yes*, no!"

"C'mon, man." Sandy leaned toward Frank, cajoling like an obsequious panhandler, "Just wanted to make things interesting, you being new and all."

"Don't you think we ought to be focusing on work?" Frank offered, but he sounded like a Boy Scout at a Hell's Angels rally.

"Shit, no! Not at lunch!" Sandy laughed at him, a familiar boom going off like a musket, such a broad band of sound that it made the elderly women turn in their chairs and look across the room at him. "Why, not even *at* work do we focus on work! What do you think this is? High school? Man, you are green!"

"Thanks, man. I'll pick my own companions."

Frank, annoyed, shifted his weight and stood up. Wyatt Little, an African American man, who worked near Frank, whispered, but not entirely out of Sandy's hearing, "He does this with every new guy. Man, he's swum in about all the waters of the veritable computer pool, so to speak, but he's never had nor ever will have a chance with *that* lady! He's jealous Dina noticed you."

Frank smiled knowingly. So that was it.

"Wise up, Wyatt. When's the last time you scored?" Sandy snarled softly, animosity curling around his jawline.

"I've got a girlfriend *outside* the company, thank you very much. Get a life, loser. This isn't the fifties anymore!" Wyatt complacently scratched his new flat cropped "Arsenio" hairdo until hostility pulled him to face down Sandy's rebuke. Both men stood now, Wyatt clenching his fists and Big Sandy leaning forward. They looked like a toy poodle and a pit bull blocking each other's way. "Women aren't conquests!" Wyatt shot back.

"Knock it off, you guys! What d'ya gonna do? Start a goddamn fist fight in the lunchroom?" Andy Meltor, a computer programmer and another of Frank's office friends who also worked on Boyko, stood near Wyatt and touched the black man's arm. Meltor laughed—comic relief in the wash of testosterone.

There were nods all around in agreement. Sandy looked furtively from side to side, slightly nervous about severing his splendid reputation with the bosses over this belligerent quarrel, although he had wanted to take down Wyatt for a long time. Even against this slight humiliation, he silently catalogued his revenge against Frank. He eyed his competition warningly as he collected his lunch tray. Frank did not glance back at Sandy or see the foreboding look of the giant man, but his heart sank. Christ! There's one in every company! And on the same floor!

"Oh well, *whatever*, as they say," Sandy said cockily. He had been in bad scrambles before, and he didn't need this aggravation. Better to plan it out clandestinely. "Good luck, bro! May the best man win the skirt in the end."

A small voice, Andy's, muttered, "Yeah, not in your lifetime, for all your clout and money."

Seething inside but untouched by any facial clues, Sandy departed, categorizing his shenanigans. Perhaps an email gone awry or a missing sales report—or worse. He didn't like being second; he was raised to be first. It was rumored about him that he was behind a plot two years ago to set up a lady's attention for money. He had paid a female coworker to perform for a certain man, Sam Gingerman, who worked in accounting. The plot had gone well, and it held Sandy's amusement for a few weeks until Sam fell in love with "Sandy's whore," as the office called her. The plot thickened into scandal, gossip, and heartache, ruining Sam. He fled from Sandoval to escape, no longer able to tincture the gaping backstab wound that Sandy had inflicted. Smitten and humiliated, he even left the state as well, and he was now rumored to be married but unhappy. Stepping on Sandy was like stepping on a Gila monster.

Sandy took pride that he remained unscathed during the fiasco. He lapped up his juicy scenarios as he had others. How did he do it? Life's little decencies had never fixed right in Sandy's head, as his relatives used to say. His tactics had ostensibly left the mischievous "hijinks" category and seemed to nestle in an uglier realm. Somehow, the heartless blowhard managed to dodge sexual harassment and Cupid's arrow. Except for Dina.

So a tense thread between the office and Big Sandy was growing thinner. Frank couldn't possibly know that he was standing—rather, working—in muckraker territory without boots.

As the men moved en masse to deposit lunch trays, Sandy was far ahead now, but his voice could still be heard rambling on to some poor sap about "that vixen, Sarah, who just started in human resources, and Glenda was her trainer. And those two-total opposites in personality! Can ya believe it!"

Andy and Wyatt flanked Frank as they moved to drop their trays on the moving belt. Wyatt nudged Frank with his tray. "We're glad to have you aboard." He nodded at the retreating Sandy. "Think of that blow-ass there as, well, you know, something like an uncorked volcano that spews lava which passes as vocabulary and personality. Tolerate it and try and stay clear. For myself, I guess I stupidly made an exception today. At least he doesn't work in our corridor, even though he's still on the sixth floor with us and continues to kiss his way upwards. Maybe he won't be on our floor long. We can always hope. Anyway, if there's anything else I can help with, it's Wyatt Little, extension 2340. We met the other day, but I just wanted to remind you I'm only two cubicles over."

"Thanks, I'll remember that," he said gratefully. Wyatt hurried away, leaving Frank with Andy, who now pushed an arm around Frank's shoulders and spoke conspiratorially.

"And if you *do* end up dating her, you're one lucky bastard. She's genuinely as kind as she is beautiful. And keep that fact to yourself, you know. As much as I'd like to know the details, as any single guy around here who would kill to date her, it's an office of *ears* around here. That's just what that schmuck is banking on." Andy winked and moved away. "I'd say 'see ya' but, you know, I'm on another floor—but I hear I might be working with you soon. He paused and then added, "Beware Sandy's reputation. It's company wide."

"I'll remember."

Frank pondered it all silently during the long walk back to his desk. He hadn't really given Dina much thought, but who was he kidding? Of course, she was gorgeous and desirable. Perhaps he more interested in the mystery than in anything else. He was way beyond intrigues.

CHAPTER 6

Karen strode into Dina's office Wednesday morning, owning the world. She flung her body against the wall, a tall statue but for a voice that was heard several cubicles away. Her eyes took in the bric-a-brac on Dina's desk as she moved forward and pointed at a photo "Who's this? I don't remember you having this before."

"That's the problem," Dina remarked sarcastically. She was tired, and it was too early for Karen's sarcasm. "You never remember anything— even the stuff on your own desk!" Her hand supported her chin, her face changing to a slow impish grin, her expression turning dreamy and lazy, not ready for work. She pulled the photo lovingly toward her, stroking the frame. "It's my grandmother Roberta, and this time you are right. It wasn't here before. My mom just gave it to me. Word was, Grandma was psychically gifted."

"Oh, one of those terrible Irish relics!"

"No, not necessarily. Mom said she had a sad life as a child. And, yes, of course, she was born in Ireland. Emigrated here with my grandfather. Do I look like her?"

"It is hard to see. The photo is a little gritty, but maybe." Karen took the photo and squinted at it. "She's not living?"

"No."

"And your grandfather?"

"No. Deserted her when Mom was very young. Mom does not re-member him. As I said, she had a very hard life. Grandma, Mom told me recently, 'saw' things ahead of time, if you know what I mean."

"Wow … geesh! I don't want to know how, but you're not thinking of all that today, are you, sweetie?" Karen put the photo back and folded her arms. Karen scooted a nearby chair under her and unleashed a banter of her all-to-familiar advice. "What are you going to do with the office newbie? Those looks, too unbelievable to leave alone. I'd kill my sister for him, if I had one. Besides, if you don't accept his first date, I will!"

Dina half-smiled, picturing Frank, virile and so masculine, with the ribald and quasi-suspicious Karen, who was a loyal friend and a good worker but whose ability to drive men out the door of her life was un-rivaled. This flaw, coupled with her usual routine of "I'm not serious. Were you?" She was a joke cracker, who was inclined to put herself in a storm of self-deprecation, usually losing some poor bastard because he didn't understand this kind of personality. And it wasn't her looks, really—although she didn't manage that chimney stack of red hair very well. It didn't seem suited to her tall, spindly frame; her hair was too lush and come-hither for a body lacking the necessary feminine curves to complement it.

Time and time again, Dina watched as Karen headed some sorry boyfriend down a path that ended in a fork in the road with a sign that proclaimed: "One way. *My* way."

And so it went. Some misguided quirk in Karen's personality seemed to run out of options, as if to lay claim to all bad habits concerning men. Dina would never know. She could only guess. When she attended occasional suppers at Karen's place, they were often attended by some woebegone man Karen had taken a liking to but who was somehow gone without a trace by the next week.

Karen's last, husband number two, was left like her first hapless hus-band, simply because Karen could not fix the erratic and self-absorbed path of self-affliction or stop the rote behavior that came with it, which included the vices of overeating, drinking, and possibly purging. At no closer to true love when Dina met her, her bad-choice lifestyle was a dichotomy to her loyal, unswerving sweetness. It was Dina who believed Karen would rather see her friend's success than her own. At forty-two, she was thirteen years older than Dina, qualifying almost as a surrogate mom to her friend, never more than in the workplace.

"You seen Hendricks?" Dina asked. "I gotta ask him about the Boyko project."

"No. So, let's get back to a more interesting subject. Do you think the gorgeous Italian stallion, Frank, that hunk of a new employee, will ask you out?" A microscopic inspection of Dina's eyes for clues revealed a clear hesitancy.

"I-I think, I don't know." Even when screwed in knots, Dina's face was beyond beautiful, Karen thought.

"*Oy vey*, don't confide in me with anything. God forbid! I am only your lowly friend who's worked with you for five years!"

"Okay, okay. Give it a rest! I'll go if he asks."

"But of course you'll go, and you'll let *me* know first so we can plan the finest outfit. Say, you abandoning your self-inflicted company policy?"

"Karen! Yes, I guess so. Frank's different."

"I Immm ... you refer to future sex, honey? Put those not-so-innocent eyeballs back in your head! Wel-l-l?"

"Are you taking anything these days for that redundancy and over-attentiveness? Can we say *nosey*? Because, Karen, you know, you are *something else!*"

"Oh, yeah, I know, and if *only* every guy I dated would keep that in mind. Me? I'm exclusive to everyone and answering to no one!" Karen now was sitting in an adjacent chair, twirling it around and batting her lashes at some absent Romeo.

"I'm glad you said that, not me."

"R-i-i-ght. I know when I'm not wanted. You'll come crying to me, Dolly, when he asks you out for that special night, and bingo! You have nothing to wear! Then you'll come a-begging: 'Can you go with me to Saks?'"

"Oh, lighten up. I don't need fashion advice."

"Just so I don't miss the newsflash, you secretive beauty, maybe you are just like your grandmother, hiding the 'unknown!' So if he does ask and I don't know—"

"As if," Dina muttered, but only half-convinced. She knew exactly who her beauty could propel in her direction; genuine modesty, however, did not allow her to sound so conceited.

"Well, if I am *not* the first one in this blabby little office to find out, I will never go to lunch with you again, even if you bribe me with your Potbelly Sandwich Works tokens!"

"Like I said: *As if! As if!* And you won't miss lunch with me, not hardly!"

"Cool it, Juliet." Karen's voice cooled to a low-fire warning. "Just don't be too fickle with this one. Remember ol' Jeff? And Huey? Whom you used to see? Don't move in on Romeo too quickly! Can we spell haughty?" Karen was at the door now, hand on the doorknob, her body pirouetting gracefully, exaggeratingly into the hall. Her mind, Dina decided, was by now temporarily unglued.

The office was left unusually quiet following Karen's stridency. Computers hummed well beyond Dina's silent cubicle, the low buzz like the warning of a bee. To Dina, it seemed like an odd premonition hovered there in the space, then flitted away without a trace.

CHAPTER 7

When Dina awoke that morning, feeling extraordinarily pleased with the day, she barely minded that her cat, Mellencamp, was anxiously biting her toes in an attempt to get his breakfast. It was mid-May, not too hot or cool. The weather cooperating; thus, she would not have frizzy hair. I was important, because today she was to focus one-on-one Boyko with Frank.

She could picture his godlike features, hair as black as a funnel cloud, and he was probably just as wild sexually. Dina shivered at that and tossed the cat aside, bounding out of bed. It was no longer just a rumor that Sandoval was helping settle a big contract with Boyko Industries, and the project of suave finesse would be in her capable hands—and that of the new man. She had heard from Mr. Hendricks that Frank came highly qualified from his last job. Dina knew about Boyko and how hard it had been to hook them before, and how opportune it was that she, the lone woman, and perhaps a few other men, would be working with Frank.

Aside from work, she sensed the mutual attraction. Once, while both of them were exiting an elevator, his smile had sent a beam of light into her orbit, like a rare exploding star meant for only her temporary viewing. This magnetic force, she sensed, would not lose its grip anytime soon.

After dressing carefully, even down to the color of her eye shadow, she slipped on her highest heels, usually reserved for date nights. *I'll probably be sitting a lot today anyway,* she argued for the stilettos. She turned herself around several times, preening in the full-length mirror while Mellencamp licked his paws. She stopped to give the animal a kiss on the head, then bolted to her car and drove breezily down the sunny Chicago streets, allowing herself to woolgather what the day would bring. Excitement, a bullet lodged inside her, brought so much anxiety that she almost missed a stop sign.

Slow down, she chided herself, but she knew this was exactly what she wouldn't do. *I've always been the one in charge with other men.* Yet Frank did not seem like a pushover. Today she felt she would rather not lead.

Dina drifted into her favorite parking garage beneath the giant skyscrapers sprouting above. Usually, in good weather, from there she hiked the three or four blocks to work, as it was the least expensive lot. Today, however, with her stilettos, she hailed a cab. *The wind better not ruin my hair!* Her mind on Frank, she decided she would encamp slowly. After all, she was *not* like other women. Hurrying was not her intention. Better to savor. Besides, she counted on her looks to give her a sense of equanimity, a sort of spin control over romantic and teasing conversations. Even if to the rest of the world this immutable security was artifice and transient at best and overblown in proportion to her real character at worst, somehow, she failed to regard this today. A child of ten never can look forward and see themselves as fifty or sixty.

She got into the cab, chuckling about Karen's previous warnings. Of course she desired him the minute she met him. Had Karen seen too much? No matter. Dina knew that she and Frank belonged together, like a lost button finally being reattached to a coat that she could now close around her forever. And she was sure Frank knew it too.

"My, you're in a good mood for such an early morning," the cabbie commented hesitatingly, not sure how his passenger would take his intrusion on her thoughts .He had a toothpick between his teeth. Russian icons littered the dashboard, and he peered through them to glance occasionally at the rearview mirror.

"Yes," she agreed softly, "it is a good day."

Frank eased himself down on a chair near Dina's desk, all legs and languid attitude. In reality, he hoped she wouldn't notice his hands were slightly shaking.

Stop! he told himself. *She's like any other girl you've wanted in the past.* But she wasn't! And that was just it. Her soft cascading hair not quite blond, and that face. He knew he had never seen such a stunning woman. Up close, her looks were even more intimidating so that he felt almost out of his league. Then, after some discussion, she laughed, green cat eyes crinkling up, inviting as those of a child. And he eased up.

"So, my guess is you're here to see me about Boyko? Hendricks sent me an email. By the way, no one calls him 'Mister.'"

"I-I have some other notes on Boyko—new information."

"You do? Where'd you get them?"

"From the computer, from some files Wyatt rooted out for me. I found some new tips I'd like to share." Wyatt Little was Frank's friend now, and he had also been selected to be on Boyko. Charming and witty, the African American seemed to know obscure minutiae about Sandoval, which amazed his coworkers. However, like Frank, he was somewhat of a newcomer himself, having worked there a little less than a year.

"Some of those files are out of date. Shame on Wyatt! Probably only the computer ones are relevant."

"So you've known about Boyko for some time?"

"Yes, they've wandered in curious from time to time, but they always retreated from our offers. This time, we're going to nail them!"

"Sounds like Hendricks wants it done."

"Oh, Hendricks. Yeah. You figure him out yet? Such a softie. Not exactly a martinet. Probably why the Boyko approaches have failed before. This time, I am in charge, and Boyko will want … er … come begging for us!"

"That so?"

"This time, he's appointing five of us, including you and me, to take down Boyko. And we *will* succeed."

Frank smiled. There was a pause for a moment, during which he stared directly at her. Written in her eyes was neither business nor Boyko. Dina, coquettish and embarrassed, leaned down to scratch her ankle and kick off one high shoe, which was killing her. Frank heard the thump and said, nonplussed, "Eh, you believe in getting comfortable." It wasn't a question.

She blushed and handed him a new set of papers she had just pulled from her desk drawer. "I think you'll find these useful and relevant."

Frank had taken in her roomy and private office, noting she was a superior at Sandoval. He was impressed but not overwhelmed. Most of the employees on that floor, except for Karen and Big Sandy, had small cubicles, including him. Her power did not escape him; it only added to his sense of attraction. The Italian in him wanted to protect her, but above all, his masculinity wanted to ravish her as soon as possible. Too many fish and guppies in the sea had swum by; she was his marlin.

When he went to reach for the papers, he covered her hand instead and crushed it lightly in his own with familiarity. "Don't let us fool one another." His stare gave her a rush inside; she felt lightheaded and overly warm. Her pulse raced, although she longed to remove her hand for protocol's sake.

He leaned forward, and without compunction or fear, said huskily, "You want me. It's true. I know it. You know it. When can I see you?"

"I-I …" she stammered, trying to be both flirtatious and helpless. This was not the Dina of old, who dealt with young men like they were stodgy old dotards who needed to be pushed back into their rocking chairs since they were not ready for the likes of her. She was beyond surprised and could not answer.

"When!" His demand was like a bark. "Did I guess wrong? About your feelings for me? I doubt it. I don't waste time."

"No," she whispered, letting her hand stay there, grateful that there were no side windows in her office to reveal anything to nosy outsiders.

The back window faced out to Michigan Avenue, with a sweeping view. She could even envision Karen outside her door now, giggling.

"So? When can I see you? Outside of work? Look, I'm not good with flowery words. And even though I am new." He paused, looking down. "Well if you're not attached, I would want you for my girl. Yes, I know it's sudden, but we'd be swell together, as my dad used to say in the '50s, when he dated my mom. He told me the phrase, and I liked it." He leaned back in his best Jimmy Stewart expression.

Dina smiled shyly at the nostalgic reference, her heart jittering. "T-Tonight?"

"I won't let you down. I know you don't know me, but I can read people pretty well. And I can see you *more* than like me."

Dina's head began to spin. Lost was her power at Sandoval. Lost was her ability to crack hearts like ice cubes dropped callously in a glass. Lost was control, indifference. Instead, her head hung like a small child's, and when she lifted it, she heard him announce, "I will be like no other guy, no other relationship." His eyes were gleaming with anticipation, almost demonically, she thought. "And forgive my boldness, but we Italians get what we want! I got this job, beating out eight others, so you see, I don't want to spend the next six or seven dates, if they happen, in a game. I want you to realize how I feel, here and now, and how I expect to feel about you later."

Dina had trouble believing it all was happening this fast. Yes, she had heard these same offers from other men and had almost become jaded to the words and the false sincerity that accompanied them. Frank was different, so direct, and she loved it. She desired him so much right now she could hardly form the words. She coughed a bit.

"Be at Higgy's at five thirty. It's close. You'll buy me dinner, and we'll … talk. And no, I am not going to bed with you tonight. But I may, and often, after that. For now, I have to make sure you're not a psycho or something. You're awfully pushy."

Frank laughed and dropped her hand at last. He stood up, and Dina smiled at him. "So?"

"I'll be there, and by the way, I won't disappoint you."

"Hmmm, what's that supposed to mean?" She grinned, mysterious and catlike, relaxing her hand in her hair and giving it a toss. Frank had edged toward the door but turned abruptly, hand poised on the doorknob.

"Anyway you want to take it. Gonna get those files now."

When he was gone, Dina wilted. She could still smell his aftershave, a scent as bold and unapologetic as he was.

CHAPTER 8

The following day, Dina sat in her office, continuing to work studiously, occasionally swiping at the heavy locks of hair that fell across her cheeks. She licked her lips in concentration, her hands moving and adjusting papers, which rattled in the soft breeze of her partially opened window. She had jutted the door open as well.

Frank observed her and felt something tear at his heart, something he thought he had almost forgotten—a reeling infatuation. Here, in this small space on the sixth floor, it was as if her office took on a jungle-like heaviness; she, a blazing fire, impossible to approach. At last, her eyes lifted quizzically, surprising her with a view of him as he had appeared suddenly framed in her doorway, his body a slumped question mark.

"Oh!" Dina's expression was not one of surprise, and she dared him to look away first. "Business, pleasure, or both? To what should I attribute this second visit of yours?"

Frank tried to sound nonchalant, but he only felt sheepish. They had talked for several hours the night before at Higgy"s 'and he had walked her to her car. She had disarmed him with her personality, both passionate, shy and antagonistic all at once. She was someone who, like a pampered thoroughbred, had always found her way to the winner's circle and was used to that same attention.

"Well, since I'm here." He looked around theatrically. "I guess it's business."

Frank tossed his body at the door jam, hand in pockets, but he missed ever so slightly and slipped a little. Regaining his footing, he looked up and thought he detected a smirk.

"What *really* brings you here, Frank? You know, of course, we've already met."

"Yes … Dina, wasn't it?" he said, attempting a playful tone, but his voice quavered, and even now, blinded by her beauty, his innuendoes went bouncing out the window.

"So again, I'll ask, what business are you here for? More Boyko info?" Her gaze twisted back, away from him, like unwoven yarn, settling upon her papers. Frank tried to convince himself that perhaps she also was awakening to the reality neither of them could stand being away from the other. But when her eyes did not immediately return to him, Frank then thought she was being subtlety arrogant. Why did she act so enigmatically? What did she sense? And lastly, why was he willing to throw himself off cliffs after her?

"A-a-ah …" Frank burbled. What damned dog had gotten a hold of his voice?

At last, she looked up and leaned back, chuckling, and scooped back her hair with her hand, a gesture that was not coy but somehow hidden and perverse. Feeling officious, she helped him out by saying, "Are you really asking for a second date?"

Frank sensed his window of opportunity, but before it shattered, he lied, protesting, "I am still new at this." He quickly corrected, "I mean, w-with you." He had laid down his poker hand and sensed Dina's hesitancy. From behind her heavy lashes, her eyes fired a cannonball look at him. With a wry smile, she shrugged. Her office courtesy returned, and she was all business.

"Well, will you go?" he almost squeaked.

"Of course." She dropped the papers now, stacked them perfunctorily, laid them down, and rose from her chair. "You're the man. You decide where."

She moves like an angel, he thought as he watched her stand and glide across the room. At the door, however, she stopped and only touched his shoulder to turn him gently away from the door frame. "Now that you have your answer and apparently don't need any further Boyko information, go back to work. Employees are watching." She pointed, and the rise of her arm sent a splay of her perfume wafting up to him.

Frank wanted to close his eyes and lap up the scent. With his heart half splitting, he took a meat cleaver to his humility. Pressing his hand spoke-like on the door jam, he stopped the momentum as she slightly shoved him. "You know, I really wasn't … it really wasn't about Boyko, I mean," he mumbled quietly, hoping she would be inclined to accommodate the pesky little boy in him.

"It wasn't? What?" Dina said a little too truculently.

"Never mind. I'll call you."

Dina's eyes softened to the color of soft Fraser fir. He knew he had her.

CHAPTER 9

The wind that blew Frank's love into Dina's life was not discretionary. Hesitation was collateral damage, the fallout, for she invented hopes and excused her own unhealthy emotional behavior. These excuses to herself rose sharply in her mind as she and Frank spent languid days under the Chicago sun, testing and tasting each other, like drunk sailors who can no longer pay attention to their ship's passage. But unlike seamen, the spell they frolicked under was fueled not by alcohol but by their own eroticism. For Dina well knew Frank's unique caresses, the fingers that curled around her hair and lowered to her body, the hands large and only slightly calloused, whose movement sent a pressure in her stomach, a jolt of recognition that she was being held, being made love to like no one ever had before.

Her vision of Frank was pure but unstructured. Her fevered thoughts about him and their purported destiny blotted out her foresight, a gnawing and constant warning bellwether. The romance could not possibly draw to a close like some Shakespearean tragedy. In short, she was lying in wait for more illusions to come. Whether she saw them as such or not didn't matter. He could not possibly break her heart. Like a lion tamer, Frank had cordoned off her soul on his own golden chain, then he knotted it slowly and unfailingly around her, caging her into a sexual funnel where she was grateful to stay.

Once, Dina did try to tell herself to resist falling in love. Maybe she should reinstate the desultory pace she had with her former heartthrobs, she thought. But her own advice was short-lived, and she wallowed deeper into that safe foxhole in which all other hapless lovers find themselves. And so, greedily, Dina welcomed the accelerated pace, a powerful pull she attributed to Frank's charisma, although Karen would continue to call it more of a "spell." She saw the danger, the incautious way Dina transmuted Frank's tepid feelings into love.

"Remember last winter? You told me *you* would never go overboard with guys, that you'd play it safe. I mean, I see the signs. I remember the history. The men. None of them were right, but you talked a good game, being the ice queen you were. You had your wits about you with both Jeff and Huey. And *now* look. And what about your sworn statement about not dating within the company? Should I go on?" Karen sat across from Dina in her friend's office, only half concentrating on her fingernails, which she was now scraping with an emery board.

"Get in the mix, Karen. Jeff's a friend—still is."

"Yeah, but that elevation from lover to friend took a couple of crying jags on your part and more vodka than you knew was good for you. You were *so* not 'wanting to crush him,' as you said, that you drank more than a little, until you figured you could change the nomenclature of his status to 'friend.' I bet if I saw the guy today, he'd still be screwed up!"

"Old history, Karen, old history." Dina huffed good-naturedly as she continued to shuffle through a tedious file stacked on the adjacent cabinet—the Boyko project, not at all nearing completion.

"It's only been about four weeks, Dina. Watch out!" Karen lashed out, causing Dina to scowl momentarily. The two had already met four times this week alone, barely stopping to eat or breathe, so quickly did they assume a supine position when they reached each other's apartments. Once, they had not even made it to Dina's bedroom, forgetting to shut the front door, and they were surprised to look up from the rug, where they wound down their lovemaking, to see the neighbor's cat, who had wandered in, staring at them from the sofa as Mellencamp hissed a warning. They laughed but breathed a sigh of relief. They had not been careful and were lucky the cat's owner had not broken in on them to find his pet.

Dina continued to have carpet burns, battle scars to attest for her love. The will of effort to curtail the all-too-frequent visits to his office—for nothing that she could not solve herself—took on Sisyphean effort, and before she knew it, there she was, back at his door again. Their sexual heat burned on her skin as she thought of it now, an immolation of her entire body, for as he would draw her near, the lust on his lips making them shiny, his hands dragging through her hair and snapping back her neck like a twig to kiss her, he would further entrench her into a blinding, spinning emotion. She knew *this* was the man she could never be apart from for the rest of her life. She could feel him now, almost, how he paralyzed her with such force that sometimes Dina nearly lost consciousness, delighted and oblivious until …

"Hello! Earth to Dina!"

Karen rudely brought her back from her drifting little daydream.

So entranced was Dina into the scenario and discombobulated with the momentary thoughts of her lover that she kept missing the very papers she needed as she tediously shuffled through the copies on the file over and over again.

"You're falling in a hole! You know I don't trust Italian men!" Karen's raspy voice was startling, its dissonance ripping through the dainty symphony in her head.

"Pretty politically incorrect, let alone maybe a bit bigoted." Dina's question came out as a smirk." And I believe *you* were the one who seemed to tease me about him when he first walked into Sandoval. How do you reason with that?"

"So I was. But now I stand corrected. The whole office is talking, not that I care a whit, honey. I just don't want you to get hurt. It's unlike you, getting nuts over him, and it is all so … so …"

Dina finally pulled a file from the rift of copies lining the cabinet, which was a hodgepodge of blueprints, coffee cups, and so many abandoned pencils thrown asunder on its surface that they looked like some weird psychological puzzle waiting to be solved.

"I *know* you," Karen continued to preach. She picked up a Sharpie and pointed it at Dina. "You get that look in your eye, and then *pouf!* You are out to lunch, and just because you brag *you've* never been hurt doesn't mean it can't happen!"

Karen cocked her eyebrow at her and continued, "You're usually so nonchalant when it comes to guys, *and they* get the shaft. I-I don't know. I just have a bad feeling about this bad boy." When no argument came from Dina, Karen sighed. "I see, however, that it's becoming impossible to get my motherly advice through to you."

"I have a mother already."

"But you need a friend—at any cost!" Karen hurled the Sharpie back onto Dina's desk. "Will you at least have a drink with me tonight at Higgy's? I promise, girl talk and gossip only. No lectures about Frank."

Dina laughed slightly and clutched a file to her chest. There was still so much work to do on the Boyko project—phone calls, appointments—that she was glad Karen was making moves to leave. "Well, I'm supposed to—"

"See Frank again!" Karen interrupted. "So, I am right to be a bit worried. No time for a friend. That guy monopolizes your time."

Dina hung her head, deep in thought. "Maybe you're right. I'll cut it off with him tonight. I can see him another evening …"

Her sentence drifted off.

Karen, her arms akimbo and hearing the forlorn little acceptance, refused to renegotiate on her offer. "Good! Then I'll see you at five thirty."

As she sauntered down the hall to her own office, Karen smiled with satisfaction as she heard the dull click of telephone keys and Dina's low voice. "Hi, Frank. Baby, I've got to cancel—"

Half-hidden by a corner of a cubicle, not six yards away, the corpulent frame of Big Sandy stood listening and half nibbled at the corner of paper in concentration, as if it were a sandwich.

CHAPTER 10

As they lay together one day on the bed in her room in mid-July, Dina smoothed back Frank's hair as gently as she would a child's. Frank turned around to her, his eyes examining her with piercing lust, cooing softly and pleasantly, reassuring as a doctor to a patient. She so longed for his diagnosis, his commitment of love. He felt it now too, didn't he?

And how had she ever existed before without ever letting in this exquisite feeling? It was as if she had been caught, suspended in time, like an acorn ready to drop to the reality of earth, where the exigencies of life would cruelly take away these sexual moments, which were so lurid and heated as to be unearthly. Yet, then again, her life would play out at a monotonous pace, drafted away from their euphoria: eat, drink, work, sleep, and wake to do it all over again. Those moments then were unendurable, that ennui of the day-to-day, where she was only merely sustaining, pacing herself, and counting the minutes until she was alone with him again.

For it was not enough to glance casually at him in the workplace, perhaps over the frame of his cubicle, or to allow his smile to arrest her as he traveled through the halls while she sat lonely amidst the grime of her work. She wanted him completely, especially his word of love, pronounced to her at this moment, which would placate her heart until they could again meet, would stave off the mundane hours she drudged through at Sandoval, mostly out of his sight. These things, this work, however boring, she knew she could do, would do forever, as long as she heard those words from him.

Yet Dina knew she had given him as many tomorrows as she could as she waited in anticipation of his proclamation of love, gazing at him like a relay runner as she approached and passed him her own love, brimming with angst and torment, straining to hear those words—"I love you"—but then inexorably fall back, their mutual baton never exchanged, no sound but her heart dying once again, footsteps slowing, waiting yet again for that ultimate admission.

She made no sound now as she gazed out the window of her room at the sky, a pale, gray morning light, and yet, she could not look at his face, perhaps more prurient than pure love. She knew she had told him she loved him—twice, at least—her offering coy and shy, but as yet, there had been no similar reply.

Lightning from that pewter sky flashed through the room, illuminating her body, graceful and dewy, as well as his darker skin, corded with virile muscle as he balanced horizontally on the bed. At that instant, her eyes winced from the light, scouring his face for an answer to her passion, but there was only the pain of neglect, excruciating to her and one-sided.

At that moment, she loved him and did not care, her feelings born those hot summer days as they had sat on the grass and he told her about his past. Or it was revived at the lake, where he galloped toward the water amidst shrieks of children and plunged in, diving under and swam rapidly as her breath caught in her throat more than his even as he resurfaced and gasped for air. So magnificent was he that her mind played these moments as major events, reeling out all over the surface of her brain, until there *was* no memory but him—where he had been, what he had done, and most importantly, what he was like when he was with her.

Frank seemed to follow her melancholy thoughts as she lay quietly next to him and deftly, with a hard kiss, shattered her reflections with a demand she had to meet. Their bodies were like molten glass, a concoction of lust to be poured out, molding them together as a statue with no air between them. Hundreds of memories of unsaid words dotted her mind now but quickly flushed out, as did the sweat as it dripped from their bodies. Dina received him and all his movements as every flash of lightning only heightened their experience, and all the callousness, cynicism, and reluctance drained away from Dina, hopes siphoned down to an empty well, down which she dared not look. His possible feelings of love *should* turn toward her own life, which had seemed lately like some vapid piece of crockery, waiting and sad. But this mottled collection of thoughts now fell backward in her head, temporarily forgotten and excused as she succumbed, fell to rolling and licking, kissing, penetrating.

"Frank?" she murmured as they lay silently for a few moments afterward. He turned toward her, and she smiled feebly and gave a small laugh. "I forgot what I was going to say."

The admission of this was easier than the excuse of fear and the real question that lay unsaid on her lips like a deflated balloon: "Do you love me?"

"Then don't say anything." His voice trailed off lugubriously, his mouth forming a small, twisted smile. His eyes were solemn, as black as olive pits, the eyes of an animal lurking in obscurity, seemingly triumphant.

Dina shuddered, the look silencing her. His eyes were a tempting, coy come-on. She had faced that look a few times as she reached for the prize of those three heavy words only to come away disappointed, collapsing into an awkward moodiness as now she did, everything out of her grasp.

No! With Frank, she could not make *that* mistake. Had it been too soon? Was she too quick? In too deep?

But can I wait? she warily questioned herself. *Does it matter now that he is here and with me and …?* But she knew that although it *did* matter, she could really do nothing to accelerate his love. His passion, that was another story. *But I don't want it all to be about the carnal,* she rationed, *and why can't I just enjoy and not prod and plead?* Would scheming be next?

With a sigh, she got out of bed, feeling a bit more confident. After all, they were in *her* bedroom, her "home court" advantage to her dignity.

"Frank?"

He looked at her standing by the bed, and his eyes were not panther black anymore but warm brown, twinkling and mischievous like a little boy's. He did not answer her, and so, slowly, she dropped back onto the bed, submerging her mouth onto his masculine territory, willing her own surrender to his wiles and inveigling. As her tongue teased him, she reached out with her arms to pull him down onto her, for he was ready. She would run apace with him for tonight.

CHAPTER 11

It starts with a flick. In mid-August, high up in the trees, a cluster of leaves have suddenly changed. Yellow and lambent, they hang like a group of small, bright bells. Then the ineluctable consequence: autumn is coming.

Change.

It's usually slow, but sometimes, as one holds his breath, it occurs overnight.

Like love.

Suddenly one notices, slow growing or not—it's here. With a flick of the hand, an eyelash, a straw.

***

"Dina's sick today. Wanna go to lunch?" Frank hollered across his cubicle to Benny Trossman, at twenty-five, the youngest member to be appointed to the Boyko project. Benny was intelligent and good looking and had risen up the ranks of Sandoval rapidly.

"Afraid of sitting by yourself, as in *loner*, or is that *loser*?" Benny jested as he turned to face Frank.

"Naw, c'mon!"

"Surely I am happy that you picked me, sire, a lowly peasant, since you are without your queen today." Benny rose quickly and the two ambled down the corridor like a pair of tall pines swaying to some invisible breeze.

Lunchroom scents brought forth a plethora of enticing edibles—chicken, hamburgers, pizza—and after scanning the fare, they took their seats, opening their colas with the aplomb of men who are sure of their place and even more confident of their attractiveness.

Before he began to eat, Frank looked around nonchalantly as if not knowing what to say to Benny. The distraction of work was not available to them, allowing them to duck back to their desks when conversation lagged.

"You catch the Cubs game last night?" he ventured.

"Nah, I follow the Bears. Should be out of Bourbonnais from their practice soon. Home preseason game's on the twenty-eighth. Say, what's Dina got? Is it contagious? Did she get it from you?" Benny laughed, but Frank looked up from the pizza irritably.

"No, you jerk! It's just a bad cold. Should be back tomorrow or the next day." He turned back to his lunch and the men were silently grazing.

Suddenly there was an insect-like touch at the back of his head. Frank brushed the back of his hair. Maybe a fly. Then it came again. This time it hit his shoulder, and an empty straw wrapper slithered down his suit and landed on his tie. Frank crumpled it quickly and turned around.

Grinning at him and holding in place at her lips yet another straw aimed at her target was a petite young woman, who now flipped her luscious hair to smile at him. Frank, seeing the gesture of waterfall elegance her hair made, was immediately reminded of the beautifully groomed thoroughbreds scurrying across a meadow that he'd seen on vacations to Kentucky as a child. Their tails had plumed out graceful and danced in the sunlight as hers did now.

"Don't you think that's a little high school?" he said bluntly to the straw-holder.

"Not if I got what I wanted in high school. Did you?" she replied tauntingly.

"I wasn't popular in high school, but I'll bet you were."

Frank was half-turned in his chair, the pizza forgotten. From behind, he heard Benny murmur, "Steady there, pilot."

Frank did not turn back, but the admonishment made him smile, and the woman immediately read it as a signal to approach. She had been sitting alone, and now she rose. Her gait in her pencil skirt rocked more than a boat on a windy day. Her eyes bore into his, as black as a starless night.

"Well, did you?" she asked again as she sashayed forth, reaching their table. Her presence was cloying, taking up too much personal space, Benny thought. "Get what or *who* you wanted, that is. You still can." She extended her hand. "I'm Antoinette-Toni Spaulding, and you must be the gorgeous Frank. Don't believe I've had the pleasure of meeting you. But I have seen you often—with another girl, that is."

Her way of speaking, her inflection, made Frank lasciviously uncomfortable, but he extended his hand, looking up at her, and she held his gaze staunchly. She had the iron grip of a sumo wrestler.

"Frank Ciarelli. You're in a different department?"

"Oh, you know, Graphics. Tenth floor. The nose-bleed department, although I'm looking to transfer. Hey, maybe I'll end up working with you. You know, I must have been out sick or something the day Hendricks took you around a few weeks back. Or so my coworkers told me. Well, I should've gotten down to your department sooner to introduce myself, but before I knew it, the 'fly paper' had caught you. How is Dina? And where is she?"

"She's out sick."

Benny again tried touching Frank's arm in warning, but he waved an impatient hand at him. Toni now bumped their table on purpose, hoping to show her body to its advantage. She raised her arms, which accentuated her breasts as she flicked an invisible piece of lint from her top. She lowered her lashes as Frank's eyes took in her body while she looked askance. She was a small woman—compact, voluptuous, and pretty, with lush raven-colored hair. He felt as if it were a rope pulling him toward her.

Frank felt like panting. As if she had just noticed him for the first time, she said off-handedly, "Oh, hi, Benny."

"Hi, Toni," he answered through gritted teeth.

"Well, I am sorry I hit you with that straw wrapper. You see, well, I was aiming for you. To introduce myself." She was a woman who did not fear anything. Could probably even use her charms well beyond their expiration date. She no doubt already had Hendricks wrapped around her little finger, Frank thought. He'd probably grant her any kind of transfer she wanted, even if he had to cajole Graphics.

Toni continued to gush and stand there, like a prize fighter taking shots strategically, both speaking and maneuvering in just the right way. She drew perfectly manicured fingers along Frank's shoulder now. "You didn't mind being a target, do you?"

"So affected, Toni. So *film noir,*" Benny complained.

"Oh, Benny, shut up, will you! Let me have my fun in this boring place." She sighed impatiently and reached into her top between the ample breasts to grab a scrap of paper and turned her words back to Frank. "If you ever get tired of …" Her lips formed a perfect kissing pout on the word "if," and she drew it out insouciantly, "Well, my number. Anyway, I'm done with lunch." She tucked the slip into Frank's suit pocket, arched her neck, and threw her twenty-two inches of marvelous hair backward and stalked away on her stilettos, looking back only once to smile (or was it a smirk?), for she knew Frank was still watching her backside retreat.

"Load a crap!" Benny growled "You got a real prize with Dina. Don't listen to her!"

"Why?" Frank, with Herculean effort, turned himself back to face Benny, his face open and curious. Yet even through the lines on Frank's face, Benny could discern the interest there.

He's smitten, intrigued, Benny thought. "One word: reputation," he warned.

"For …?"

"Man-eater. Don't go near the water, friend."

CHAPTER 12

Dina was trapped in a dream now, observing a background of flame while a disembodied voice was repeating, "Evil's Excuse!" The stentorian warning rose as each word kept repeated like encroaching tsunami, water gushing toward her, blackening her sight and then suddenly blotting out the dream to wakefulness.

She shook her head on her pillow to dislodge the image, and suddenly, almost violently, she opened her eyes.

What the …?

The alarm jangled as she quickly dismissed the nightmare as useless. Surely it was not prophetic, so she did not contemplate its meaning anymore. It was a foolish hobgoblin of the night.

Lately it had come to that: she was ignoring all the telling signs that embodied much of her decision-making. The odd words of caution were a hazy dream that made no sense even if she bothered to unscramble them, so she surrendered her feeling to the day, which would be expanding to a more exciting level: Sandoval's field trip to Old World Proprietary Industries (OWPI for short), in Naperville, Illinois.

As she hurried to get ready, she envisioned Frank, waiting for her, later sitting next to him on the bus, nuzzling like young colts when no one noticed. It was getting late, so she hurried her self-assembly, going over each preparation from makeup to shoes as if she were going to a solitary recital.

Damn, that alarm must've been ringing forever. Why didn't I hear it earlier? she thought as she eyeballed the second hand, wanting to rip it from the clock's innocuous face. *I've got to hurry!*

She reached Sandoval only to see that she was really late. Employees queued around the building like attenuated train cars, trooping slowly into three buses. Dina was unhappy to see that Frank had already boarded another bus without her. She could see him at the window of the second bus as her line snaked around to the third bus. He was not looking out the window, and from her vantage point below, she could see he was engaged chatting with someone next to him. Who? Wyatt Little, maybe? Or Andy?

Suddenly Karen's rangy figure appeared in front of her, cutting into the line. "'Scuse me." She sidled tightly behind Dina, bumping another girl, who threw both women a rude expression. "My friend, ya know."

Karen popped her gum at the woman, as if *she* were the one who had cut into the line. "Have you seen lover boy?"

"Yeah, he's already on the bus." Dina nodded to the window. "I was late, but I'm surprised he didn't wait for me." Her voice trailed off dismally, a low train whistle suddenly gone silent in the beyond.

"Me? I'm always late. The company has grown to expect that of me now," Karen laughed. "Well, you'll catch up with him as we tour. This line sucks, anyway! Jesus, all we need is for Hendricks to give us nametags and matching T-shirts so they'll know us when we come. Hey, ya think they'll serve lunch there?"

The woman, who had been pushed aside overhearing her, rolled her eyes while Dina continued to crane her neck to the second bus window.

"Aw, c'mon people! Let's get on!" Karen whined obnoxiously.

OWPI was as stuffy and antique inside as its name—Old World—implied. The words were painted with a sad-looking script above the entrance. There were cracks along the door frames which must have dated back to the '20s, and the floor was concrete instead of tile. But as airless and unhopeful as the atmosphere was, OWPI employees, by contrast, laughed and chatted happily as they blanketed the corridors (some of these were tile, although yellowed by age). Offices were meager and scantily furnished. To the Sandoval group, it all seemed depressing, but more so it was confusing, as the OWPI workers acted as if they were in Disneyland.

Inside now, Dina shook her head as the dream's words came again unexpectedly.

"What's wrong? Flies bothering you in here?" Karen's voice was the elephant in the room as she complained loudly, "They never heard of Raid? Ya suppose this company ever had computers even? Looks like the walls could use a paint job, too, among other things. Geez! It's 1991, not the dark ages! Can we say 'janitor' about this floor?"

Dina smiled, but only half-heartedly. Frank had not come back to stand by her, let alone seek her out with his eyes. What was wrong? Laughter did not exist inside Dina; she remained confused about Frank's unnatural lack of attention to her.

Then the Sandoval group, about ninety-five employees, moved out into another larger, vaster room. Now that the large group was spread out, Dina again searched for Frank. She immediately spied him and moved herself a little closer, squeezing, then thrusting herself in a zigzagged manner through the crowd like water from a shaky hose. Karen remained behind, babbling aimlessly to disinterested coworkers.

Mr. Dobson, OWPI's CEO, introduced himself to the group as he stood behind a large, dilapidated platform. The room felt more like a warehouse than an auditorium, and it gave Dina the impressions of a corral with everyone loaded inside. This particular room was vast, so why did she feel like a trapped steer?

Did this cloying feeling have to do with … something she should know? Pay attention to? It almost felt like … something *starting*, but …

The CEO's voice carried over elevator music everyone seemed to ignore (how could OPWI employees work with that din?), but the

Sandoval group seemed uninterested in the speech. The drab pipsqueak's over-inflated speech came forth as if from a tunnel.

"Welcome, Sandoval employees! I'm here today to …"

Dina was just a bit behind Frank now, getting ready to whisper something silly into his ear when she noticed his hand holding another hand, which was attached to a short, pretty brunette by his side. She recognized the woman as … what was her name? In a stupefied, trance she noticed the woman's hair—thick, dark, beautiful, and partially piled up high. Like Marie Antoinette's.

Antoinette … Toni! Toni Spaulding. That was her name.

Frank leaned forward and whispered something into Toni's ear, and she chuckled softly and playfully punched his arm. Dina's outstretched hand, with which she was going to touch Frank, became suspended in midair, her face unmoved in its pain as if sunburned in the sunless OPWI room. She banged down on her heels from the bad ballerina pose she had assumed in order to reach his shoulder and watched, horrified, as the two grasped hands, and sidled closer together, shoulder to shoulder, locked in an oxen yoke. The brunette's head, petite and acorn-shaped, almost too delicate for the massive hair, leaned ever so close to him, as if there were no one in the room and she were about to kiss him.

What in God's name was Frank doing? A high, whining sound dimmed out the surrounding noise. She opened and closed her fist, like a pugilist ready to pounce. An abrupt cautioning thought brought her back to sanity: *This is a business trip, and the boss and everyone else is watching. Don't make a scene! Not here!*

Finally, the pompous CEO stopped speaking, and the employees moved cattle-like into another room to observe something else. Karen was suddenly at her side, her humor gone as she quickly sized up the situation with Frank. Dina, however, did not move, and as the crowd crushed forward to follow, Karen had to tug her friend's arm. However, Dina remained immovable, her face blanched, her hands at her sides, curled into such defiant fists that she reminded Karen of a stoic Joan of Arc on the burning pyre that she saw once in a movie.

Frank and his companion were moving forward, unaware of Dina and the Sandoval employees squeezed through the next door. The room now held only the two women.

"Clearly he never wanted to be with me," she whispered.

When the company was out of earshot, Karen gave vent to her anger. "Oh, my God! The bastard! Honey, are you okay? Dina?"

No soothing thoughts came to her, only a nightmare, a tight, choking in her throat. Her breath came in gasps, her body using all its strength to contain her tears. In another minute, the employees would return. Already, OWPI kitchen people were moving around them, setting up tables for lunch. Dina stood devastated amidst the rattling plates and scraping of tables being maneuvered into place. Karen remained beside her, her voice low, offering chastisements against Frank and soothing encouragements to Dina.

A few steps were taken, and gradually, Karen, taller and stronger, was able to move her companion toward the washroom, appearing like an ocean liner moving a tug through the flotsam and jetsam of tables and chairs.

CHAPTER 13

Dina rushed into her office and slammed the door, Karen right at her heels. The disgraced feeling of having watched Frank all day and sidle up to Toni had made her sick. She stumbled over the leg of her desk and lurched forward inadvertently, quickly holding her side at the pain shooting upwards to her hip. Karen was immediately at her side, her advice more trumpeting than solicitous. She touched her shoulders, shuddering under her embrace.

"Sweetie! You've got to get a grip! It's not the end of the world! Toni's not the last girl he'll admire. You'll see. There'll be others. He's a player! He's constructed that way. Types like him don't want to change. Kiss him goodbye! If only I could've convinced you earlier—"

Dina whirled around, facing Karen, eyes bleeding tears. "You don't understand. It's not just that I love him or even that the sex was unbelievable. It's ... something else! I have never *had* this feeling! I simply can't live without him! I feel connected to his soul! It's like I'm responsible for him, almost as if he were my own child or ... or sibling!"

"Oooh, honey," Karen moaned in a whisper. "Dear Jesus, Mary, and Joseph Christ!"

But Dina had heard it. "No! Oh, Jesus ... you! I *knew* you wouldn't get it! You can't understand!" Dina's voice now was hoarse, and since other coworkers would be filtering back to their work spaces from the bus trip, she lowered her tone. "Just get out of here! I think I might be sick, and I just want to be alone!"

"You're wrong about me not understanding," Karen said hesitantly.

"You mean because of course you've had the experience of love in *so* many marriages!"

Karen forced down her shock at Dina's sneering comment. "Oh, no. You don't mean that. You're upset."

Dina stood trembling, hope slowly ebbing away. Her chair was nearby, so she slumped into it. "Sorry, Karen, but I-I *can't* get over him. It's impossible! He is as different from my old heartthrobs as Earth is to Mars. I have to think of a way to lead him back to me. Maybe sabotage Toni? Cut her off at the pass?"

Karen stepped toward Dina. "Smearing someone at work isn't your style. Why risk your job and good reputation on that clown with big hair? Toni's just one of those sluts whose purpose to grab. And it is more perversely suited to her nature if she scores someone else's guy. Wouldn't matter even if it were Big Sandy. If you're dating him, she wants him! I've seen plenty of women like that, and they make me ashamed for our sex! Listen to what I'm saying, and—"

Dina interrupted her, twisting her face around angrily. "Frankly, Karen, it would mean less to me to lose this job than to lose Frank. And I am sincere about taking one big risk to get him back. Yeah, that's a risk I'd take."

"You don't know what you're saying! It won't work!" Karen pleaded. "Frank would never take you back then! Your meddling would get back to him. Besides, the end doesn't justify the means. Just shut down your thinking on that lame plan."

"He never even looked at me the whole day! Who does that? Like I didn't even exist! That scheming slut deserves it!"

"Causing a catfight at Sandoval? I won't let that happen! I won't!"

Dina shot up now from the office chair. "If you try to stop me—"

"Okay, okay, relax! I'm in your corner. I *am* trying to understand this fixation on Frank. I don't understand why. Why *him?*"

"I don't honestly know myself. I feel it in my bones that I am here … to protect him. He belongs with *me*, not Toni! It's a weird feeling—that I need to try to *save* him. Does it make sense?" Her innermost feelings about Frank would sometimes come frothing out—during the day or in the night—like a rain of confetti. *Somehow* she was meant to be beholden to him as he was to her. She did not relate these last feelings to Karen. How *could* Karen have understood?

"Oh, honey! Protect him? And who protects you?" Karen said again sorrowfully, her hand reaching out for Dina's.

"I-I think I'll head home early. Now. The field trip exhausted me just holding in all that anger. Just talking about it, I relive it all."

"Can I drive behind you so I know you got home safe?"

"No, really. I'll be fine, okay?"

"Will you call me later though? So I know you got home okay?"

"Yes."

"You know, it's just a guy. Just because you have had luck of never being dumped, this privilege doesn't extend to *all* of that sex. You picked one that happens to be shitty; that doesn't mean there can't be others. You're just starting later than most of us girls."

"Now wait—" Dina hurried to interrupt, but Karen pushed on.

"And one more thing. You are wrong about me not understanding. Although my last husband took me to hell and back, sometimes, on a beer-sloshed night, I still find myself wanting the moron back. I get it, but do you?"

Dina raised her chin, affronted, and with a cold voice said, "It's not the same, believe me. Your feelings aren't like mine for Frank."

She sat silent for a while, listening to her coworkers outside her office take their seats and regroup after the field trip, although this last hour before the end of the workday would surely be spent loafing instead of doing anything constructive. And of course, there would be lots of digs and comments about OWPI and the people they employed.

"Well, it must be different somehow."

Karen looked at her skeptically, as if she wanted to fling something meaningful at Dina, something that would catapult her in with all the other millions of heartsick women who suffered at the hands of male flippancy. But right now, Karen didn't have the energy. It was close to five o'clock, and she was tired, so she whispered, "Call me," and slid out the door.

Dina turned and gathered up her purse and a few Boyko papers, just in case she wanted to go over them tonight to distract herself from the heartache. (Who was she kidding? She'd be lucky if they ever left her coffee table.) Vile thoughts about Toni caused her to mutter, "Bitch!" It never occurred to her that perhaps she was baring her teeth at the wrong victim. Frank should have been the one her fury was meant for, but in her mind's eye, she—having been exempt from really facing full-blown, low-down blues—had placed the target on the other woman's back.

As she left, she slipped on sunglasses to conceal her puffy eyes and called out to coworkers Wyatt and Benny, "Hey, I'm going home early! See you tomorrow!"

Luckily, Frank had not yet returned to his desk, which was near Benny's. Perhaps Frank was still talking to Toni at *her* cubicle, she surmised. As she hurried on by their desks, the two men looked at each other, and despite Dina's hope that the office had remained ignorant of the attention Frank showered today on Toni, Benny and Wyatt nodded.

Neither had to say a word.

CHAPTER 14

As she sat in her bedroom that evening absentmindedly petting Mellencamp, Dina continued to try to revise her opinion of Frank as a man who simply enjoyed female company. After all, she *was* late. Why shouldn't he have set with someone else? His actions seemed all but justified.

Justified! How? I can't be taken advantage of! He ignored me! Should I confront him? Or should I give him the benefit of the doubt?

But what about you, a little voice chirped.

She squashed it down, too manically in love to let the OWPI incident get between them. The relationship was too important. *Maybe not important enough to sail along without confronting him?* She couldn't control the churning in her stomach. The agony of seeing flippant Toni was made worse in that the blow to her pride had been more than stunning. It was a slap.

<hr />

Frank's cubicle was adjacent to Wyatt Little's and Benny Trossman's. The shared overhang of personally decorated Mylar reminded one of leaning over the fence to chat to one's neighbor. If Dina wanted a word with Frank, whom she noted with anger, had not sought her out first, it would have to be done on her own territory. She pushed the button on email to summon him.

Frank moseyed in about fifteen minutes late from the time Dina requested, unapologetic and not at all diffident. He greeted her but said nothing about OWPI. He grabbed a chair without asking as Dina herself rose with slow grandeur out of hers. It was her symbol to demonstrate both that her legacy with Sandoval overshadowed his *newness* and that she possessed enough inner strength to chastise him. Regardless of all that, she was still shaking.

The nerve of his insouciance! She was still feeling the jealousy, yet she could not completely hold his nonchalant stare and looked down, saying nothing.

"Hey, babe! How's it going?" Butter dripped from his words. "We gonna see each other Friday night? The usual?"

Dina gripped the back of her chair momentarily for composure. "Frank—" she began haltingly.

"Something tells me this is not about the new Boyko project." He lifted his eyebrow, giving his come-on look.

She tried to ignore it and left unsaid now the stern speech she had rehearsed last night in her room. Instead, she retreated into a stark foxhole, where bullied lovers seclude themselves, giving up the war for the sake of an argument.

"Yes, of course," she replied, glad he hadn't brought up Toni. The room was quiet for about thirty seconds.

"So? Well, what then? Why email me to come to your office?"

"I wondered why you didn't come by me or even sit with me on the bus trip yesterday." She sounded like a fifteen-year-old with a crush.

"Huh?" His other eyebrow shot up. He was playing it cool, she thought. *More like deceptive.* "Does it matter?"

"W-well, yes. Especially since I am your girl, as you have me believe, and everyone saw you holding hands with—"

"Hey!" he interrupted, getting to his feet, "you *are* my girl. And Toni?"

She's new to our department, transferred and maybe assisting with Boyko, I hear. I thought I'd be nice and stick by her." Frank had an odd smile. "I can't help it if she … well, the guys, you know, say she has a crush on me. I just placated her by holding hands—"

"Placated her? That's an interesting choice of words!"

Frank stepped over to Dina and touched her hair, smoothing it back from her cheek, letting it ripple down her shoulder. "Don't worry. What we have, well, we don't *have* to be joined at the hip all the time."

"It didn't look all that innocent to me, and you didn't even acknowledge that—"

"Hey! Give Toni and me a break! She may need to get up to speed on this project. We spoke mostly about Boyko—and OWPI. She needed a little bit of an edge, coming from Graphics as she did—"

"Hmmm." Dina stepped back from Frank's touch. "You don't know for sure that she's going to work on Boyko! She seemed *familiar* to you!"

"Look at her! She's twenty-two if she's a day. She's barely got more experience about our department than a student intern!"

"She's no intern, if you know what I mean. Her behavior toward you didn't look that naïve. Why, even Karen—"

Frank stepped forward again, interrupting her speech by putting two hands on her shoulders. "When are you going to stop thinking about what everybody else thinks and start believing in *me*? We've been so tight these days. I'm sorry I didn't come by to wave or acknowledge you at OWPI, but she really monopolized all my time with questions."

Leaning in, he lovingly pecked her cheek. That's all it took for Dina to give in to his unconvincing argument. Frank corralled her closer, not letting her escape his clutch. Before she knew it, he was whispering in her ear, "Don't let that *little girl* get to you. I'm all yours, babe."

"You sure?" She turned her head and looked him in the eye, and he nodded—almost a little too quickly.

"Well, I guess I'm on for Friday. It can become like a henhouse around here with people pecking out each other's eyes—and hearts. I've seen the fallout. It isn't pretty. Employees with angry words dismembering Sandoval's serious projects like tinker toys. We've got to be strong and true to one another, Frank, if we're going to make this work. Both us and Boyko!"

"Absolutely!"

It almost sounded cynical. The word hung in the air like a helium balloon that she longed to tear down, revealing its intended meaning, but her heart did a sharp U-turn, and she dismissed anything hidden in his affirmation.

"Now, darling, is there *anything* more?" he cajoled.

She longed to say, "Yeah, the world and all your faithful and undying love!" Around Frank, she knew she wasn't the Dina who tossed men aside on account of a fractured word or look. Instead of further reprimanding Frank, she merely shook her head. "No. I'll see you at the Boyko committee meeting this afternoon."

"And Friday, don't forget."

"Lunch today?"

"Er … I promised Benny I'd meet him today. Okay with you?"

He was sidling away, his hand moving forward eagerly to the doorknob of her closed office door.

Why does he look like some feral animal fleeing human touch just now? she thought, but she pushed the niggling thought away.

"Yeah, I'll eat with Karen."

CHAPTER 15

Early in their romance, Dina wore her love for Frank like an invisible crucifix around her neck. New extremes were required daily to preserve the romance. Crusade-like, she would willingly march into his disquieted moods, pardoned his slipups and unfailingly embraced everything he espoused, whether it was a sports team or a rock group. She ignored his negligence and unfalteringly admired his successes. In short, he was achieving status no less than a deity in her eyes.

But gods topple.

Gallant sacrifice took savage holds on her personality, demanding her attention, creating disdain from her friends, namely Karen although thankfully not yet Mr. Hendricks. Sometimes she questioned it all in the dark of night just before sleeping, but then she thrust it all aside and gave in, and so the one day when she spotted a crack in her "statue," she chalked it up as sort of a damage control all relationships have to weather, even while it plunged her into a kind of painful jealously she could barely conceal. If there was a chink, she would patch it.

The chink was caused by the sledgehammer, Toni Spaulding, who trespassed onto Dina's holy ground with her iconoclastic and overtly sexual behavior. Her surreptitious winks, her sideways leaning against Frank's arm, as he explained the pitfalls of the Boyko project, which she now was officially assigned to assist on, to Dina were tantamount to blasphemy. The curl of her lip, jackal-like, smiling so coyly at Frank, was undermining Dina's belief in fidelity. She could hardly stand to be in the same room as the petite black-haired witch. Constantly on guard and jittery, Dina felt the Boyko project falter under her touch even while it rose seemingly like a phoenix under theirs. Excommunicated from Frank's attentions, falling down on the project, it became evident to Dina, like a truism she didn't want to face, as the three worked every day for hours in Sandoval's conference room on Boyko, that he, the once faithful, could become fallen away or misguided by her effort of trying to painstakingly reinforce a hold on what now felt like only an ideology … or a fantasy.

❧❧❧

"You directed the funding here. When you did that with the Thompson Company before, they folded on execution. You told me that, so don't let that happen to Boyko." Toni pushed the syllabus forward, tapping it with her pen, and stood up, flanking her chair.

Frank gazed up at her from his chair with a look Dina tried to tell herself had no other meaning than business.

He laughed slightly. "Look, we don't have to get it all down in one day. Changing structures would require a total re-dividing. It's Friday afternoon. Let's break—"

"Break! Why would we break on something this important?" Toni slung her heavy hair back and knotted it with a twister rubber band.

"Why not?" Dina asked. She was angry Hendricks had assigned the newly transferred Toni to such a career-changing project. Before, it had been only her and Frank and the three other men. Toni wasn't even aware of the ebb and flow of the Boyko undertaking. She had come from Graphics, for God's sake! Why had Hendricks done it? Even now, Dina sensed Toni and Frank had met up before, maybe even before the OWPI field trip. Were the flying rumors true?

And Frank had, at first, meted out duties to the two women unruffled by the poison in the air. After all, everyone at Sandoval knew Dina's main man. But Toni was one of those beautiful women (although her looks paled before Dina's) who took possession of whomever she wanted. In older days, Dina could picture her as a perfect cattle rustler. Here in the modern world of the '90s, Toni's *savior faire* was suffused into the small room every day. Her sexuality practically overshot the room, rippling into the halls like a giant wave, much like her overdosed perfume.

Even Hendricks noticed the tension as he peeked into the room one day. He coughed delicately, and Dina scowled at him with pure revenge.

"How's Boyko going?" he inquired sheepishly.

"Fine!" Toni answered too quickly, even though, that day, they had hit a snag where all three disagreed with one another. Her eyes were bright as a cherub's, but her glance was dripping with a flirtatious eroticism Dina detested. Toni all but dragged Hendricks into her lair, and Dina sensed now, as never before, how this weak little man had been charmed into putting the inexperienced con artist on Boyko.

"Wouldn't you like to come in and have a look?"

Her head pivoted sideways, a marionette taking control of her own strings.

Such an affected ass-kisser, the bitch! Dina thought, looking away. Maybe even a cock tease, as she preferred to think of her rival.

That Friday, the trio did break for the weekend, but not before Toni's lilting little voice threw a dagger of condescension at the couple, probably for not getting her way.

"Soooo, I guess you two will be going off for a brew. Two's company, three's a crowd?"

"Yes, it is!" Dina snapped, standing before Toni, her anger a concealed grenade. Frank twisted away from gathering up the syllabus to glance owlishly at her. "And I don't think we *should* rework it at all. We should learn from the mishandled Thompson promotion. After all, Boyko has its own guidelines!" Dina was sneering now. "I know that from studying the company—*and* from my experience! It weakens the whole presentation. It's fine the way it is!"

"Oooh," she said, her hurt-little-girl voice accompanied by a beseeching sidelong look toward Frank, "maybe Frank wouldn't agree—"

"Frank can speak for himself, but I think he would side with me."

"Whoa! Whoa! I think I *can* speak for myself, Dina." He had now turned fully toward them.

"Well, do we go with the change or not?" Dina challenged him haughtily, but deep down, she was hurt that he did not respect her enough to agree with to her comment. Why was he giving the bitch a shot at all when he had talked to her in private days earlier about the difficulties of making changes on Boyko? She didn't want to downplay his importance, but Toni was rubbing her raw. She felt the sting of his words burned on her face as if hit with a blowtorch.

"I-I think it's best decided on Monday," he offered diplomatically but lamely. "After all, everybody's tired."

"Not me! I'm just getting started! My thirst needs quenching at Happy Hour at Higgy's right now." Toni boldly yanked at her blouse in front of Frank, pulling up her bra straps to readjust her large breasts. Frank was watching curiously, and Dina fell into a purgatory she had never known when she saw the look.

"C'mon, Frank, let's go."

Dina extended her arm to him, but it felt leaden now when he touched it, as if it might fall off.

Suddenly defiant, Dina pulled herself out of her gloom and shot Toni a savage look. "After all, ahh ... maybe you can get Randy to take you." She smirked. She knew she was being unkind but didn't care. Randy was the nerdy mailroom man who almost everyone at the office, Big Sandy included, had bet on being a virgin.

"Cute," Toni shot back, chaffed. She collected her documents and pushed deliberately between them both and as she exited winked at Frank only. "See ya on Monday!" Momentarily she turned "Oh, and Frank, make sure you get plenty of sleep." Her brown eyes slid away to Dina's green ones, and the beauty countered her look with a stare of one-upmanship. But before she could think of a fitting retort, Frank spoke.

"Yeah, see ya."

He shrugged. He lacked the businesslike tone that Dina expected. Suspicion was driving her to analyze every little nuance. Coldly and without a word, she walked down the hall without him to her office to collect her things.

"Going home now?" Karen suddenly materialized at Frank's side. "Or are you two going to Happy Hour at Higgy's?"

Frank smiled. "Don't know yet. I'll leave that to Dina."

But Dina didn't hear them. Karen's further inquiries to Frank on Boyko were only a wash of background noise since her head was pounding. Witnessing the tawdry exchange of banter between Frank and Toni, the floating innuendos between them all day, day after day, Dina was afraid. She had been ostracized from Frank's favor in that room, and although she thought she again heard that inner voice that spoke to her urging her to *flee, move away from danger*, she again chose to ignore it, even though today it was louder, sharper. Something could—would—materialize between the two, something to befoul them all.

CHAPTER 16

In observing Dina, Frank noticed that the periodic upheavals of her past, for example, the death of her father, measured low on the litmus test of her emotions. If she was ever wistful about his passing, she didn't show it. This was a poor albeit odd example to weigh human feeling against, but in harking back to it, Frank decided that Dina would be the most unruffled by his flick of emotion; her suffering would be measured on a lesser degree if they broke up. As to the histories she would often relate to him—of reigning supreme, never having unrequited love—he found this fact helpful to his exit.

He could maintain control over the situation with feigned sympathy if needed, preserving his own kind of smash-and-grab personality. Better yet, she might drift away on her own, like a lost ship. He remained cold, all the while taking the temperature of their affair. He needed to leave her, but he might need help. He might need advice. He may have been mercurial, but he was guarded.

As the days lingered on, he became more uneasy around the two women with plenty of polite mannerisms and coquetry for Dina to spare, but they were growing effete too, only a crust on top of a pie obscuring delicacies not so sweet about a personality he would rather not face.

He often wondered why women were attracted to him as he whisked his way through drama like an eggbeater through life, everything in him so mixed up and undetectable that there was no way to sort out the *real* Frank. To the women who caused him pain, he was adeptly able to shut the lid perfunctorily on those feelings and longings over time, and while not as callow as Big Sandy, Frank could have been, in that respect, a distant cousin to the Texan.

So Frank waffled on and remained stagnant in his relationship with Dina, continuing to two-time.

Eventually, like many cheaters, Frank didn't want to continue the charade forever, and yet, there seemed to be no one to confide in when it came to letting Dina down easily. Should he simply keep showing up with Toni, let that be some kind of a symbolic statement? Should he see Dina less and less? Toni would eventually protest. She was already whining for exclusivity. There would be no disrobing, no sweet ecstasy of sex, without it. These were terms she said he had to adhere to even while he really wanted the sweet, seductive Dina more. She had what he was looking for, and as farcical as it was, she would take him, as he was without change.

His dilemma deepened. Who to talk to?

It was the fortress of Karen he feared. He realized that if he gave Dina up, *she* would be in his face, in his office, in the corridors, like a squeeze of grapefruit in the eye. Dina? Avoidable. But Karen? Ubiquitous and full of contempt. The worst thing in a woman.

The first time he had met Karen, he had emphatically climbed out of his office attire and shrunk to the level of a little boy. Her eyes had sized up his extraordinary good looks and challenged him to mistreat anyone she knew. Men come and go, her blue orbs seemed to say, but women friends are forever. Even Big Sandy seemed to avoid her, slinking and ducking out of sight when she strutted down the corridors of Sandoval like a confident cat staking out its territory.

Karen's strength, Frank surmised, was constructed from a tremendous combination of cold nerve, previous hard knocks, and fiery protectiveness, the latter a feature Frank likened to the color of her burnished hair. When she opened her mouth, it was all wisecracks and jokes, but when she stopped performing—and this Frank could not know—her insides were trapped with pain, a festering that lashed through her body like a laser. If Frank had only known the similarities, they both maintained as they masked their real selves for different reasons and for different outcomes, he might have developed more of camaraderie with her.

Those who can't assimilate joke about it.

The gathering office gossip was continuing, extruded through every email and corridor whisper. This could not be good for his career, so when he drummed up the courage to enter Karen's office, he questioned and re-questioned himself.

Could he do it? Actually seek advice on how to break up with her friend? Or was he just fishing for the trapdoor? Karen no doubt knew the air-conditioned feelings he was giving Dina these days. He nervously he licked his lips, wet his hair, and with one icy hand, grasped the doorknob.

Frank, ever the schemer, ever the seeker of appetizers while foregoing the relish of the actual meal, muttered to himself, "Coward!" closed his eyes, gulped, and walked into Karen's office.

CHAPTER 17

"Hello?" Frank edged into the office. Karen was at her desk. And with his ducked head, slumped posture and how he repeatedly screwed his tie around absentmindedly with his hand, Karen, merely in observing him, felt like an overly controlling teacher.

What does he want? I'm not working on Boyko. She narrowed her eyes with suspicion and she swore she heard him gulp.

"Uh, can I sit down?"

"Yeah, you got an ass! Sit!" Something deep inside her warned about Frank's complexity; she really couldn't have known if he had hurt other women, but nevertheless, she came by the knowledge from some profound perspicacity that cautioned her at other times. It was the same shortwave that encouraged her to abandon her two marriages. She smelled a rat in Frank, and she didn't like the looks of this visit.

He sat down in the adjacent chair and didn't hesitate. "Uh, you're good friends with Dina, my girlfriend, right?"

"Ah, *ye-ah!*" she retorted, not bothering to hide her cynicism. "What are you doing here? I didn't call any meetings. I'm not on the Boyko project, so this can't be business!"

Frank, humiliated, pressed on, "I-I need advice on, eh, Dina."

"Why? You getting married? It's only been three months! What *do* you want anyway?"

Finally, although a bit intimidated, Frank sighed. "I-I know how much Dina loves me. And for me? She isn't … right. I need to know, well, you know her best, er, how to let her down easily?"

The hurricane blew in. "When in the history of men has any guy ever needed advice, let alone with my best friend, on how to break up?" Karen kept her voice from booming but barely. Frank was reminded of the disembodied head of the Wizard of Oz. "Don't you men kind of have a similar *modus operandi*—just stop calling or take the lady to a busy restaurant so she is too embarrassed to make a ruckus? Why are you asking *me* anyway? You know, Frank, you gotta work here, but like that bullshitter Big Sandy, I don't *have* to like you! And right now you've thinned the borderline between like and hate!" Karen crossed her arms furiously.

Frank straightened, ready to argue for his gender. "Yeah, so you don't have to like me. My only concern is Dina—and yours should be too!"

"It *is* for Dina, unfortunately. For myself, *I* don't want to go to jail for murder in this lifetime, and that would be the only way she would let go the grasp of the love she feels for you! I *know* her! She's so smitten that I can't get a word in edgewise! She can get any guy. Anyone can clearly see that! I've always felt characters like you to be out of her league! But I can't force her feelings, and she's got oceans of them for you. I don't know why. The whole office saw you and Toni. Whadaya going to do about it?" Karen shook her head. "God, I needed a cigarette right now!"

"Nothing! I-I mean, it's wrong. I mean, maybe I'm wrong—we're wrong together! Maybe I just need to go and figure out what to do on my own. I've never seen anything, anyone, as serious as Dina feels! I just wanted some kind of advice—"

"Yeah, like you *never* broke hearts. Line of crap! You expect me to believe that? You eat women for lunch and have another on your plate by dinnertime!" She poked an angry finger at him now, Jimmy Cagney style.

"Forget it! I'd better go." Frank got up, frustrated and this time sweating in anger, not nervousness. "But I ask you, plead with you now, on my life! Human being to human being." He paused and looked down, grasping the back of the chair, and with one hand gestured emphatically. "Promise me, employee to employee, if it has to be, since you hate me, promise me you'll *never* let on, *ever*, about this conversation, to Dina or anyone, about breaking up. I'll do it in my own way. Please! Promise me, for her sake, forget this meeting. My words didn't happen. Do you promise?"

Karen stood up quickly, narrowing her eyes once more, her rolling chair bumping back harshly against the wall. "I promise."

Frank went to turn around to the door muttering. "Thanks," but Karen's words stopped him.

"One more thing!"

"W-what? I-I can't imagine," Frank said, wondering just what she wanted now. She really had been no help, only succeeded in browbeating him.

But Karen's interruption held a softer tone. She played her last card: "Reconsider."

"I-I can't. It's too late," Frank said, and he left her office.

Karen slumped back down in her chair. While rubbing the sides of her face with both hands, she whispered, "Oh God! I don't like what's coming."

CHAPTER 18

The sun slid into darkness almost too suddenly, like a fried egg sliding off a blue dinner plate. The night was a coy youngster, begging his playmates, a group of infatuated stars, to come out and wink at the moon. Two figures now lounged on balsam-colored sand beside Lake Michigan. Toni spoke now of her ill-concealed confusion.

"Why do you take me out? I mean, everyone at Sandoval says you and Dina are a couple and, well, so I'm going to ask: Why me?" Balanced on her knees, she drenched her hand as she dipped it down to the cool surface water. The sand was still warm from the sultry day, when she had walked with Frank, its crunch and crackle under the soles of her sandals still fresh in her mind. She drew up her body now, sheltering her feet comfortably beneath her while her lips framed a fleeting shooting-star smile. Frank reclined on the towel behind her, unsmiling, half leaning on his elbow and staring at her with fascination.

"I take it 'conceited' is the first word in your personal dictionary?"

He shifted his position, leaning in toward the water's edge. He took up her wet hand and kissed it, biting the fingers. "Perhaps that's it. That indescribable pride that begs to be challenged. It's not only your looks—those forever-long brown legs on that petite body, which match that gorgeous long black hair." He tousled her hair gently, swiping a strand across his face to feel its softness. "You see, everyone seems willing to fight a duel over the noble ones like Dina. Always have, throughout time, always will. Me, I keep them second-guessing. On the fly, I'm taken in secretly by—"

"The dirty handmaiden's servant?"

"Something like that."

"Something like second best, you mean!" Toni scowled. To her, second best was merely waiting in the wings. The prize for her was not snagging the quarry but unseating the champion for it. Being second may be a challenge, and she didn't expect to play nice here. Why should she? But she liked teasing Frank about it anyway, just to reaffirm her place in the scheme of things.

"Second best? No."

This time, Frank, fully seated beside her, grasped her left arm in his and extended it behind her aggressively. The cool light behind his limpid eyes was almost savage.

"Ooow! You're hurting me!" Toni twisted around and with her free hand thrashed at the lake water, sending the spray up into his face, "Let go, damn it!"

"No!" Frank laughed and shook the water from his face and hair, but his eyes remained hard as gray pencil tips. "You're worth it, Toni, you see. Sacrificing any noble image I have enough to leave Dina for."

"You would have left Dina anyway," Toni sputtered, cutting off his words, "because you're so enthralled by your *own* office successes, you know! And Dina, she is the Harvard equivalent of the women you just *had* to have her to prove to yourself—"

"And leave her for who?" Frank interrupted brashly. He twisted her arm harder, with a look that held passion and other seamier forces. It frightened Toni. She slapped out at him with her free hand and hit his cheek hard. Frank rolled over on top of her and, freeing her arm, gripped her waist tightly with his hand and jerked her hair with the other hand. Suffocating her with deep, harsh kisses, between them, he snarled, "And you love it this way! Like *this*! Out in the open! How did I know this perversion of yours?"

"Wouldn't Dina?" Toni teased sardonically. Her breath was short and hot, and she tore frantically at the buttons of his denim jacket.

"Dina's not here! Forget Dina!" Frank murmured.

Toni then jerked up, not submitting to his advances." She's all but married to you! That's all the talk! Don't deny it!" She reared up on her knees now, out of his grip. She slashed at her hair to drive it from her face so she could glare at him fully, for their scuffle and the growing wind had tormented her locks into disarray.

Frank shrugged, brushing some sand from his palms. "All talk. Like the Boyko project. It's alive and vibrant, but soon, any project, like any woman, needs to be put to bed. The people at the office will stop talking of her. Of us. Yesterday's news." Frank laughed sullenly at his own excuses. "Where's your comparison now?" Throwing his head back to the stars, he laughed harder, and when he looked back at Toni's face, he was met with a questioning look. Slowly, complacently, she closed her eyes. Now a kind of a grandeur flicked at the corners of her semi-smile.

"It's here and now that counts," she said softly.

"So you agree, my pet?"

"You're an asshole, do you know that?" she whispered.

Frank frowned, dropping the mocking look, and suddenly scooped up a gritty fistful and flung it high over the water. He gazed down the empty beach for a long time, and when he looked back at her, Toni saw his confusion. "No, I'm not really. It's just—"

"Something else?" What he could reveal, she thought, and what paltry sin or giant indiscretion beyond cheating on his girlfriend that he could confess that would make this philandering small by comparison?

"Yeah." The voice was curt, forlorn.

"What's bothering you?"

"Nothing."

"Tell me!" Toni urged, but his glance back to her was perfunctory, telling her that she, maybe even he, would never uncover the reasons.

"Some things end, I feel, and not in the way I want. I just have this

strange feeling … that my payment for my ungentlemanly behavior …"
He trailed off "Ah, what's the use? Not important, anyway. Just my crazy
hunches."

Toni waited for further explanation, but instead of providing one, he
stood up and swooped her up in his arms, cradling her like a rag doll. "I'll
tell you this: I can't understand much of this world, nor all of myself. And
that, dear lady, is all you need to know right now!"

His eyes told her now that he was through explaining, but heedlessly
she pressed on.

"Oh, so then you—"

"Shhh now," he cut her off. "Shouldn't we look for the car? And maybe
go back to your place and look for better things to do than question each
other?"

Toni curled lasciviously into his frame and nuzzled his cheek, her
arms surrounding his back like a pair of pliers tightening. He lifted her
and carried her across the beach, grabbing her sandals in an easy gesture.
Frank continued to kiss her as they retreated, the small waves popping
and smacking the sand behind them. Breezy night air was keeping all
Frank's secrets, and he wore an arcane, brooding smile as he clutched Toni
to his chest, much like a child clutching a prized souvenir.

CHAPTER 19

The nausea continued to rise. She quickly clamped her hand over her mouth. They rounded the corner of the lunchroom, not knowing that behind the marble pillar they passed was Dina. Toni's skirt hiked up higher as she reached up to Frank's tall form to lay her arms around his neck—such wicked long legs for such a petite girl! She was a schoolboy peeking under a circus tent at a peep show, her revulsion at which somehow did not force her to look away.

"When will you tell her?"

"Why should I?" came the gruff, masculine response.

"Oooh, Frank!" she whined back. "I thought you'd be all mine—"

"I belong to nobody! C'mon!" Frank barked, urgently pulling Toni out of the quiet corridor.

Would they go to either office to linger, now that no one would be on the office floor with the lunch hour in progress? Would they perhaps go further, breaking all the rules as his sexual appetite leaned her over the desk? On the floor?

"Oooh, God!" she cried out as she teetered, then staggered on her high heels, groping the column for some kind of support, but it had no ledge, and the cool marble caused her hands to slip down, throwing her off balance. She fell in a heap, her eyes watering, just as two men who worked on the floor below hers entered the hallway. Dina shakily tried to get to her feet.

"Are you okay?" one of the men responded, and they hurried forward. Then arms were suddenly around her at both sides, helping her to her feet. "Did you break something?"

"N-no, I didn't break anything." Dina knew she couldn't survive the rest of the day, offering simpering smiles to Toni as though nothing were wrong. To hell with Mr. Hendricks and his deadlines! "But my head hurts. I may go home."

Your dates have dried up, the phone calls halted, and I'm still a fool, she cursed at herself inwardly. She felt the disgust rising even as these caring, charming, and dateable men stood by admiring and fawning over her!

"Can I help you to your car?" The tall blond man at her side offered his arms kindly to her. "You work upstairs, don't you? It's Dina, right? Say, I can let your boss know."

Big Sandy was the only one who sang the praises of the imminent breakup.

"Serves her right! *She* probably did something. They always do!" Or, "Did ya hear that Frank's really serious about Toni Spaulding? He's glad she's on Boyko too. Wouldn't ya like to see *Dina* standing in line for a change?"

The men in the office were confused as to what could have driven Frank out of the bed of such a sexy woman, one who was in all of their own sexual fantasies. Why her? Why now? Why the trade-off? Shrugging bewildered and communal shoulders, they moved at last on to other fascinating subjects, such as the cute new receptionist or why Frank's friend Benny had shaved his head. No one cared about Big Sandy's ammunition; it was all sour grapes, redundant, effete.

The end of the romance was indeed sad; people noticed the lost sheen from Dina's scintillating personality. She drove herself by rote now, while another part of her was tearing at her insides like an ulcer. Her voice talked, her feet walked, her downcast eyes flitted catatonically without focus. Emotionally she had hit a shoreline of solid rock, her life unnavigable, her hopes sinking under a wave of Frank's former affection in their early days together. Better times. Smoother waters.

But Karen noticed and didn't stand by dully watching the drowning. She tried to ply her with comedy, as she watched Dina's moribund personality attempt to live a puppet-like existence, guided by some omnipresent thrust. Every pencil was stacked in place, every phone call returned, the exact and expected responses doled out by her at the corporate séance of a meeting about the Boyko project. And Dina also refused many of Karen's after-work meetups, preferring to escape immediately to her empty apartment.

"Your thinness is not lost on me, you know!" Karen was perched on a lowboy in Dina's office, playing with a small paperclip box as she watched her friend one sad, rainy Monday. "Damn office! Damn rules! Wish we could smoke without going outside. I could use one!" She snorted her distaste but continued to badger. "Did you eat this weekend, honey?" Hopping down from the lowboy, she moved toward Dina, who labored over a boring Boyko document and rumpled her hair.

"Yeah, I did. A little. Don't bother me now, Karen; I'm trying so hard to hold it in these days."

"Are you telling me lately to fuck off?" Karen exploded. "So, *I'm* to get the treatment you feel he gave you? It doesn't work that way! You don't thrash out at those who care about you just because you were left in the lurch. I'm not buying it! I won't sit by and watch you die from heartache. Anorexia maybe, but not heartache. I'm your friend, and you've got to stop breaking me in two like I'm a matchstick. I am not *him*! Others care about you too! Sue in Finance, for instance. She says you look like a ghost!"

"Okay, okay, I'm sorry! Want to go to lunch? But how about tomorrow? The lunchroom lately …"

Karen, momentarily relieved, watched Dina's eyes eagerly for some small lighthearted change, but instead, Dina assumed her lethargic stare and muttered, "I'll meet you any day. You get the cab."

CHAPTER 20

She arrived at Frank's apartment uninvited, crossed the threshold, grinding down her jaw and steadying her hands from shaking. Frank asked her in, his questioning look almost a rebuke in itself. He motioned to the sofa, and while they both sat, his face averted, playing with a Rubik's Cube, the minutes ticked by without her uttering a word.

He knew why she was here, but why was she so intense? Was it that psychic shit she clung to, leading her to claim she was more *aware* than others? He had fallen for her once, but now his interest had dissipated. His nature was of a wary feral cat that doesn't know whether to stay and trust intervening human contact or flee and scrounge out on his own.

The Rubik's Cube splayed desultorily along his fingers when suddenly she blurted, "So, it's Toni, is it? So, it's over for good? Is that about it? After all we had?"

He looked up startled at her bravery.

"Y-yes," was all he muttered.

"And *this* is how you let me know? Strutting around Sandoval with *her* at your heels? Rubbing my face in it, flirting at the Boyko meetings! Not even approaching me with a conversation?"

"I, ah, wanted a change. I'm not a noble person. Yes, I chose the most cowardly way to do it. I'm sorry—"

"A change!" she cut him off. "I love you! I'm not just something you change like a different necktie you put on every day! I thought we had something that would stick! Cohesiveness! Something on which to build a future!"

"Again, I'm sorry if I led you to believe that." He tossed the Rubik's Cube, and it clattered against an ashtray. Wincing, he drew back defensively.

"Wasn't I pretty enough? Surely more so than Toni!"

"Beauty's got nothing to do with it! Hell, beauty's ubiquitous, Dina! TV, magazines—it's all over the place. It could have been anyone. Plenty of pretty women in the office. Hell, in all of Chicago! I—"

"But that's just it!" she interrupted, gripping the purse she had brought as if she were gripping a life preserver. "That's what men want? Isn't that right? The more, the better!"

Frank looked annoyed. He wished she'd go home and leave him the hell alone. He'd apologized. Why wasn't that enough for chicks?

"The Victoria's Secret ads! Titillation! The skimpily clad models," Dina continued to rant, "and they don't put those pictures in there for women!" Her voice grew more strident. She could not let him see her grovel.

Frank noticed the tears, and although he was sitting directly across from her, he did not move to join her on the sofa. He extending a hand, but she didn't see his gesture of comfort.

"I tell you I don't understand you! I've held myself back all these years from falling for just *anyone*!"

Everything raw and oozing was trapped within her; she was witnessing her own jealousy firsthand, a foreign body invading. "I've saved my love for the right man! And it's you, don't you see?"

No, he didn't see. This petulant child in front of him was anything but appealing now, and why was she going on about her looks? Toni was averagely pretty, no stunner like Dina, but he was confused and was growing impatient. "So you *counted* on your looks to capture—and keep—me?"

She sniffed. "Sort of."

Frank looked at her strangely now, not knowing before how extremely she had valued her looks. Were they employed as some sort of mouse-trap—or, rather, mantrap? Maybe even to the point that it superseded personality?

"You'll never see it, I'm afraid." Shaking his head, he rose from his chair and stalked over to the living room window, where he leaned his hands on the sill. Coldly, he said without turning around, "I really don't know why you came. It's over. You should leave now."

Minutes passed, and Frank never turned back, his eyes riveted on the trees and sidewalk outside his walkup. The only sound was the door clicking quietly.

CHAPTER 21

It was quiet in the Northbrook Township Library on a late morning in early October. Edging herself out of her gloom, Dina decided on the distant library because one of her coworkers had once declared it to be "quaint." She'd take time out of this unbearably sorrowful weekend ahead to visit the same personal life raft she used as comfort in childhood. As a child, she often lost herself in books, even while more enjoyable things had beckoned.

The drive there was ridiculous. The heat and traffic on I-94 on this humid Saturday seemed pressurizing enough, and more than once, she thought about turning around. Where was everyone going? Perhaps for one last fling in Wisconsin, as it was the end of September. Or to soon-to-be-closed farmers markets in the north suburbs. The whole city seemed to be on the move!

At last, she opened the library door to the air-conditioned call of volumes. Authors living and dead awaited her inside. How solicitous these unread walls of tomes seemed, scrabbled words collected here on so many pages as she arrived on the second floor of fiction. She placed her hand so that it drifted wantonly along the spines. Then Frank's watery image seeped in. Quickly she pushed away his memory, her own story that could have positioned here with a *happy* ending! She stifled a sob. Why had she allowed herself to be swallowed up by him? And now, still clinging to a phantasm, she was futilely trying to rip that image from her heart. *Like tearing meat from a carcass! Yes, I am left with the bones*, she thought, poised before the shelves.

She was ripped from her complacency by a mental bizarre image of a "dead" love, visceral and grisly. *I have allowed my love not to be tasted but gnawed upon.*

A chilly gust of air blew from one overzealous air-conditioning vent above her, and feeling the frigidity in that particular spot and yet unaware of its possible portent, Dina turned and walked out of the fiction area, her feet carrying her towards the shelves of reference books, which were assembled as rigidly as if a tyrannical hand had squeezed them into place. The golden lettering on the spines of dictionaries, thesauruses, and atlases glistened at her in the morning sun. How did she get here? The nearby click of computers gave her no answer.

What *was* she looking for? Where was she going?

The reference area, yes, to find the volumes that listed companies. Maybe a new job! A way out! It didn't matter today that she had illogically sought a permanent albeit difficult option to assuage the temporary pain of a lost love. And yes, a new job possibility could promise- relief? Dina sighed. Maybe some night classes? In those five seconds of decisive thought, she was actually hunting for books, possibly the class schedules she needed, not bothering to ask the bored looking librarian to help her.

She'd show him! She'd show everyone at Sandoval, especially when she would someday announce that she was leaving for an even better company—and better pay!

Idly her hand dipped down, finger pointing at titles, scanning the various books, some of which sat on shelves, bulging and neglected, others neat and almost prissy, their newness an affront to their well-worn and elderly neighbors, who were shouldered in this territory like bad urban blight.

Dina tried to focus, but suddenly, tears splattered on her cheeks. Frank again! Couldn't she just concentrate enough to do this *one* thing?

Both hands were shaking now, and as her left hand rose to wipe the damnable tears, her right hand flung out, searching and anxious, poised in that space of air before the bookshelf.

Pick up the damn volume! Any volume! Look as if you're functioning! He'll never come back! He'll never love you! He never did! He's gone! He'sssss …!

She could have sworn the volumes were hissing at her. She almost screamed and squeezed her eyes shut to prevent it.

Thump!

A book had fallen on the floor in front of her. Her eyes flung open, uncompressed springs.

Did I *do that? Oh!*

Dina leaned down and her hand scratched the fallen book's cover. She picked it up and turned it over for inspection. What *was* this book? She looked at the title:

A Dictionary of Angels
Gustav Davidson

What in God's name? she puzzled. You mean they actually have a reference dictionary for angels? No way! Her grief was temporarily halted with curiosity and the mild shock of discovery. She shuffled through a few pages, perusing the litany of holy names and descriptions and their order in the deities: archangels, cherubim, seraphim.

"Wow!" she murmured to herself. Looking a little further, she even ventured a little laugh. This *can't* be a real reference book! But then she checked the cover plate and saw the library's dire warning stamped inside:

Do Not Remove from Premises
Reference Room Only

Fascinated momentarily, she let her fingers dawdle among the pages further, as she viewed the strange but readable text.

And then, there it was. A small section, and in it:

"A Spell to Guarantee Possession of a Loved One."

Slowly Dina's pupils inched skyward, as if coaxing authenticity from any random seraphim in the vicinity. *Would* it work? She read the text:

"Stick on the head of a girl's or woman's bed, as near as possible to the place where her head rests, a piece of virgin parchment on which you have written the names of Michael, Gabriel, Raphael. Invoke these three angels to inspire (here, pronounce the name of the beloved)] with a love for you equal to your own. The person will not be able to sleep without first thinking of you, and very soon, love will draw in his heart."

Chuckling to herself, Dina wondered, *What if?* She made a copy at the copier, slipped it into her purse, and then took the dictionary to a quieter side of the library, near a window, where she sat and combed the words over and over. Her temples constricted, her eyes squinted, and even her breath grew rapid and shallow, as if she had just discovered a furtive stash of unclaimed money. Frank's love might live again! Coolly, Dina swept her hair from her eyes, her confidence returning. She appeared to study the traffic going by on the street outside.

I'm going to try it, she decided, and she shut the dictionary.

CHAPTER 22

Dina let herself be drawn into the exaggerated expectations of the conjuration, waking for three mornings in a row, groping under the pillow like a child rooting for money left by the tooth fairy. Its presence there destroyed her infantile hope; since the paper was still there, it must not work. Her twisted reasoning, however, argued sometimes for credibility; since there existed a dictionary in the reference department, then there *must* be angels, and the conjuration within this text *must* possess invincible power, right? She was patient, although deep down, she could not deny the absence of a miracle, and she became crestfallen, even downright moody.

Embarrassed now with herself, annoyed at the fantasy of it all, she stuffed the paper back under the pillow for the fourth night in a row, far from the mouth of the wastebasket. It remained there, a crumbled scrap.

"It's as worthless as the pencil I wrote it with," she swore the following morning. She shuffled into her slippers to prepare a breakfast she wouldn't eat. The four long days had stretched out, an unfinished race, where she forced herself to concentrate at her desk. Frank had not come by. If a Bible had been close to her, she would have flung it to the floor, cursing all angels. She had sunk her teeth into a fairy tale while the spell's force foisted upon her a man who didn't want her!

At the close of day four, she believed some kind of heavenly joke was being played on her. Heaven *could* mete out cruelty. She lay in bed that night feeling like an island to herself and took the conjuration from its hiding place, the thin paper worn and dog-eared by now, and memorized the words again. "And I saw him almost kissing Toni today," she said out loud. Then she crumpled the paper without replacing it and turned over on her bed as the scrap dropped to the floor. Frank was gone, and that was the answer to the conjuration's equation.

CHAPTER 23

Scraps of leaves skipped across the ebony surface of the water one evening while Dina sat by her condo swimming pool, which had been left open well beyond Labor Day due to the warm weather Chicago had experienced. Gloomy thoughts huddled with her in the lawn chair. Yet, she had needed a place where the natural stillness of night might calm her.

Oh, I hate him! she growled. The skittish trees wriggled their leaves in response, a swaying laundry line in the soft wind dispensing more specimens that dove to their death in the chlorinated water. Her body hunched over in protection from sadness. The lawn chairs within the shadows, weird skeletal horses without heads or tails, remained unoccupied. As she stared hard at them, their shapes took the oppressiveness of her humiliation, and they appeared as grotesque, gray, eyeless seats, like mouths inviting someone to sit, calling like open graves.

She began to shiver. Was the breeze quickening? Now she heard Karen's words to her earlier that day: "Indulging yourself in misery does nothing! First you're courting it, and then you're marrying it! Pretty soon, there *will* be no other world to exist in!"

Why did I think that silly conjuration would work? she sulked. Another breeze ruffled by her like a silk scarf drawn across her face. And then there was Frank's memory, like a ragged coat, an overgarment worn raw and close over bare skin. In her mind, she lashed at his face, (like she should have done a few days ago, during her unexpected visit), fingers taut and stinging as whips, harming her heart more than his skin. She could remember the look she had seen in his eyes, sheepish and uncaring.

"Evening, Dina."

George, the elderly super from the condo, appeared at her side making her jump. He smiled but looked at her strangely, and noticing her anguish, he hesitated. In his rough hands, he held a flashlight. "Ever'thin' all right?" he drawled.

"Oh! Yes, George, just thinking." She looked down, embarrassed.

"Don't let yerself think too much 'bout anything.' Kills the spirit, ya know. Sorta like the age we live in, everthin' getting too technical, too fast." He looked away forlornly, pleased with his unwelcome, simplistic philosophy.

"Yes, I know, George. I'm sorry I'm not very talkative tonight. I appreciate you asking. Thanks."

"Ga night, then." He shuffled away, the beam of his flashlight attacking the small spaces of night, flushing out and spearing the dark shapes—a tiny mouse, a stray cat—with long, luminescent brightness. She watched him go and balled her unneeded jacket angrily in her lap. A foul smell arose, but she dismissed it as someone's cooking gone wrong in one of the adjacent condos.

She peeled off her sweater now. Only her thin nylon T-shirt remained between her breasts and the night air. She touched her hand along her breasts now, a slow, lingering reminder of Frank's fingers. Her nipples rose now under her hand, her eyes quivering behind the lids, beholding in her mind this quiet ecstasy.

Suddenly the air was perfectly still, the breeze as if caught in a jar like an encapsulated insect. Her grim thoughts penetrated the water's surface; if only she could push down the pain to the pool bottom, which was somewhat brackish now with dead leaves.

You're a fool, Dina!

She stood now near the pool, her body trembling, longing to feel the explosion of suddenly diving into this water, releasing herself. *Your beauty can't buy him back!* She recalled past loves that she could manipulate to her own needs, the masculine attention less attractive girls had to work harder for. Why hadn't Frank fit this puzzle? Why had her own perspicacity for the opposite sex failed her?

Suddenly, from the pit of the pool, a whorl of water swirling counter-clockwise and gaining speed along with a sucking noise exploded into the night. Dina staggered back and fell back into the lawn chair, her eyes never straying from the gushing whirlpool before her. This was no malfunctioning pool filter! How could the water do this without a great deal of wind?

The suction was a terrifying sound, coupled now with a long, low *om-m-m-m-m*, like the raspy rattle of a bucket bottom scraping along a sidewalk. Each note grew a little louder every few seconds. The pool water, meanwhile, continued raging, gradually rising, perfectly formed, as if its "torso" were a vase made of glass, sunk into the swimming pool.

"What in heaven …?" Dina breathed quietly, too tense to move now.

The sound grew a bit louder, the whorl tipped faster, no longer at its former water- wheel pace. It was a vortex, a thunderous suction whose midsection could only be described as a black spool, spinning rapidly as it ascended from its chlorinated container.

The black mass then stretched something like insect feelers skyward nearly ten feet, spooling and unspooling, like pulled licorice taffy, taking an inhuman form. The many-legged feet were rooted in water while something like wings sprouted from its sides. Its face was ugly, pockmarked and brutal, and it arched its indigo form forward, enabling the wings to span wider out into the night. When finished, it looked like a black, hideous gargoyle taking up now almost forty feet of atmosphere. Like some weird spawn of a monster from some old horror movie, it very slowly turned its face back to Dina, pointed a skeletal digit to the sky poked from its wingspan, and with a sonorous voice, flattened its lips and screamed, "Evil's Excuse!"

Dina could not even move. Later, she would wonder why fear never drove her away or why she hadn't even screamed. It looked like something hell had manufactured, and she wasn't even sure she heard correctly what it had said. Just as suddenly, it disappeared, and Dina swore it flew upward, but she couldn't be sure. The water settled down to a glass surface, calm in a split second. High overhead, the sound of dishes clinking came from an open window in the condo building, normal nightly noises as people went about their routines—*as if no one had heard!* The cacophony of a locomotive, and nobody even looked out a window.

"What kind of God's malfeasance was that?"

It was George's voice, not twelve feet away, his flashlight sagging in his hand, about to fall. So Dina hadn't been dreaming!

"What the—"

George stood there slack-jawed, and Dina stared at him.

Her mind emptied of all former self-recriminations but one—had *she* somehow done this?

George muttered, "I knew I shouldn't have had those extra beers. It's time I go home."

CHAPTER 24

"Shut the door, quick!" Dina motioned from her office. "Come in! Come in!" She waved her hand frantically now.

Karen darted into her friend's office in fright. "Shit, I haven't even had a full cup of coffee yet, babe. And you look more terrible!"

Dina pulled at the bracelet on her arm, ignoring the jab. "I-I think I did something, maybe created something … awful!"

"You *did* something? Oookay …"

"This is serious! Sit down."

Karen grabbed a chair, studying Dina shrewdly. Something told her this was not about Frank.

"I-I did something. It's, well, it's a conjuration, really."

Karen's smirk appeared, and she leaned forward, like a jester humoring a king. "A con—jur—a—tion? Isn't that some kind of Catholic voodoo Mass for the dead?" She was laughing, although she knew what the word meant, "Hey, is it a funeral Mass to mourn Frank? In that Gentile-run church—"

Dina cut her off, "I made a conjuration with the angels to get Frank back. Listen! But I was sent some sort of black angel instead, maybe a devil, a creature! They were called archangels, er, fallen away from God, although I don't think this *thing* really belongs in the angel category. It has appeared to me and is doing, or is going to do, bad things because I brought it forward somehow, in the wrong way. I feel *it will happen!* I-I know ..."

She ran out of breath just as Karen stood up to address her.

"Slow down! And calm down! First, what do you mean a conjuration? Brought something forward?"

"Well, it's not a particularly Christian experience. More like a pagan request. It goes beyond prayer. It's a ritual. I found in this book in the reference section of the library. Really, I just stumbled on it." She shook her head wearily now. "I don't know. The book just spoke to me, so I started reading things inside. It's called *The Dictionary of Angels*. It's not Satanic in nature. The conjuration was in the back, something young girls probably performed hundreds, even thousands, of times in the Middle Ages. It seemed so innocent. It claimed you invoke angels in a certain way, like putting a piece of paper under your pillow, and supposedly you achieve things—or people. I thought it might work to get Frank back—"

"Sounds like devil-pact material to me," Karen interrupted. "Say, this devil-angel guy who you seem to have summoned, he got an agent? My cousin Sheldon is connected to people in Hollywood."

She was again smirking.

"Stop it! It really *is* serious! I know how it must sound to someone who didn't witness it! I'm afraid."

Karen patted her arm. 'Sweetie, it's okay. Frank's gone, and sometimes the pressure of not having someone makes us—"

"Stop placating me! It's nothing to do with Frank. I just wanted him back and was willing to try anything and I found this conjuration inside. It was so simple, really. I had to write down my desire—his name—on a piece of paper and put it under my pillow. After that, well, it all began." Her eyes became glassy, faraway. "How could anything so ... so harmless produce such malevolence? And now Frank is sick, and it is all my doing."

"Sweetie, sweetie." Karen rose from her chair and came around to Dina. "You are coming unglued! Frank just has the flu, I heard. It's going around, you know. It's a coincidence. No silly piece of paper made anyone sick."

"I know Frank's sickness is a minor thing, in comparison, but now my bedroom seems oddly cold sometimes, even when it's been so warm out! This, this spirit thing …"

"Spirit thing?"

"The Friday night this evil-looking apparition came out of the condo pool … Don't look at me like that, Karen. It was gigantic and looked like a Halloween mask from hell! No actual body to it, per se. All black and … and spinning! I may be mistaken, but I believe it even had a tattoo, but since the creature was so black, the tattoo appeared … in white lettering. I couldn't really read what it said."

"Hold on! Maybe it was some kids doing a prank—"

"No! You don't believe me, do you? You *never* believe me! Everything's got to be a joke! You refuse to see things beyond your understanding; everything's got to be all black or white. Are you sure you don't have a cousin Ronnie or Sal in the shrink business? To help me?" Dina was sneering now. She held a large file from her desk and slammed it down with a *thwack* for emphasis. "If you don't believe me, get out! You know the super of my building saw it too! Everything feels strange somehow! I believe what I saw, and I feel the thing to be somehow … dangerous!"

"Christ! Hold on!" Karen now leaned back against her friend's desk. "But just think what you've asked me to believe? Ghosts and conjurations? In this century? Black disembodied angels with tattoos coming out of swimming pools, existing because of your—conjuration? What if it *is* true—and I am not saying I believe you yet, but if it is—what can you or I do? This is something the Catholic Church needs to investigate—have a séance or exorcism or whatever." But she couldn't resist quipping, "We could just slip into the nearest Stephen King novel and see what he did. Oh, I'm sorry, Dina. I couldn't resist! All this talk of black monsters. We need a *little* comic relief! Besides, this *is* how I deal when I can't come up with anything! I wisecrack, you know."

"I-I don't know what to do to stop … *things* from happening! It seems the conjuration isn't innocent at all. Maybe full of black and evil power? I'll never forget the look on that super's face! He was scared! Karen, I needed to tell someone before I go crazy. I blame myself. I brought this on."

"Okay, I believe you for your sake, although it all sounds—oh, never mind. Just try to keep calm."

There was a sharp rap at the office door. "Mail, Dina," a squeaky voice commanded.

"Maybe we can talk more about it some other time, okay?" Karen whispered. Dina nodded skeptically.

Karen opened the door to a bespeckled and pimply mailroom boy, his hand grasping his cart like the leash of a faithful seeing-eye dog.

"Randolf!" Karen gushed in her best Betty Davis voice. "Where have you been all my life? Your hair speaks volumes!" She extended a languorous and fleeting caress on his curls with her hand, then sashayed Cruella de Vil–like down the hall, all femme fatale and teasing, minus the fur coat.

"Name's Randy, Karen" came the nasally reply that no one really heard as he pushed the mail cart into Dina's office.

CHAPTER 25

Karen and Dina moved through the street, picking up knickknacks, pausing for ice cream along Devon Avenue, Chicago's eastern Indian district. The day was hot, and the odor of curried food wafted from the small restaurants. Colorful saris brushed the sidewalks of its wearers. Everywhere was the arcane dialect of Hindi—a lilt of words, up and down, like the movement of a merry-go-round as one sari spoke hesitantly, the bit of hiatus filled in by the plunge of words of the other conversant, its timbre rich and deep.

Excited by the pleasant melee of the streets, Karen was talking, smirking, and mimicking the dialect, her inflection and stories unheard by Dina, an unbroken spill of noise like a baby rattle. Dina merely smiled, her step, mincing and slow. Her eyes, following the saris, counted the cracks in the sidewalk as she sidestepped some rollerblading boys. Karen glanced back at Dina, doubting whether this excursion she'd suggested to cheer her friend was working. She only had to look at Dina's miserable expression to know that this was true. Dina was at the moment imagining Frank wrapped around Toni, their bodies locked together like Christmas paper on a box. Her downward glance caught a MacDonald's wrapper as it whistled by, and she frowned. It could be a mini New Delhi here, but before you think you're really far away, leave it to McDonald's to bring you back to the good old USA and the tastelessness of mass consumption! She sighed despondently at the scraps of paper.

She felt a jab to her arm. "You've heard nothing I've said at all, have you?"

"Wh-what?" Dina looked guilty.

"I've just accused you of robbing that bank we just passed, and you nodded and said, 'Yeah, right.' In fact, that's been your answer for the last three blocks. We are supposed to be experiencing the city, our *ethni*-city program, you know, not playing in a Bollywood romance gone wrong!"

"I'm sorry. What were you saying?" They had stopped on a side street under a tree, where it was shady and less populated.

"Saying? I've been doing *all* the talking! Sometimes I wonder why I ... oh, whatever, Dina. I'm hungry. We missed lunch. I could go for some—"

"You know very well what you wanted and what you did for that *want!*" The interruption was accompanied by a thin brown hand reaching out at Dina's elbow, the touch icy, the voice, watery deep. "You *always* know what you've done. Come in!" The hand let go, and a beckoning finger streaked by as Dina stared at the crooked digit.

Karen watched the woman now and in her rudest snarling voice said, "Hey! Excuse me! What are you doing?"

The woman ignored her and poked her head further outside the doorway where she had been standing. A slightly damp house smell floated at them, effulgence that seemed to hang like wall paper around her meager frame, enveloping Dina and Karen and sucking them inward.

"You need to know." The old woman's eyes, little and as brown as burnt toast, carried urgency. She again extended her arm to Dina as if to pull her in. "Now!'

"Look," Karen spoke authoritatively, "you soothsayers are getting more aggressive. We don't need your *psychic ability*. Now, if you'll just leave my friend alone, I'd appreciate it. You know, the city of Evanston has an anti-panhandling law now, and Chicago may pass it too—"

"I ... I ... I ..." Dina hesitated, fear compelling her to investigate. The woman's stare bothered her. What did she know?

As if reading Dina's mental question, she answered, "They watch you, you know."

Dina moved closer. "What?"

"They are everywhere, so suffocating, so close, as if they were woven into the air like tapestry threads. *He* is woven into your life also—the man you know and covet so much." Her voice lilted upward, its inflection ascending and descending. A voice to be admired, feared, obeyed. The arm reached out again, cloying, winding around Dina's shoulder and gliding her forward. "You see, you *must* know."

Now the old woman smiled, the wrinkles on her leathery face panning out like marks on a sundial, telling the story of her life. Her isosceles triangle eyes were bright; she was permanently toothless, her manner suggesting wariness and welcome all at once. Around her waist was a colorful sari. She wore no earrings, and a dull silk scarf held back her heavy black hair. There was no "gypsy fortune-teller" look to her. Her face, in its ugliness, carried beauty.

"All right," Dina said. "I'll go."

"What the hell! We're not going to stop here! They're all the same! Take your money." Karen glared at the Indian woman. "And kiss that twenty goodbye if you get off that easy. All this mumbo-jumbo! Look, if we're going to get a taxi soon for the ride back, eventually."

She followed Dina anyway down a hallway into a kitchen filled with cats. There was no crystal ball or tarot cards, only a Mylar table, scrupulously clean countertops, and small modern appliances all around. The cabinets and floor were scrubbed shiny, and the only mysterious thing about were the slanted eyes of the many cats perched in every possible spot, on the microwave, refrigerator, countertop, and floor.

"Hey, Dina! Did I ever tell you I was allergic to cats?" Karen mumbled in Dina's ear, followed by a fake sneeze. Her friend ignored her and sat down on one of the plastic chairs. The look on Dina's face instructed Karen to be silent.

"You! Red hair! Sit down too! I make tea. Your friend needs to know this!"

"What's she need to know? I told you, we're not interested," Karen started up again but then stopped. Dina's unnatural silence worried her, so she complied and scooted a chair out with a loud squeal on the linoleum and sat down.

The woman busied herself with the tea, and as her back was turned, Karen waved a few fingers in front of Dina's stoic face, "Hey! Earth to Dina!" she whispered. "What are we doing here? Just say the word, and we'll go before one of these cats puts a spell on us!" But Dina had seen the old woman's eyes, as dark as knotty pine holes and full of mystery.

The Indian half turned. "You know, beautiful girl, what I mean."

"Of course, she must be referring to me," Karen wise-cracked, fussing with her hair.

"All angels are waiting like the film of an egg, only waiting for that small crack in the shell to seep through to us. *You* have made one of the cracks to expose them!"

"Now *you* wait." Karen was half on her feet, ready to do battle. "You see, Jews don't believe in angels, and since we're God's chosen people, we must be right! So cut out the angels business and—"

"Except, of course," the woman interrupted. Turning swiftly from the sink, she caught Dina in the grasp of her look, "while you let a few into our world, some angels come in and some are … not so good. You've witnessed one."

"I-I what?" Dina mumbled.

Karen slapped her own cheek. "Jesus fucking Christ!"

"And you know how!"

"The, the conjuration?" Dina's eyes flicked away from the Indian's face for the first time, and when she looked back, the sari nodded. Behind her head, an ugly gray cat dug at its ear with a paw and yawned, its mouth wide with fangs that looked like a snake's. The woman brought two steaming cups for her visitors.

Karen took the opportunity to nudge Dina. "Christ, she looks like a cross between the Wicked Witch of the West and Snow White's stepmother!" she whispered. "Who'da thought?"

Dina looked blank and scooted the cup over to take a small sip.

"This is no place for laughter!" the Indian set a sugar bowl on the table and looked directly at Karen. "You friend will experience much danger! It will circle! She may not even be aware of it!"

"How'd she hear me?" Karen muttered.

The room grew silent, and no one spoke for a minute. Dina stared straight ahead, unresponsive. Karen laughed shallowly for a moment and then, unable to stand the lack of conversation, whispered irritably, "What's going on, Dina? Conjuration? The one you told me about? With the slip of paper? How'd she know that? C'mon, let's get outa here! And does your tea taste … okay?"

"My name is Pramod," she said in a commanding voice. "I have much to tell, not all today. Will you come again? You are Dina, they call you? You were *meant* to come here, to visit here today."

Dina nodded. How did she know her name? She turned to Karen. "Shh, let's hear her out!" She slid her cup closer, her look suddenly nonchalant as if it were an everyday occurrence for a stranger to know all about her life.

"You must watch out for … an *evil one*."

"Evil one, huh?" Karen snorted, still not trusting Pramod, even though she had not asked for money. "Does she mean Evil Kinevil, who jumps the motorcycles? For *this* hocus-pocus, I gave up lunch?"

Pramod continued, "He moves through lives like a sieve. He chooses what and who, and he takes his time."

"Oh yeah, sure, babe." Karen slapped the tabletop with her hand. One of the cats resting nearby jumped in fright. "This bugaboo! Old lady nightmares—"

"And passes generation to generation, and none of us is immune!" Pramod continued, rolling her eyes expressively. "From the last person of evil, he travels through the connection of us like electricity, stops at one, hovers, and moves on … selecting … selecting.."

"Oh, I know! I get it! Electricity—Dina unplugged! Is that it?" Karen smirked, daring the woman.

"Silence, Red Hair! Of this danger, this evil *may* stop at her, but the conjuration was its entry—"

"I've had enough!" Karen cut her off. "We're leaving!" She wrenched her chair out then pulled Dina to her feet.

"What!" Dina's eyes were on Pramod, her gaze begging. "Tell me!"

"Sit. I speak."

"No, we *no* sit," Karen said, mocking her English. Due to her religious background, she was niggled at the insult of the remote possibility that these angels had any sort of control in the human realm. She herself did not believe in them and thought anyone who did was a fool and belonged in a league with Hummels and Hallmark.

"Evil doesn't always exist. It only needs an excuse." Her words were meted out lethargically, her voice like the low grating of steel against iron.

"Tell me!" Dina pushed Karen back, almost yelling. Her hands suddenly knuckled the chair back, her eyes blazing and frightened. "Tell me what he … it … this evil looks like!"

"A spool."

CHAPTER 26

She glided down the small hills of the bike trail, soaring under sallow-tipped leaves and red oaks. Her helmet perched low, she accepted the abandonment of the world's cruel pain. Braving the climb known to bikers and joggers as Suicide Hill, she shifted gears and began to level back down the other side, almost feeling in her body the rushes of Frank's orgasm and her own, the memory nearly blinding her. Riding back down the hill caused an exploding rush of air, a momentary panic, the squeamish loss of control, not unlike a shot of whiskey. Passing low beneath a yellow-leaved elm, she closed her eyes in sorrow, recalling not only Frank but also the other day—when Sonja died.

Sonja Luvanovich, who immigrated from Serbia more than five years ago, had attended college in Illinois and was now working at Sandoval. A pariah who sat at the lunch table alone, she was often seeing playing with her lanyards, braiding away. Why? It seemed almost a childlike distraction. When Karen and Dina were in the lunchroom, Sonja would occasionally glimpse from under her jet-black bangs, piercing Dina alone with her raven claw gaze. It was a wordless stare, telling and troubled; she would let the plastic pieces in her hands drop, eyes unmoving, and a conversation without words. Unnerved, Dina would hurriedly look away.

However, one time, she did give Sonja a meek smile, yet it went unreturned. Where was her family? Back in Serbia maybe. She seemed so young, twenty-two or twenty-three perhaps, but in her silence, she seemed so aware, her stillness and isolation somehow sheltering a deep understanding of the knowing world—and the unknown. Dina looked up again to smile, but Sonja was grimly gathering her bracelets and moving away from the lunchroom. No one ever saw her eat, as if she were a ghost, never needing to nourish herself.

A few days later, Dina passed her in the narrow hallway. Sonja's desk was far from Dina's office, so it was odd that she would use this hall. Dina's arms were loaded with books and files. In the hall narrow, however, Sonja made no attempt to let her pass. Instead, she stopped, bracing herself before Dina, forcing Dina to stop also. She was shocked at the woman's rudeness, but Sonja's pale eyes with darker centers ensnared her. Dina jerked when Sonja spoke; her voice was low, otherworldly.

The Serbian pointed to Dina's left. "You have angels on your shoulder." The accent was mysteriously calming. "One is fair, but one is dark. Beware!" Her inflection ascended on the last word. Then she glided away so silently in the direction she had come that Dina got the feeling that Sonja had never been there at all. Effervesced.

Now Dina's bike moved recklessly, forcing her to shift quickly, the gear rasping painfully. She felt the chill of air on her shoulder.

Was it the recollection or just the downward shift of wind? No, she should have simply worn a warmer jacket for October. Her thought hurried back again to that day. Last Friday. Why did she have to witness that? First her handiwork with the conjuration, then the ghost in the pool, then this ominous suicide from a woman whose only words to her were about angels on her shoulder.

Her mind flew to that Friday, when she was exiting Sandoval, pausing at the top of the steps that led to the sidewalk. In the streets, the cars moved quickly under a cinder-colored sky, their headlights lit up like pieces of an electric train, locked close together while rain sweated on their doors and hoods. Windows of the vehicle were obscure. From that distance, they looked almost driverless, and every car was hurrying.

Then the stop light changed.

Like a power surge, Sonja appeared on the street corner out of nowhere, enveloped in that weird light of traffic, her clothes surprisingly dry. Dina had been glancing her way as she fumbled for her umbrella tote. Sonja had not waited for the light.

It was Dina's belief that Sonja *knew* she was stepping in front of traffic, stepping in front of death. *As if she planned it* in timing with the moment that Dina was then walking out of Sandoval, just so *she* could be a witness to it! In a flash, Sonja's eyes skewered her, her head raised, her lips clearly mouthing, "Beware," and then the sedan struck, hurtling her over and over.

Dina screamed. A coworker, Maddie, exiting shortly behind her, said, "You okay? What happened?"

"Y-yes ..."

She pointed to the street and heard Maddie's scream.

Soberness instead of sadness overhung the office for days, no one quite knowing the victim well enough to be overly maudlin. Sonja's department manager, Hendricks, and some coworkers attended the funeral. Dina did not, instead cowering in her office, feeling shredded into pieces. Maybe she should have gone to the funeral. She did owe Sonja that, since she had *warned* her ...

About what?

"Small funeral, closed casket too. I guess the body was, well ..." Karen sauntered into her Dina's office. "You didn't miss much. Didn't see any of her family, at least not anyone who resembled her. Some Sandoval people from *her* department were there—Les, Tracy, Hendricks, of course. Frank was there ..." Dina glanced up at her, then back down to gaze solemnly at her desk.

"The most gorgeous coffin I've ever seen, as though it was pure gold! With no family to speak, where d'ya suppose the money came from for such an ornate ceremony? And the flowers, gardens of them! You Gentiles waste all that dough on death." Then Karen vanished out of her office.

Next, Dina heard the shuffle in the adjacent office and pieces of conversation "Taking up a donation in memory of Sonja to give to the Suicide Prevention Association."

The words trailed off, and Dina, aware that the donation-seekers would be upon her next, was already reaching into a locked drawer that contained some emergency dollars and small change. A scrap of something brittle brushed her hand as she reached in. Opening the drawer further, she ducked her head down to look. There, at the bottom of the gray metal drawer, mounted in front of the money, was a colorful lanyard bracelet like the ones Sonja had assembled. Dina examined it. It felt oddly warm, almost hot.

The next instant, the donation collectors were there. "Hi, we're here on behalf of Sonja—"

Dina jumped, dropping the little bracelet.

"I I know."

She handed over the currency.

"Thanks! That's really generous, considering …"

One of the collectors raised his eyebrows at the fifty-dollar bill she had given him.

When they had gone, Dina scoured the entire floor. She was never able to find the bracelet.

The bike coasted slowly. The sudden sight of an odd tree made her stop. Had it been here before? She tried to recall. Experienced cyclist that she was, she knew the trail like the back of her hand. In its rarefied state, the tree seemed to have several jutting branches v, perhaps skewered by recent lightning. It was malformed by nature and spirit-rendering to observe it. She shuddered as she walked toward it, her arms firmly grasping the handlebars as if they contained an invisible curtain that she could hide behind.

The poor tree was twisted strangely, bearing not a single leaf this early in the season, whereas most trees were a showcase now of colorful half-fallen foliage. What *was* so special that she had made her stop? The denuded spectacle niggled at her.

Go home now!

She gazed at the gnarled limbs. Would they sprout eyes like in the cute cartoons she had seen as a child?

Get on your bike and pedal fast!

The trail was getting darker and now. With the sun setting, eerie shadows formed that seemed to not to have been there before, branches finger-like and arthritic, whose digits pointed skyward in such an extreme way that a carpenter couldn't have pounded them there with any kind of tool.

I know *this tree was not here before!* she told herself. *I have traveled this trail a hundred times, and I have never seen it!*

But was it an oak or elm or … what?

It's dark and late and my mind is playing tricks, she thought. *It has been about ten minutes I have been looking at this dead tree, and yet, no one has passed me on either side of the trail! I'm tired and hungry, and my water bottle is empty …*

Still, she inched forward. What *was* that? A noise. Was it wheels squeaking? Gears clicking?

Get on your bike and pedal, damn it!

She knew where she was—Beaubien Woods, a particular section or trail she loved so well, knowing every mile, every bump, even to the larger stones along the asphalt. She never rode with a Walkman CD player; she *had* to hear the birdsong, the squirrel twitter.

A loud unusual clicking noise drew her attention. She could hear no bird or squirrel now. Only that click. No leaves rustling in the wind, no jabber of other bikers' conversation. She looked down at the chain of her own bike—at the gears, the wheels—and straddled the bike and moved it forward. Okay, the click was *not* bike gear noise. Her eyes rose up toward the branches. Everything was eerily silent. The click came again, and she stood up quickly, grabbing at the handlebars, knuckles white.

Did the sky seem suddenly darker? Had she even heard anything? It had to be the wind and she was losing her composure, what was left of it. All this hocus-pocus and conjuring, angels, Pramod, jealousy, fear—what did she expect coming to a dark, clammy woods at sunset, punishing herself?

A second, third, then fourth click came forth. The forest was no longer beauteous with dying sunlight and russet leaves. The air felt cold, unfriendly—like hell.

Now she turned the bike back up the trail and pedaled with every bit of stamina she could summon.

Get home! Get home! She followed the mantra unquestioningly.

Left in her wake, in the dark branches high above the forest floor, its oily body suspended from perpendicular branches, a ghoul as large as a church spire had lodged between two trees like a spider on a glossy black plastic lanyard. Dina had not seen this monstrosity because it had been behind her, and she had not turned around. The phantom's red eyes stared down at Dina's departure, carefully observing. It never moved on its own, although the slight wind, which had now picked up, swung its greasy strings back and forth like a multi-tiered hangman's noose. The branches clearly had been mutilated by this blackened entity. No human endeavor or force of nature, such as lightning, could have accomplished such destruction. The ghoul depended down now, the red laser eyes observing the wheels of Dina's bike as they moved, whirling away.

Never unwrapping itself from the braches now. The colossus remained so transfixed on Dina's departure that it appeared to not even know that its own jaw was opening and closing involuntarily, its ochre canine teeth grating harshly together in one hideous mechanical sound. Like chains and pulleys being hoisted!

Click. Click. Click.

CHAPTER 27

Dina stepped gingerly into the doorway of Pramod's house, sidestepping a cat that lay sleeping there. The animal looked at her in disgust with a perfunctory "meow" and quickly slipped away to other quarters.

"Pramod?" she called her voice doubt-filled and empty as a genuflection before icons. The long hallway lurked before her. She moved down along the walls sheepishly. "I-I know you're not expecting me ... The door was open."

Evening made the walls much more obscure, so unlike that bright September afternoon when she and Karen first stumbled upon this doorstep. It smelled now not so much like tea and incense but more like a curious musky vanilla, as if she had walked into an old hippie shop from the '60s that her mom spoke about.

"The smell would get you before anything else. It grabbed you from the sidewalk!" her mother would gush, her eyes focused back on an era Dina found it hard, if not impossible, to picture—that of her sensible parent strolling down Wells Street in Chicago under colorful and funky psychedelic signs, not lined with the yuppie boutiques it was today. "The places would be full of candles and bongs, with the low FM radio station in the background. Sometimes I found it hard to leave."

Dina would smile at this, shaking her head, saying, "Oh, Mom, not *you*."

"Oh yes, me! I was a poncho-clad hippie who practically lived in head shops, as they were call back then in 1968!"

Where was Mom now that she needed her for strength? And what would she think of her now, visiting some voodoo Indian woman, going down an eerie hallway when she wasn't expected? What if she got to the room at the end only to find some séance going on?

"H-hello?" she tried again.

"I am here," the voice tumbled back to her, rushing at Dina with urgency. "Come in the kitchen." Dina advanced upon the bright light at the end of the hall, which was small and wobbling before her like the approach of a train light in the darkness. She tiptoed, expecting a hail of bats any minute.

What am I thinking? It's close to Halloween, but I'm a grown woman! I'm just here to get advice about, about … what? Angels? Monsters? Or was it really about … *Frank?*

At the hallway's end, Dina peeked cautiously around the corner. She was assaulted by the bright kitchen light, which reddened her face with the warm comfort of the familiar. Rubbing her cheeks, she noted that the oven ticking in the background had perhaps attributed to the heat on her face.

"Hello, Pramod. I-I hope you don't mind the intrusion." The Indian sat at the table, looking smaller than Dina last remembered.

"I know you are hungry, child. I bake today because I knew you would come back."

"Y-you knew? How?"

"I know already you are worried about … danger. Sit and rest."

Dina sat down on an adjacent chair, replacing a skittish cat who scurried away in fear and joined two of his companions in front of the oven, where all three remained staring at her with inquisitive green eyes.

Pramod scooped up yet another black-and-white feline from the floor by her chair. "See, even the cats know you are afraid." She laughed softly as if the reason Dina had come wasn't all that serious. "If they could speak, they tell you what you *really* witnessed—and they know why."

"They do? They are? I mean …"

The cats did *look* friendly. The cloying kitties made her mind dart oddly in another direction. Maybe she should get a companion for Mellencamp?

Another animal? Who would depend fully on her responsibility for its existence? Was *that* why she lost Frank? Because of trust? Responsibility? Dependency? No! Her mind was spinning out of focus, roaring angrily out of its wistfulness for her pet and back to reality.

"Yes, child. Animals read you mind better than soothsayers, holy men, why, even your own mother. But that's not why you've come," Pramod observed, "to talk of animals. At least not the everyday domestic kind. Would you like some baked bread? Some tea?"

She was struck by the dichotomy sitting next to this small, dark, Indian woman, swathed in a sari and offering her bread and tea like some kindly English country woman, while she here to address a swirling demon on high, who seemed to leap into her face from a pool, from Sonja's warning, from a slip of paper! Like a befuddled child given too many options, Dina couldn't distinguish the truth from the unreal, and she slumped peevishly in her seat. The heat, the cats, the smell, and Pramod's speech discombobulated her. She tried, however, to drown out her swelling panic.

"Tea only, if it's not too much trouble."

"I tell you what you want to know—rather, *need* to know." Pramod tossed the cat off her lap with one hand and raised the teapot on the stove; the other grasped two slices of warm bread. "About what you saw, the suicide of the Yugoslavian girl—"

"You know about Sonja? Ah, did you hear about it or read it in the paper? Because of the traffic jam, her death was the result?" She felt suddenly protective of Sonja. "I thought they didn't publicize suicides in the paper."

"No, child, it is given to me. Close to my soul. Things I need to know to help you. I do not control those things that come to me. I only know *when* the calling is very strong." Pramod poured Dina's tea, looking directly at her. "And I hear only the parts of the whole picture. Evil things, unfortunately, I hear loudest of all, but then, it is why I was given such a gift—to help. To warn. Now that young girl, she experienced a great evil in her life."

"*Who* tells you this?" A light electric shock was trilling up Dina's spine.

Pramod ignored the question. "You were ... very fine to try to help keep that girl alive with your small kindnesses, and even though you failed, the effort is not unrecognized."

Dina shifted in her seat, ignoring her tea. "What has all that got to do with that evil thing that, that ..." She didn't want to raise the issue of the monster again, hoping that Pramod would bring it up and explain it away. Instead, they were getting off the subject.

"It *all* has to do with evil. You came about the dark angel. I know that. I am getting to that, you see. But, you are still unsure you want to know, aren't you?" Pramod tapped the table with a long fingernail. When Dina didn't answer, too confused now to speak, the Indian woman leaned back against her chair, her backbones touching the wood slats and snapping softly like the crackling of a wicker basket when handled.

The house was quiet, even the street noises seemed hushed. Dina touched her hair distractedly. Why was the old woman talking in riddles? Maybe she was insane.

Or I am! Why did I come?

"When something that old makes itself known in the modern world, there's always tragedy. *You* brought it forth, as I mentioned when we first met. This dark angel doesn't belong here. It's not happy. It knows of your unhappiness, was built upon its negativity, and it enjoys now, as you Americans say, 'making a mess of things.' Your coworker died trying to face the hell she was in because she attempted to free her mother from her country and was not successful."

"I-I thought she became suicidal because she was depressed over being so ostracized at work." How *did* Pramod know all this? Now Dina felt sick with fear, and she started to get up to leave.

"Wait! There are things humans do not understand in this world—and in other worlds. Please sit. It will all make sense, *if not now.*"

Dina complied. Something in Pramod's face compelled her. Maybe belief?

"You will ... *know* evil and how it touches someone you know directly. You will comfort strangers, if only with your interest, like a good angel who holds one's hand in the face of trouble. My comfort against evil is my own knowledge. And my responsibility is to tell these things to you. Soon you will learn of my *personal* history, and afterwards you will go on and finally face evil in your own way." Pramod sighed, a sigh that held the reality of an immutable past.

"So, my listening will help? Okay. But what do I care about evil? I just don't understand all this." Dina's head was pounding. It seemed as if Pramod was wailing. "Look, I just want to know why I saw a monster in my swimming pool! All these clues—"

"So, it arrived in a pool of water. This I did not know. Your face gives away many clues, especially your fear. It was greater than any fear you had before. The pool's monster is an embodiment of what you face! But you can render it helpless by your own good deeds, sort of a salvation. You must understand that I do not know where the knowledge comes from, as I have said. I only know that I must bring it to you. I hear it ... inside." Pramod pointed to her head and leaned in close, whispering, "You *must* trust me."

Trust. Was she hallucinating or what? Yet Dina willed herself to stay in her chair, hear her out. "Okay. But why me? I can't believe all of *this* spilled forth from a silly little conjuration! Come on, this is the 1990s, not the year 900!"

"It isn't going away. It never really does. That's the bad news. The good news is *you* have the power to recognize or even prevent evil in *your* world. Only time will tell if you succeed. It is something like … you opened the book, the dictionary, you close it."

"Me? I have power? And you hear all this inside? Is that how clairvoyance really works?" She wanted to laugh.

"This is all I know. All my soul will tell me. You believe, so you came. You believe in that conjuration while others laugh. You do not know yourself or even trust what your eyes have witnessed. It is *more* than just the loss of a boyfriend. You cast your line out into the universe, and you caught this specter. Now you must ready yourself to repair that tear that this evil has crawled through. The evil, after all, has no excuse. *You* are only a block to prevent its spread, prevent it from making its own excuse to exist."

"Let me understand this. So, I let this thing out somehow through a conjuration of my own making, and if I, let's say, succeed with some *good deed*, I'm preventing more evil?"

"It affects you most directly," Pramod said calmly.

Dina shook her head, refusing to accept such a crusade. She was exasperated and sad, her mind off evil and back on Frank. Pramod hadn't given her any solace about that!

As if reading her thoughts, Pramod clutched Dina's hand, a motherly touch. "You must listen to me, as I will soon reveal all I carried inside me. From listening, you will gain strength. It is and was a pity and a horror, my own denial of facing an evil that stayed with me all these years. It has swallowed up a part of me. In telling, it will help you *and* me." Her black eyes darted around in shame. "Part of me, my family, I have never revealed. I have no children, no husband to tell, only my knowledge of the things beyond earthly realm. That is all I have. Yet this shame troubles me. I want to confess, so to speak. Will you listen?"

Dina nodded, surprised that Pramod would readily relate such a profound confidence to her.

"Please do not question why I will one day give you my story. Your *other ear* will hear the devastation in my life, and somehow you will correlate, assimilate, and understand—just as you *heard* the Yugoslavian girl."

"But I never heard! She said very little about her country. I-I really didn't help." Dina wanted to mention to Pramod that the country was no longer called Yugoslavia, but she didn't want to embarrass the old woman. Because Pramod had been talking about her own past, perhaps she was *still* there in it somehow and that was how she remembered its geographic nomenclature.

"You heard with ears that were your heart, which is what evil despises."

"Oh. Okay."

Well, if the old woman felt better prattling her story to her, what was the harm? In her mind, Dina envisioned that perhaps listening to someone else's misery would somehow assuage her own pain over Frank. Nothing had worked to purge it so far.

The Indian's eyes were grave, but she continued to grasp Dina's hand. "You *will* avert evil. It will be gone, but maybe, like mine, not without some suffering and loss." Pramod hung her head, as if she were popping in or out of some trance—Dina could only guess. *And what loss? I already lost Frank! How does she know I'll come back to see her? What is she talking about?* Dina was almost dizzy with so many warnings.

"Okay. I mean, all right. I-I guess so. I'll come back."

"We will talk another time. For now, I am very tired."

Pramod waved her good night and shuffled off to another room. Dina remained sitting there for a few moments, her tea with the warm bread grown cold.

CHAPTER 28

Dina was asleep, and the dream started up, detaching her from her bed as if she were suspended on a pendulum watching a stage. She heard a whirring sound, like the winding of a sewing machine bobbin. She twisted the sheets and heaved from side to side.

She tried to yell but couldn't. Sonja appeared. The Serbian was sitting, crouched almost, and her hands were busy braiding. The scene focused on her hands, from which coils and coils spun along her fingers until the tails of this black weaving fiber leapt up, swirling and ascending through her digits. The fiber became blacker, and Sonja's controlled hands kept feeding slack until, finally, two serpent-like creatures merged from the long skein, transforming into one large, odious monster. The braiding continued on, an angry spool of black hurling itself around the room of its own volition until it reached the throat of Sonja.

The dream switched next to Dina, as she saw herself in her office, working quietly at her desk. The threads entered the room now, lashing around her like whips, the spool transporting an unctuous black muffler encircled her throat now, cutting off her air. Dina, in her sleep, coughed and choked, dizzily trying to wake herself up, but she could not. The dream seemed poised to destroy her too, like Sonja, who had destroyed herself.

Suddenly the black neckband surrounded her. From far off, radio music was humming, crackling.

"Ha! Ha! You'll remember this one, I think! Especially all you baby boomers!"

Dina jerked open her eyes, fear hitchhiked away by the rock and roll. Fully awake now, she thought about the lashings and the hideous creature they were attached to. *Did I really bring this embodiment forth? With my conjuration?* Pramod's admonishments sat heavily on her heart. *Did I miss my chance in* not *helping Sonja?* She hung her head ashamedly, silently cursing the dream that had seemed to start her day now with one of self-accusation, along with, of course, the inevitable observation of Frank gushing over Toni during Boyko meetings—a death-knell reminder of Sonja, a death knell for her hopes of reconciliation with Frank.

CHAPTER 29

"Your life is out of proportion, and I don't recognize you anymore! This lack of function is going to affect your job, and *then* where will you be?" Karen shouted to Dina. She had stopped by unannounced at Dina's condo to check on her friend on a warm October afternoon. Dina sheepishly let her in; deciding to ignore her would only make Karen more combative. Putting up a false demeanor at work all week was exhausting. The last thing she needed was scolding, and she wished only that the lanky redhead would just go away. Dina remained slumped back in her easy chair, staring out a window without seeing, barely hearing Karen's sermon. "Get a grip! I think that encounter with that voodoo woman—what's-hername—did more harm than good!"

Dina angled her face away from the window, reluctant to mention her other visits to Pramod. "Everything's so far down inside me, this feeling ..."

"Uh, that's called nausea."

Dina smiled now. It was the first time, outside the exigencies of work, that Karen had seen her grin. "No, Frank needs me, needs my help. Pramod has nothing to do with the feeling. She just awakened it."

"Why? What?" Karen had been standing with her arms crossed, and now she relaxed her posture and slumped toward a wall surrounded by a door and some shelves. She picked up a trinket from the shelves and pretended to examine it.

"I don't know that either. I'm afraid I really don't have an answer. Maybe you should just go," Dina said dejectedly, "since your arguments won't get anywhere with me."

"But, babe, I worry!" Karen threw the trinket back on the shelf and moved forward with arms like two welcoming tree branches.

"No need to, really." Dina stood, accepting the embrace. "You've seen me functioning at work. No need to mother me."

Karen unclasped her arms now and stepped back. "I won't accept this answer. It's like he's put you in prison, and you're only too happy to stay there with your tin cup, groveling! You've got to unshackle yourself from him!"

"I *want* to be in prison." Dina's voice was low, like a cat's growl, her eyes determined. The unearthly look chilled Karen.

"I-I just don't know you anymore, I—"

"Here's what you can do." Dina lifted her chin sullenly. "If you're my friend, do what you can *when* I ask for help. I know this sounds strange, but I feel sometimes, in an odd way, that I may just need your help one day. Even if what I propose might seem awkward or … dangerous!"

"Babe, you know I'd give my right arm for you. Are you mixed up in something because of all this ghostly stuff you saw? Although I can hardly believe you saw more than dead leaves and maybe a lost bikini top come out of that swimming pool!" Karen joked.

"That has nothing to do with it—and yet it does." Dina looked away "Maybe *all* things are connected in some way by some force. Even so, I know what I saw in the swimming pool. It was real!"

"The Creature from the Black Lagoon, er, swimming pool?" Karen touched her friend's cheek and turned Dina's head back so their eyes met.

"You didn't promise me!"

"I—"

"Promise me!" The command was filled more with fear than urgency.

"Okay! Okay! I only promise not to incite any more arguments with you. But I can't promise that I won't worry, however hell-bent you become. I'll be there for you."

"I think I am going to wait it out," Dina said decidedly. "Toni can't last forever. I'm hearing there's a possible conference in December at Boyko headquarters. She won't be there, and maybe we could … re-connect!" A glimmer of hope was in her eyes, but Karen knew well that Dina had probably been strategizing about this for days. "I'll be there if I have to crawl."

"Yeah, great," Karen said with a surly smile. "Even though we're still in October, honey, the witching month. Just what we need, you and your preternatural behavior about winning Frank back. By the way, I feel that ghost you saw in the pool was a sham, you know."

"Was it? You appeared to believe me when I told you about it that day in your office," Dina said defensively.

"Hey, well what has gotten you but all the bad dreams you seem to talk about, which means probably no sleep and, most importantly, no Frank! Am I right?"

"Time will tell. As I said, I want to wait out Frank's, er, indiscretion. Believe what you want."

"But I *do* remember the voodoo Indian indicating that something was bad. That angel paper you wished on?"

"Bad only if you look at it in certain ways. In other ways, it's telling."

"How telling? The only thing it's telling me is the world is messed up! You can't really think a scrap of paper caused anything bad!"

"Yes, Pramod did say my conjuration was bad. But maybe it's only bad for some people, people who aren't really so nice." Dina was starting to sound crazier by the minute, and Karen was beginning to think it was too extraordinary an autumn Sunday to listen to any more lunacy.

"Maybe I had better go. Do you at least have food in that refrigerator? And get out of those pajamas! I don't want my non-functioning friend slumped around her apartment with her bed as her best friend and not me. Humor me a little, will you?"

"I will, and I do have food."

Karen was backing toward the door. "Gotta go, but I promise to help you any way I can. Feel better about yourself, girl. You can always count on me."

CHAPTER 30

The days of October did not fall neatly into a pile; they were as leaves tossed from trees, scorching her heart. Leaves that were meant to fall on her grave? Or someone else's? Dina took no pleasure in the welcoming coolness, the riotous colors, or any kind of joy that accompanies seasonal change. She viewed her life as one giant comedy/tragedy, likely to end badly and ironically loaded with absurd characters: Karen, the crazy clown; Big Sandy, a wicked and evil employee; Mr. Hendricks, a fumbling and inexperienced jester not wise enough to somehow excuse the former lovers from a project that welded them together; Frank, a bona-fide romance-book cad; Toni, the superficial vixen; and finally herself, the unrequited and blasé lover.

Frustration loomed every day, and as the completion of the Boyko project approached, Mr. Hendricks innocuously poked his head in to address Dina, singing out, "How are you doing?" He was so ignorant and frivolous! Didn't he have eyes or ears? She wanted to throw the files in his face, stuff the contracts down his throat, and then, following this rampage, go on to stab a letter opener into Frank's heart. Wouldn't that make the news! It only comforted her for a few minutes until finally she simply laid her head down on her desk to shut her eyes and welcome the blackness.

"How do I get rid of this, this longing?" she had asked on the next visit to Pramod.

"One never 'gets rid' of anything impacting our lives. Even life itself, as you know, continues to evolve. The trick is in the harnessing. You are talking about your depressed emotions, I assume?" Pramod sat at her kitchen table, the usual place for their talks. She was dressed in a golden sari and had a yellow cat on her lap.

"Yes, I—"

Pramod stood to let the glowering orange tabby out a small back window. "Of course, I knew the moment we met that you were one who had trouble putting aside overly strong feelings to conserve, say, good mental health. Only objects can be emulsified. We can throw away cans, glass, and scrapbooks—these tangibles gone the moment they leave our hands. But emotions, ah: good, bad or apathetic, they are an ever building tower. Some emotions form a foundation, some walls, some even broken windows or stagnant moats that surround us. Emotions are ever moving, suspended in time, never to go away. They only transmogrify into memories, and the emotions hold fast to those memories, much like a diamond stored in a safe."

"Oooh," Dina said sadly, "can't I *do* something—"

Pramod interrupted her, "Some would point out pain as being a necessary evil to advance ourselves spiritually. But pain is the greatest of God's amusements—unequal, indiscreet, lurking at the fringes of a beautiful day that we want to enjoy. The laughing crowd we see, perhaps a group of merry people. Imagine it! Close your eyes—now!"

Dina obeyed.

"Can you see it? Feel the crowd? The park? Where people gather?"

"Yes."

"Keep looking. These people have not a care in the world—"

"Well," Dina muttered sarcastically, "now, that is not always true."

"Shhh! That's my point! When you yourself scan the crowd," Pramod's voice, low and lilting, somehow coaxed the image into view, "you want very much to have *their* fun, *their* gaiety! Desperately you want this! You find yourself wishing to *be* them! It is because you are at your very lowest—and then! The realization comes rolling forward at you, like a tidal wave!"

"What? I-I don't understand!"

"Your own special foresight, that 'special knowledge' of yours, tells you everything. You just don't want to admit it to just anyone. You are *not* like those everyday individuals! You *more* than sense that someone in that crowd has pain as deep and as sharp as death! And you can sense that that atmosphere of evil lurks above him like a talisman. Oh, I can see it. I can always pick that *one* out of a crowd, no matter how hard they laugh, how big they smile and fool everyone."

"I am?" Dina looked doubtful. "I mean, you can? How?"

"Because, somewhere, that pain will be, as I remind you, a part of that person's anatomy, for lack of a better word, absorbed into the body and into all its actions. Although a person *could* have chosen to lean toward the face of goodness, learn from hurt. That is the mystery. Don't look to compare to others." Pramod paused here. "As pain can turn evil. Forces tell me. It will come."

Frightened a little by Pramod's tone, Dina asked, "How do you know? Your psychic ability? You *know* I feel things, although only they come at me like some vague miasma."

"And I knew it all about you from the first, as you recall. Although what I know has less to do with psychics and more to do with psychology. Soul reading, I call it. A reading directly from the heart." Pramod paused. "Although I am sorry to say your pain will continue a great deal longer. Many months. But it will pass in a glory whose importance you do not yet understand. You cannot fathom it ... today."

"In glory?"

"You will understand one day. Let yourself *really* live day to day, even though you feel like dying inside. This is all I can say."

Pramod whisked her sari close to her, stood up, and let in the contrary cat, who stood at the window meowing, having changed his mind about the outside. Dina knew their meeting was over, and she walked out into the darkness, once again confused.

❧

Later on in October, Dina gave in to another visit. When she arrived, she would first sit quietly listening to anything the old woman had to say, talking about weather, the neighborhood. The place possessed a cathedral feel, Pramod's voice, like a good Sunday sermon. Although it had been many months since Dina had attended Mass, she felt these visits were better than the hypocrisy surrounding her in the pews of a church. As a teen, parishioners exited the services whispering about their neighbors and their lurid, corrupt ways. Why bother to come?

Pramod studied her.

"You already caused a storm in the heavens. A stairway. A path where either good or evil could reach earth. Unfortunately, evil has won this time—with your conjuring. Evil found its small but lucrative advantage in you. Be careful!" Pramod's eyes widened, then abruptly narrowed, like Venetian blinds hiding dark, ominous pupils with enigmatic meaning. "So many incidents are filling your mind. The dead girl. The swimming pool. Your ex-lover. The conjuration." Dina leaned closer, caught up in the power of Pramod's quick perception of herself.

"God, the Holy One, the personification of good, or whatever one believes, He has the full capacity of kindness, but is not only benevolent. He can't be. He is an armed warrior, ready to take on the evil. It has gone on through time. This evil has you transfixed. You don't know where to take it, what it means, who to trust, above all, who would believe—am I right?"

"Yes."

"Child, you need to know about other things in life, which I cannot tell you about right now."

"Why not? You keep hinting at telling me about your past. I might need the information," she protested, although she couldn't understand herself or Pramod right now. Nor could she understand why she felt this way, so lost, untrusting. Perhaps it really was that hazy harbinger inside her, as familiar as one of her limbs, trying to scope out the reasons. "All this and about Frank," she whispered now, as though the mention of Frank did not seem as lofty a subject as the things Pramod was trying to explain.

"You *will* know, child, eventually. Now we must speak of other things."

There was a long pause, and Dina leaned back and dropped her arms into her lap, a gesture of despair, knowing the subject of Frank had to again be pushed aside.

"I need you to know the vehicle evil uses right now."

"Why?" Dina complained, frustrated with the allegories. She didn't care if Pramod connected all these things in weird hyperboles as long as she could feel a little solace when she left. She felt sullen and sick, wanting to leave Pramod's and go, where? Instead, she stayed.

The Indian sensed her anguish, but instead of reaching for Dina's hand, she actually chuckled. Dina looked up affronted, but Pramod merely grabbed the teapot to refresh her cup.

"Ten thousand, twenty thousand volumes have been written, and still more coming to ascertain—what? Why the need for pain? Dina, you have a weapon against your personal pain as well as the evil you brought in."

"Stand up against evil? You referred to a vehicle. What are you talking about? I respect you are older and wiser because of the life you have lived and all the things you've experienced so far from my everyday world. You seem to know ... unforeseen futures. I believe this, but it is not really why I came ..." She trailed off melancholically, and because she sensed something profound, yet elastic between both of them, she changed the subject and boldly asked, "How old you are?"

"I am nearly eighty."

"Eighty! And yet you told me once you've had no cancer, no serious illness, no osteoporosis, Alzheimer's, arthritis, or even an upset stomach! I thought you would be decades younger!"

Pramod seemed almost astonished at this revelation. "Why God couldn't give me the distraction of an illness! It would take away the time and energy for all I have to do for this world!"

"Then ... but ... why? Why tell me? Why not tell others? Speak to the whole world, let people know—"

Pramod chuckled. "But that would be egotistical, as if I were demonstrating my sensitivity to show off my importance. Enlightened people *never* have to be ostentatious. You can claim your own entitlement to your gift; however, your incredible beauty does make you a bit ostentatious. Beauty *should* make you humble, as it is a gift given to those fortunate enough to know not to manipulate with it. Others have beauty. You are not unique. Take care not to overshadow this obvious gift of clairvoyance. This and kindness are part of a package you received at birth. It is almost like armor. Beautiful people *can* be evil, but kind people, like you, well, it is not seen."

"I know I am undeserving of these so-called gifts—my looks. And yet, possessing them, my life is even more troubled! Attractiveness is meted out so randomly—*by a higher power*. Why me? Why isn't everybody—?"

Pramod interrupted, "Use your beauty for higher good! You must be responsible for it. The gift was given as a reason! I know so!"

"How?"

"Child, all your life, you have been using your beauty unwisely. Why don't you think people would want to hear from you, learn from you, a beautiful, deep-thinking woman? Of course, there will always be ne'er-do-wells who judge you and believe entitlement to beauty suggests callowness in everything else."

"But—"

"Beauty really isn't truth. Truth is a tool that you turn into a help. And is it not an unconscious effort that society puts the most attractive people on TV to give the news? In advertisements? We are *all* vehicles. That you cannot deny. Stay strong. Be what you are and nothing *worse*."

Dina shook her head. Pramod felt she was somehow *chosen*? Because of her looks? It was surreal. The ghostly light of the kitchen, Pramod's creepy words made her squirm.

"Know that sometimes, it is unexpected to learn that a beautiful woman wants to shrug off all the compliments and give back—in a different way." Pramod took a photo from beneath her sari and nodded. "That woman grows tired of compliments and realizes her power *within* is the *real* compliment. Here is a photo of my mother when she was young."

The photo, dingy and obscure, showed an unbelievably gorgeous woman. The chiaroscuro of shadow along the angular planes of her face and her jaw line gave her a look of intelligence and serenity without artifice or smugness. It was the kind of beauty that made other pretty women look away in deference, knowing there was no comparison. Dina gasped.

"Beauty is on this earth for nothing but to impart good. Human beauty inspires, but it has a duty also to mankind," Pramod said solemnly. "Work with it, outward and inward, a treasure for all time."

Dina thought she knew what Pramod was trying to say, that beauty was really only a help. A *tool*. Did Pramod's words somewhat imply that she might *never* have Frank? She turned to leave.

"Wait!" Pramod said, "Your tool keeps you running, you know, to catch up to yourself. To *protect* it all."

Dina gasped. Now what could *that* mean, and how had she somehow heard her thought?

"And soon you will run for yourself but stop for others," Pramod finished solemnly.

Dina shrugged and kept on walking to the door, dismissing the Indian's strange statement as again yet another of her confusing mantras.

CHAPTER 31

Plunging into the placebo of work, kidding herself about Boyko, whose advancement was desultory at best and infinite procrastination at worst, Dina decided, with November now approaching, that the project needed her undivided attention if she was going to maintain the schedule of implementation. She worried that her lackadaisical attitude toward the completion of Boyko might delay it, or worse, expunge her from participating in it altogether, and that she couldn't bear. At least being able to encounter Frank was better than nothing at all. Futilely, she tried to wrest her thoughts back to the many phone calls and paperwork at hand to be attended to. Had Hendricks become aware of her turbid pace? She was scared.

Finally, one late October afternoon, she shooed away Karen's quizzical and disapproving looks as her friend put on her coat to leave. The redhead knew of Boyko's limping pace and thought Dina was gunning for more stress with this self-appointed after-hours work.

"Are you going to pamper yourself forever with uninterrupted thoughts of Frank while the Boyko idles even more, even in these late hours? Do you really need to stay on after five and work? What is it?"

Dina did not answer her friend but only glared. She wouldn't waste after-five hours woolgathering! She would work! Be proactive! Karen left, shaking her head.

It was now the second of these nights that Dina stayed behind. The cleaning service had come and gone. No one so far had noticed except Hendricks. There was nobody to bother her amidst the quiet cubicles outside her office—or so she thought.

The tap on the door of Dina's office was so slight that the staccato click of Dina's computer keys buried the sound until, finally, the deep voice that had opened the door broke through her typing.

"Hello? You working late too?"

She rose up, back straight in her chair with a jerky kangaroo hop to her feet, the chair bumping backward against the plaster walls. "Jesus, Sandy! You scared the hell out of me!"

"Sorry." He shrugged and ignored her ominous glare, which she'd hoped would send him away quickly, but he lumbered into her office anyway. "It's just, I get a little lonely on my side of the world, if you know what I mean." He picked up her grandmother's photo off the desk and fidgeted with the frame, rubbing it a little too indolently, almost lasciviously. Dina was disgusted. A shy grin came to his face, purely sham. Behind his eyes, he was breathing her inward all to himself while he replaced the frame.

"What do you want, Sandy? I'm a little too busy for this 'lonely' nonsense!" Dina demanded testily. She scooted her chair back into position and detachedly raked her chestnut hair back with one hand. A pencil was perched behind her ear, and she removed it now and tossed it on her desk in annoyance. "I only need about fifteen minutes to wrap up." She glanced at the digital read on the computer. Eight o'clock. "Then I'm calling it a day. I'd really like to talk," she lied, "but if I get this finished, I can probably find a cab at this hour and leave my car. I'm too tired to drive."

"Can you now?" Sandy interrupted, shifting his bulk from side to side, leering at Dina despite her arrogant attitude. She despised this colossus in her office, his elephantine shape wedged into her world, messing with her head. Like the discovered refrigerator box disregarded in someone's alley when she was a kid, Dina remembered warning other neighborhood children against entering it, dared them not to intrude upon her refuge.

To her, it was safe, semi-dark, and close, but the kids would inevitably come barging in anyway, destroying that obscure nest of solitude that she wanted all to herself. The difference now was that her displeasure had fear sprinkled in. This was her four-walled world. What could Sandy have to say?

"Y-yes," she stammered, "so excuse me. If you just go, I can finish. Perhaps I'll talk to you, ah, ah, tomorrow?"

"Why put off tomorrow what you can do today? A stitch in time, so they say."

Sandy's smile was a smirk. Why was he dallying in these stupid aphorisms? She wrinkled her nose at his comments as she conjured up Ben Franklin. Sandy even looked like him, without the white blowsy hair and bifocals. They both had ruddy complexion and squirrelly blue eyes, but Ben, she had read, had been a real man for the ladies, knowing women and their finer points, their highly tuned sensitivity to flattery. Sandy just left women with a bad feeling. She remained standing, impatient for his exit. Sitting back down would signal some compromise.

"Why don't you sit down and be comfortable?"

Had he read her thoughts?

"I only want five minutes," he whined, leaning his arm on the wall. With his sleeves rolled up to the elbow, the elevated bicep exposed … What was that? A tattoo? She had never seen him with his sleeves rolled up. No one in the office had. His white "sausages" with downy hairs repulsed her. What *was* that thing on the tattoo?

Sandy never budged but moved close enough to extend his other arm, and with his hand, picked up a curled brown strand of Dina's hair and examined it tenderly. "Dina, you're so beautiful. I just thought you may need a shoulder to cry on, you know, since Frank. Well, you know, friend to friend, nothing more." He hoisted his shoulders back, a movement trying to show he was earnest.

"No, I don't need anyone, thank you." Did the man have no shame, proselytizing his friendship as if he were hawking papers on a corner? In her shakiest voice, she pulled the curl of hair away, saying icily, "I'll thank you not to touch me. The office rumors are none of your business." She leaned over and shut off her computer and gathered the Boyko papers. "You know I think I'm going now. I can finish this tomorrow."

"I'll go with you." The hulk moved in front of her, barring her exit.

"No, Sandy." She pushed him slightly, trying to unblock her way. A fleeting impression crossed her mind just then: she as a small, colorful flower in the inexorable path of a Caterpillar road grader tractor. She shivered but kept collecting the papers while his tattooed arm came forward from its place on the wall and took up one of her own hands as if to kiss or caress it. His manner was obsequious, his breath smelled, and Dina recoiled fully, trying to get her hand back.

"I could make it worth your while, you know. Just one date. Really, nothing more. Give me that chance. I've admired you so much." His eyes glassed over, softer, but Dina wondered what was behind them. Something treacherous and foul? With her own wall of pain to contend with, she didn't want to examine *his* baggage. She finally got her hand free.

"I—"

"I know you are so sweet and nice. You don't deserve a schmuck like Frank. In fact, I know you're the nicest woman—ah, person—here at Sandoval. I know you look beyond everyone's faults, so it's not my appearance that makes you hesitate. I really don't want to sleep with you. We could just talk. I mean, I can't ever hope to be close to you like that. You know, I have plenty of money. You could be taken to Scoosi and all the finest places on Rush Street and Michigan Avenue. We'd have fun. No one at the office would have to know. Not even that red-headed shrike, Karen. No one would have to know. Unless you told them—"

"I-I can't," she insisted in a quiet, bottled-up voice. She now noticed that his eyes had a distant focus, as if he were not really looking at her. He seemed to be watching something else going on in his brain, something internalized that wasn't normal.

Sandy *was* watching some other vision, and it was not the thrilling, good-looking lady before him. He seemed to be robotically turning around a panorama, unfolding it now like a map, and he no longer saw or sensed Dina. Before his inner eye, in that split second, he saw the vile ugliness of his past, of his childhood. Without being aware of it, he pushed himself directly in front of Dina now, his belly forcing into her breasts because of his size.

"Be nice, now," he slurred almost drunkenly, and in a semi-daze, reached around and gave her breast a squeeze. With the other hand, he fondled her ass.

The room felt airless. A coffin! Dina cleared her throat loudly but did not move away, eying Sandy cautiously with an ugly sneer, as if he were a violent aberration to be spat upon. Through gritted teeth, she ordered, "I said get back and get out! *Now!*"

Big Sandy gave her an obsequious look that made her queasy. Where *was* he now in his head? He did not move. Was he mentally in the room with her at all? His smile remained, and his eyes pivoted slightly.

Dina growled, "You know there have been sexual harassment suits thrown at people in this office before."

Big Sandy's mouth went rubbery. He did not look ready for a tussle, but not because Dina's words stopped him. He harked back to that faraway look and appeared not to be looking at her but down at his arm.

The look alarmed Dina so much she could only stare. The big branchlike arm fell away from her body, and she was able to step quickly aside, but not before she saw what he was doing. He was intently studying his tattoo, an image she could discern now, scribed with fiendish and ghoulish figures displayed. The eyesore reminded her of the hideous gargoyles she'd seen on the churches in France on a college trip, only the tattoo's figures were a hundred times worse.

That monster in the pool had tattoos!

"Evil's Excuse," the writing said amid the garish figures. The drawing was as black as coal and seemed to almost surround his arm, as if it were crawling up.

"Evil's Excuse … Eeee! Yeah," Sandy's mucilaginous voice came out of the box of a man, a Frankenstein's monster sound, ghoulishly framing every syllable. He ignored Dina now.

Quietly she minced toward her desk so as not to disturb Big Sandy's quasi-catatonic state, grabbed her purse from the drawer, cradled the files in her arm, and ran.

CHAPTER 32

The next morning, Dina thought about calling in sick, since an encounter with Sandy might be unavoidable, and she couldn't bear the insipid innuendos he'd toss at her. Before he was a headache, a necessary inevitability that she had to tolerate; after yesterday, she saw the slime and evil he truly was.

Big Sandy had a history with the firm and a chumminess with Mr. Hendricks that made her question bringing up sexual harassment issues, especially since there were no witnesses. She knew Sandy would bluster, playing down the incident, put blame in her arena, and the whole thing sickened her. Still she argued with herself, chastising her cowardliness. What and when Big Sandy doesn't get from a person, he remembers, and this cold thought caused her to hesitate pursuing a lawsuit.

But facing Frank? Today? After what happened yesterday? Both men seemed to be driving her to madness, but mostly she felt like Sandy's target, and this realization made her suck in oxygen in quick gasps, the air feeling brittle in her lungs. Where once romance had been lofty, full of pleasurable power, pain was a foreign thing, an outsider invading her world with a simpering smile of welcome.

So screw Sandy! The buffoon! Why was he sniveling over his arm? Of all the horrible things she remembered about last night, that blank abandoned stare he had on his face as she fled the office was the most disturbing, the way he was fixated on some thought *behind* that tattoo! What did it all mean?

And then there would be Karen. Dina debated whether to tell her about the attack. The redhead would obviously go commando on her, insisting she wind the noose around Big Sandy's neck. "Finish him off for good! Rid the office of him! No one likes him. He could be fired, and you'd be doing us all a favor. Besides, I warned you about staying late." She could just hear Karen's chastisements now.

She pulled a cover up over her shoulder now. The room seemed chilly, Big Sandy and Boyko far away. With the pain came rage. Was Frank the kind of man whose love life was spent as a passerby? She thought back to the meeting in the conference room, Toni's mellifluous voice saying, "I'll just talk to *our honey*, Frank, to okay the final details of this research." Had she really called him "our" honey?

For today, the casual ebb and flow of the office seemed like sudden quicksand to step delicately around. She decided that the best plan on this cold, gloomy morning was to remain buried deep under her bed covers, a handful of tissues in her grip. Let Big Sandy pontificate and conjecture about her absence.

CHAPTER 33

On the Saturday morning following the attack, Dina remained quite shaken. Big Sandy had scared her, even beyond the brief physicality of his implied intention; she feared the unspoken threats from so big a colossus as the most frightening. Her world felt upside down, and yet she forced herself not to think of retribution.

The one image that hounded her. That tattoo. What was he trying to proclaim? He was certainly a scary and intimidating enough individual. Why promote such a thought? What was his story?

She decided to go to Pramod's, because while talking about the flotsam and jetsam of human inclinations, Dina found the woman's voice soothed her, seeped into the insecure cracks of her own nature, warming them, effacing them, and perhaps even changing them by way of Pramod's indirect way of interpretation. She now knocked on the Indian's door, yoo-hooed her way out of the rain and thunder, which had suddenly blown up and sent Devon Avenue shoppers popping into doorways and queuing under colorful store awnings. Immediately she felt the warm welcoming milieu of incense, the familiar sidling of a cat against her legs as she entered. Pramod was there, of course. Almost as if she knew Dina would come, she had the piping hot tea in both her own cup and another across from it.

"Welcome. You are troubled." It was a statement rather than a question.

"Y-yes, how did you know?"

"I know."

"I'll get right to the point, Pramod. As you know, I am upset, and this time, it is not about my, er, ex-boyfriend. It's … something else."

Pramod jerked her chin at Dina to sit down. "Go on."

"I-I was attacked. I mean, we have this heavy set creepy man in our office. I don't even know his real name, as he was working there long before I started. They call him Big Sandy because of where he was from and because he is so fat. Well, like I said." Here, Dina paused to withhold her stuttering by gulping some tea. It was surprisingly just the right temperature and did not have to cool. So odd.

"He's a rather miserable man who no one likes, maybe in his mid- to late-thirties, and there's something suspiciously threatening about him. I mean, he's big—not in the jolly Santa Claus way—but mean. Nasty somehow. A person who you would meet just once and not want to ever be around again. He takes advantage of people's weaknesses. He's sullen and seeks revenge on people who don't do things his way or, like me, shun his advances. I'm afraid and …." Dina trailed off. Pramod kept nodding, her face trance-like. Dina could not read any emotion. "Well, anyway, last night, I was caught off guard, being in the office late, and all of a sudden, he was just … there. And although he didn't really assault me—"

Pramod interrupted "He did not hurt you?"

"N-No. I got away. He touched me once, inappropriately but it wasn't the advance so much that bothers me. When he moved to grope me, he had, well, this tattoo on his arm that said." Dina paused. "Evil's Excuse."

Pramod recoiled a bit, her posture ramrod straight. Her eyes pierced Dina's own, and she said in a low voice, "This man is extremely evil, I must warn you. You must stay away from him at all costs."

Dina blinked twice, dumbfounded at her friend's sudden body language and ominous tone. "How is that possible without quitting?"

"Just avoid him."

"B-But why would anyone wear a tattoo like that? What is it saying about the owner's character? And he needs all the help he can get. I mean, I've seen dragons and ugly faces and skulls on people's arms and legs and all, but there was something about *this* one that totally unnerves me. It all harkens back to the ugly tattoo I saw on that swimming pool creature and the sound it made, that moan. I think the words were the same."

"You don't want to understand. It is almost a sign—no, a prophesy. There is an emotional nature to evil. And he who wears this warning embraces it, embellishes it! This is no dragon or skull. Those depictions are paraphernalia worn by people who are rough and tough or want to appear so. Big Sandy adorns himself with this warning because it is in his soul, and he is not play-acting. It is a mark of evil, and I must make you aware of how people like that come to excuse themselves *and* their actions by it."

Dina was fascinated by the explanation, which seemed creepier than Big Sandy himself. The room was quiet for a bit, and then she spoke. "You act like you know about this evil personally. You spoke once about your mother in India and that she was killed. Did that have anything to do with—?"

Pramod interrupted, "Let me tell you further about this excuse. Please, promise me you will be wary of this man. You see, people have infinitesimal ways of giving their own evil-doings an excuse. They say, 'The boss was pushing me so hard, so I shot up my coworkers.' Or 'My upbringing was terrible, so I took it out on my wife and beat her.'" Pramod let out a sigh. "Or 'The order came from Colonel Dyer, and he was in charge—so we killed.'

"The truth is, evil *has* no excuse. Evil is evil. No one knows why it worms its way into one human heart and not another—even in the same family, with identical backgrounds. Evil is not a breaking point. It is a turning point. One person shuns the evil and musters on through disappointment, sorrow. The other *creates* his own behavioral explanation for wrongdoing. These are the people who give evil its excuse. In your case, Big Sandy surmised, 'Dina was tempting me,' even though you were not.

Or 'She inveigled me, forced me into attacking her because she did not recognize my need to possess her and that only I should have her!'

"The excusers know this and fall back on all their own malignant deeds in the world. To them, they can excuse anything. The rest of us cannot. Our outlook is only for the good of the human race; we can only stem the flow, try to harness the evil by staying to this side of goodness. But evil flows as water. It goes where it wants and seeks its own level, which is always downward. It is abominable and frightening as well as exhausting to control it."

By the time Pramod finished this explanation, Dina looked worn out but wary. She reached out her hand to touch her friend's arm, feeling a little more comforted. The two women did not speak for about a minute, and Dina felt a surge of good connected through their touch, like a gentle electrical shock.

"I *will* promise to try and stay away from him," she whispered.

The old woman nodded slowly, as if it were immensely tiring just to speak about the subject. Dina noticed how drained she looked and was mystified by the sudden change. It was a good time now to leave and go back to her apartment. Outside, the rain had abruptly moved on and the sun was out. Dina could even hear birdsong from a nearby window cracked half-open.

"Will you tell me about your mother soon?" Dina offered as she rose to leave.

Pramod nodded.

❧❧❧❧

The next time Dina returned to Pramod's, it was nearly Halloween. She sat sullenly and not too patiently across from the old woman and whined, "Why do we talk so much about evil? Our talks sometimes get too heavy, depressing."

"But it is why you come."

"I-I do?" Dina shook her head in confusion. "You said that I brought this ghoul into the world. I'm scared for Frank, but that's because I don't trust Big Sandy's jealousy. Nothing really out of the ordinary has happened. I think it's over."

"It is *not* over by any means." Pramod clasped her hands and leaned in close, her voice lowering, serious. "No, not at all. You must know the evil beyond the realm of mere monsters and ghouls. These identities are merely trappings, vehicles to represent man's evil on a lighter scale, to scare for entertainment. But your creature is viable, *real*. It wants to go where evil is."

"Big Sandy?"

"Yes, he is dangerous evil, the worst kind." Reading Dina's quizzical look shot from across the table, Pramod replied, "You know why."

"I-I don't."

"You do, however. Because he, Big Sandy, is … death-like, and death is always what surrounds us. Lurking. Close to us. Big Sandy is just making the choice to *whom* to make this diabolical and unholy gift." Pramod stopped speaking for emphasis. "For his own pleasure. He relishes this, as many leaders did before him—Ivan the Terrible, Attila, Hitler, Genghis Khan, and others. Big Sandy will sometime stand among them, though not in their historical light, much as he imagines he would."

"Death-like? Meaning what, exactly?"

"Big Sandy is a master. He does not want to annihilate the whole population. He *selects*." Pramod folded her hands and looked away far away out the window, as if the starlings flying by the high kitchen window now would give her the strong words she needed to let Dina hear. "But you have knowledge. This knowledge becomes a sort of segue way to aversions, a prevention of sorts."

"How?"

"With knowledge. Big Sandy *is* evil, but you are one step ahead of him with what you know. What you know about him. You have felt it."

"I don't remember feeling anything about him except disgust now, and do you really think Big Sandy is capable of … killing?" Dina asked.

"*Is,*" Pramod breathed out, "and probably *will.*"

Dina jumped to her feet, tingly adrenaline washing into her arms, legs, and even the roots of her hair. "Oh, my God!" Her hands fluttered, the gesture childish but somehow ominous. "Are you saying he will kill me?"

"No, child, sit down now," Pramod commanded sharply. "It is not you. He is too smitten."

"Not really a relief!" Dina whined, but she did sit.

"Be aware."

"Tell me what to do! Who—"

This time, it was Pramod's turn to stand up and interrupt, angrily defending the cryptic message that allowed no answers. "I tell you, I do not know these things! Not everything. You must see your way through, as you will play a part." Her eyes were hard but full of worry. She hesitated "I am not privy to know the who and where. Only the act. As I have said, things come to me bit by bit. I do know it involves the supreme act of evil and could be tomorrow or ten years from now."

At that moment, a scruffy cat curled against Dina's legs, and she gasped, more at the old woman's words than the electric touch of fur. "It's unfair to let it go like this, as a warning and not…"

She was flustered enough to want to shake the truth from her friend, hammer it out, whatever it took.

"Stop! Now I begin my story. Amritsar. In India."

"Where?" Dina shot back crossly at Pramod. "But evil! Big Sandy! You give me this information on a plate, like, like you were calmly serving it up for dinner. But I am confused. I must know *where* and *when!*" Insanity was licking at the lateral parts of her brain that still contained reality and equanimity, not the dire warnings of this possibly crazed woman. This information was a ticking time bomb, a confession, a harbinger.

But then Pramod began speaking airily, as if she had never referred to anything as dire as murder. Her voice was soft and pitying. "Evil. So many forms. Maybe you even dated someone sinister without knowing it."

Determined not to move into an area where Pramod again digressed didactically into a lecture on evil, Dina blurted, "How can I stop Big Sandy or anyone like him, for that matter? Just talking about evil here, well, there are all kinds of psychology at play here! It's kind of a moot point—"

"Knowledge. I *need* to finish showing you. I know you are resistant to hear again about evil and how knowledge can conquer it. And I *will* show you, child, a picture of my past, to demonstrate that I met up with evil and I am no stranger. It was when I was a youngster in India. The assimilation will help us both. You see, evil was an emotion for me so foul that day that I was sure everyone could smell it in the air. It was not the fires set later that burned and flared our nostrils. It was evil. Yes, evil was under his fingernails and of every soldier too. But mainly him. It was the word of one man. I was the one who lost to evil. I lost my mother, and she was my world. In Amritsar, in 1919. I was only seven, but I still remember the horror."

Pramod stopped here, wheezed out a sigh of sorrow, and dropped her shoulders like a balloon losing air.

"Amritsar?"

The old woman resumed, not looking at her companion. "It was proved to me that day that evil is everywhere, and it can shatter what we know of goodness. Evil. Not only when we look under a rock do we see its underbelly, for it cannot hide under or behind an excuse. Colonel Dyer or Big Sandy."

"Colonel who?" Dina got the impression that the elderly woman was carrying a weight she could never shrug off.

"I know well of Amritsar, but I cannot tell you of Big Sandy's excuse. You may have to find it. This evil that scares us does not scare them. It is an embellishment to their personality, and being so, they look upon it as an excuse, as if you were a cripple and couldn't walk and people would somehow excuse you a forgivable handicap.

"This is the way evil people think; they excuse their traits within themselves. These traits are not afflictions but justification for this badge they wear. And that is their excuse."

Pramod proceeded with her recollection.

CHAPTER 34

India, April 1919

Amritsar is and was a beautiful city, erected many centuries ago in the Punjab territory of India, a segment in the northwest corner known for its fertile fields and abundant growth of crops—cotton, corn, and many more, much like the Midwest and southern United States.

Most of the region had Sikhs, a religious group residing there, especially in the early part of the 1900s. A beautiful golden temple was erected there by the ruler, Ranjit Singh, and Amritsar was a holy Mecca for the Sikhs. In construction of this temple, pure gold was employed in some parts. Amritsar was a walled city with only five gates to exit and enter and was bordered by the adjacent Ravi River. So romantic and compelling, it called to mind a castle with a moat of medieval times. The large, airy courtyards and gardens were perfect for the celebration in spring, called Jallinwala Bagh.

"Bagh" means "beautiful garden" but the massacre that occurred there nineteen years into the beginning of the century was anything but a rustic retreat and would forever be marked by the Sikhs and all of India. That day in 1919 would be a harbinger of the British-Indian split, and more incidents over the next years would further strengthen this possibility.

Because of all that went on that April day, Mahatma Gandhi, who had earlier been restricted from entering the Punjab territory, was heard to proclaim that he "no longer had affection for an evilly maintained government." Jawaharlal Nehru, who ruled India later, decried everything British, beginning his retreat back to his roots by disdaining the British, who he once revered and went on to burn his British inspired clothing in a great bonfire.

British Parliament would later admit this Amritsar atrocity as only "an error in judgment" and simply relieved the man responsible, General Dyer, of his office.

Because of Indian work stoppage at that time and other protests and unrest directed against the British, as the natives fought to maintain their control, the city of Amritsar had been ordered not to stage public meetings or gatherings. Unfortunately, the command was lost on the ears of the Sikhs who resided in villages too far away to hear of the order and who entered the city anyway to celebrate their special feast. After all, it was Jallinwala Bagh!

CHAPTER 35

She never wanted to go in the first place. Geeta had been pushed and persuaded by her husband, Sajjan.

"It will be fine, much like a carnival, many booths and merrymaking and food. It will be fun! You will see," he argued.

"And what about Pramod? She is so small, even for her age. The crowds! She could get lost and—"

"Stop worrying! All will be fine."

"No! There is so much unrest with the British. I fear the worst. No good will come. There is evil. I feel it in my bones! This, this event seems more like a protest. Your wife and child don't belong. Can't you go alone?"

"No! I will not at all! And Amritsar is too far to walk alone. You must go." Sajjan's voice softened. "The British have their excuses, but I think India is turning. Much is changed now." He reached to touch her hand reassuringly.

"No! I do not believe it is changed all that much, except more un-rest—and the rumors!" Geeta's voice spilled over with fury. She dropped her hand away from her husband's touch and clung to her silken sari.

"I do not believe the rumors!" Sajjan put his fist down hard on the table where Pramod and her parents now ate their breakfast in their small house. With that sudden violent move, his daughter nearly jumped from her place.

"Calm down!" Geeta warned. "This is not right. I will argue it against the life of my child!"

"And what of your own life? You do not care about that? Or mine?" Sajjan roared, and Geeta immediately ducked her head as if waiting for a blow. Her arm shot out protectively and cupped the head of her child, but she said nothing. There was an edgy quietness for a while, the three of them eating almost disinterestedly, although Geeta was seething, and she could hardly keep her breakfast down.

Sajjan started up again. "You will see. All is well."

"I go but against my will," she said, and she added under her breath, "I would sooner go to my grave."

But Sajjan heard it and now laughed. "Such nonsense about graves! I will hold Pramod on my shoulders, and she will be taken care of. We will have a feast on the holiday of Jallianwala Bagh, the time she remembers from last year. Right, Pramod?"

His daughter didn't answer, but her eyes grew big as she looked out from under her mother's hand. Sajjan's eyes, however, were lit up with excitement.

He is fooling no one, Geeta thought to herself. She knew he cared more for the sweet treats the vendors sold than for Pramod's entertainment.

They started walking very early, as their small village was about four miles from Amritsar. Upon arriving, they soon found that the crowds were indeed thick. There must have been close to four thousand people there.

"Where will we sit? All the grassy spots are taken," Geeta complained, sighing loudly as if this fact would change Sajjan,s mind about leaving.

"Then we will stand—over here." He had already purchased the prized sweetmeats he had been longing for, and now the three of them stood loitering on a gravel path, tucked between two grassy spots, which were filled with the many revelers. It was hot and dry, and there was an air of hesitation, suspicion, and warning in the air. Geeta was sure she could feel it, but Sajjan, smiling broadly as he hoisted Pramod off his shoulders, sensed nothing.

Her senses came to her as if they were throbbing, pulsing harder, her pores filled with fear and she clutched her lucky star that was around her neck, as if that gesture alone would make the feeling subside. She took up Pramod's hand and squeezed it so hard that the child squeaked in pain. They began to walk forward, moving slowly with the crowd that bumped and parted them, but the surge of people did not have its usual sound. Suddenly, there was no happy trilling of women's laughter, no men guffawing. The very mood of the crowd seemed anticipatory.

Geeta's heart stopped. She looked alarmingly at her husband, sure he felt the tense unstable mood, but he simply kept ambling along looking at the sun, his face like some bright clock with his moustache as the hands.

Pramod now felt her mother's fear, the hand that held hers grew ice cold and she looked for protection from her father, who had now stopped to remove a handkerchief and mop his brow, oblivious. Geeta's breath came quickly now, and she raised her hand to touch her husband. The crowd, which was so heavy now she could not see beyond, suddenly, as if on command, huddled more cloyingly toward the trio. Claustrophobia now gripped her, and she moved to impulsively shield her child with her body.

And then there was a shot and a man's voice ordering, "Fire!" The screams started, and there was more gunfire. Geeta still could now see the brigadier soldiers, who knelt in a line with firearms. Hysterically she ignored her husband and wrenched Pramod's arm trying to duck to the grass, hoping that the shelter of the lower angle would shield them. But others had already had that plan, people diving down so that the ground quickly became a carpet of frightened festival-goers, and there was no room, so Geeta scooped up the child and began to run crazily forward hearing Sajjan's call from behind, "Wait! Geeta! Do *not* run!"

And many were already running.

Geeta could see the evil in the sudden gush of blood in the dirt. A feeling of desperation surged through her and she knew the child sensed the unholy wrongness of the scenario, although Pramod remained quiet as she was jostled about in her mother's sweaty arms, her sari flying.

Pramod knew. The evil was in the air. It was the British General Dyer's excuse, although she did not then know his name, this commander whose shouted order would rip apart so many bodies on this beautiful April afternoon, without so much as guilt or compassion for this crowd of villagers who had simply gathered to observe their holiday.

She knew what would happen, and Geeta knew it too, so she kept running, the small star on her neck flying backward. She did not even duck when she received the bullet and went down, the child ejected from her arms like a canon, rolling and tumbling on the blood smeared grass across bodies which were torn by bullets, their mouths screaming in agony, or not at all. Meanwhile the shots went on without stopping.

Why? And where was her father?

Pramod's small frame came to rest under the twisted torso of an old woman whose eyes were rolled back in her head. Pramod knew that look; she had seen it in dead dogs in the road. Too frightened to scream, she extricated herself from the slippery, blood soaked body and crawled crazily on all fours back to her mother.

Geeta did not look like the dead dogs in the street. Her eyes were fluttering, and then they stopped. She was peaceful, although blood continued to gush forward and spill onto the ground from a small hole in her chest.

The child shook her mother. "Mama! Mama! Wake up! Wake up! Guns! Hurry! We must run!"

Her urgings were unheeded, the body laid quiet yet cold and getting colder.

After shaking her mother several times and finding the effort useless, Pramod turned from her crouched position and stared at the firing infantry. They had begun to lower their guns now, almost sheepishly, embarrassed for having fired for almost ten senseless minutes at unarmed helpless people, simply following the orders of their maniacal general. And it was he, General Dyer, whose eyes Pramod observed, for he was not too far away, and the look he fixed was beyond the misery, torment, and carnage before him. Her eyes rounded in shock, even at her young age, at the stoic composure of the man who mused to himself that he had done well and who later would even be awarded much money and a jeweled sword for having massacred a harmless crowd of festival attendees. He was a brigadier who the British would revere. He would not be chastised; in fact, they would laud him moreover for his "cleaning up" of civil unrest.

Pramod saw it all now, the impending British inquiry into the melee which would upturn British and Indian relations, the Indians never really forgiving the act of harrowing violence on a town most famous for a sacred golden temple. The Indians in other cities beyond her Punjab home would retaliate by protesting and burning in honor of the nearly 400 dead and 1,600 wounded that day.

Dyer, who looked upon the crowd as a disturbance, almost a riot in his mind, as body after body went down, women and children, felt smugly reciprocated, for hadn't these people heard that the British had, after all, enforced a law banning crowd gatherings for any purpose? What he did not know was that the villages far from Amritsar did *not* hear about any sanctions against collective meetings, and they came to celebrate as they had year after year. To Dyer, the tangled bodies, the motherless children, the arms, legs, and torsos pocked with bullet holes needed to be "taught a lesson."

Pramod sensed it all in those icy eyes, and if she had been older, she may have wept for yet the future bloodshed. Only now she sensed the entire vision and felt Dyer's *excuse* so much in her heart that she quivered and shook as she stared at the man standing in the sun, a supercilious smile, "Cease fire!" and "Retreat!" on his lips. She felt his hauteur, louder than any screams of torment, and above all, she saw the utter contemptuous satisfaction of a man who had bought on this evil, since the act of splintering bodies was his alone.

Pramod had witnessed his look; she would remember it forever—the infantry slinking off like rats offering nothing as much as a bandage to the wounded. And why?

Her mother's body was frigid under her small hand.

Evil. The man, the deed, but most of all, his reason for the butchery was justified, as many past megalomaniacs have excused themselves casually by way of reassurance for what called out to the rest of us as sadism and annihilation. The tragedy was guided by Dyer's own intrinsic form of vengeance, for he was only following orders, wasn't he?

Dyer had enjoyed it. This Pramod saw.

The child dropped down on top of her mother's body as the troops moved backward in retreat. Victims were still trying to scale the walls, frantic and fighting to survive, since the exits had been gated off and Dyer's troops had blocked the only remaining way out of the walled city. Many others were trying to stem the flow of their loved one's blood by their smashing hands against wounds. Here in the hot, still air of 1919 was a horror, a mere lack of communication had forecast an excuse to murder. These shots were against innocents, some diving into a deep adjacent well only to drop to their death in a dried out cauldron.

In the future it would be called the "Jallianwala Bagh Massacre," although to Pramod, referring to it as a massacre would not label it right. It was open calculated pure murder that was on the soul of its commander, she told herself, as if Dyer had fired every gun. No warning shot in the air to disperse, just the insane shooting, as if picking off deer in hunting season.

Pramod, her head in her hands, continued weeping, but no one came to help her. Where was her father? She felt so weak. She needed him. So weak. Dyer's excuse was emblazoned forever on her heart, and she would feel and sense evil *before* it happened for all time, and unfortunately, in all formats.

When Pramod's story had finished, Dina quietly cleared her throat, as if this would clear the air of all the heartbreak and misery. The old woman's words hung like blood dripping in the air, condensed, a feeling not yet mourned, an atrocity unforgivable. Her hands were folded, looking into her lap for some rejoinder for the profound, pathetic history which Dina, whom she had grown to greatly admire, would now have to remember. Pramod's childhood had been hijacked by these past events, yet her faith in humankind remained oddly unjaded.

The old woman had always remained kind toward Dina, and because of this growing closeness endured over the last few weeks, she felt her companion's pain solemnly, even though Dina could not raise her head up now to console. What *could* one say to ameliorate this sorrowful history?

For a long while, Dina kept her eyes glued downwards, hearing the clock tick, a cat purr nearby. Finally, she raised her eyes and tentatively said, "What did happen to your father?"

Now Pramod put down the cat and the animal immediately went to zigzag against Dina's legs, seeking another customer to administer attention. Getting no notice from Dina, it dashed again up on the Indian woman's lap. Pramod petted the cat's fur gently, as if every stoke erased another year she had to remember. "He was never found."

"Then you assume he was k-killed?" Dina asked softly.

"I know it sounds strange that he was never found. It was the regime, you see, and no one really looked into it very much. Perhaps he tried to scale the walls that so many festival goers tried to do to escape and he made it and ran away. For me, I think he ran away out of guilt—because he forced my mother to go to the Jallinwala Baugh when she didn't want to and in his guilt, maybe, he felt he caused her death. He was a coward and could not face it. I was raised by my grandmother and my father never tried to find his mother-in-law to take me back. This is all I know. I could *feel* his desertion, even at the point of my mother's death."

"Y-you did?" Dina was dumbstruck. How could she have known so much? At only seven years old? It was beyond belief, yet she had heard of cases of crystal clear clairvoyance in very young children. "This General Dyer got no punishment? Nothing? Shouldn't he have been put in prison?" Dina had never learned about this part of Indian or British history. Like many American children, what they were schooled with at that time was more about the Great Depression or World War I than Great Britain's dealings in India.

"The opposite happened. The British extolled him. Evil personified with no excuse." She paused slightly, then repeated, "There *is* no excuse."

"Oh oh, like the tattoo on Big Sandy's arm," Dina whispered, piecing together what Pramod really meant.

"This whole story. My history. It was told to you because I wanted you to be aware of evil. Some people are stamped with it. Recognize it and go forth making others more aware."

Suddenly, the cat leapt from Pramod's lap, as if the creature did not want to be around the subject the Indian had again brought up.

Dina slumped against the back of the chair. "But what can I do, other than avoid big Sandy as you advised? Which is obvious, and by the way, aren't people who are driven toward goodness going to be that way naturally? And the others, well ..."

She trailed off quietly, and she was not prepared for Pramod's sudden bolt from her seat, knocking her chair to the floor and waving her hand, her eyes hard.

"Yes, it is true, you can't do everything. You can't absolve evil, but you can always do *something*! The nature of evil is *not* in its excuse! It is not disease! It is not personality, background, or innate! It is active, whether cultivated or taken on a slight whim! It is a *thing, a noun, a person*! And now, unfortunately, as you have seen, a ghoul manifested has decided to work you into its sorry world. And I am not happy to say," her voice softened, "it may win. It is trying."

"Trying?" Dina said.

"It is not coerced by Big Sandy, but both man and evil ghost are on the same mine field. It is attracted to the weak, the desperate. Your love of Frank, for example. The haloed light you put him in weakens you. You feel he belongs to you."

"That is exactly what I feel!"

"And what you think you deserve!"

"Yes, but what is wrong with that? I-I—"

"You have to stand in your own light and examine what you are headed for. It may bring much pain. And I know this is hard to hear but evil has already gotten hold of the circumstances and—"

"What are you saying?" Dina interrupted nervously.

"Do not chase this man. Work on chasing evil away."

"But—"

"There is misery coming and we cannot change it."

Sparks were now going off in Dina's head. "That's it!" She stood up, the two women almost face to face across the table. "It's Big Sandy! He wants to harm Frank! I knew it! I gotta help him!"

"Settle down." Pramod waved for her to sit. "You are not helping anyone, least of all yourself with hysteria. What will happen will happen. Only if more evil takes hold. I know your heart is hurting and I know you saw him as your husband. You came to me for comfort, for answers. I do not have the answers, but it is more important you see the bigger picture, the recognition of evil, the lesson here." She turned slowly to the side and back again, knowing how her next words would sting. "You know evil can be *your* pride too. Your desperation for possession. Obsession at its darkest form can be evil too."

But Dina barely heard her, her mind fishing for a solution to save Frank, if she had to, not necessarily to save evil from the world *or* herself. "I have to go now. I feel sick with all this scary and bloody talk," she blurted. She wondered if she would ever go back to Pramod's again.

"The ghoul is—"

Pramod's words were rudely cut off, as Dina rushed out into the October evening.

CHAPTER 36

Mrs. Harrington stepped out of Saks Fifth Avenue and hurried forward to her car. Clutching her packages, she opened the rear of the RV, chucked in her purchases and slammed the trunk, sighing heavily. She was glad to be of help searching for silver metallic pants for her oldest daughter's Halloween costume. *Why she had ever wanted to be a robot, of all things, a pretty girl like Kaitlin, was beyond me,* she thought to herself.

It was five o'clock, Halloween night and already dark. She knew Kaitlin would be upset having to answer the door for the trick-or-treaters, patiently trying to put her makeup on before her sorority's Halloween party began. A Northwestern University dorm on campus was Kaitlin's home in Evanston, but she had stopped by her parents' house in Skokie earlier in the day. Finding nothing of use for her costume by rummaging around in her mother's closet, she had enlister her mom, who was more than happy to search the adjacent mall for her daughter's supplies—that is, if Kaitlin would stand in for "door duty" for the collection of trick-or-treaters who would come hour after hour this night. And now Kaitlin would be late because of her mother's dawdling to look at gewgaws for herself at Saks.

I'm horrible, the older woman thought, *but, hey—silver pants indeed!* Yet who would have thought Saks Fifth Avenue, of all places, would have a Halloween department complete with kooky masks, tights, decorations and every imaginable thing for grown-up Halloween costumes. She had profusely thanked the woman at Nine West for suggesting Saks.

Now, jamming the gas down a little too forcefully, she pulled out of the parking lot with a screech. Just as she was heading west, her car phone rang, arresting her attention from the road and bare branches overhead, their skeletal frames hoisted like crooked girders in the moonlight. She was passing through Harms woods to get home and the wind, which had blown gently before, was gaining in strength, and now tree limbs swooped eerily back and forth above her car like a hangman's noose. She shuddered at the likeness as she put the receiver to her ear.

"H-hello?"

"Mom!" the voice caroled back with an undertone of frantic panic. "I owe you. Are you on your way? Did you find something? Could you hurry?" Mrs. Harrington had just gotten one of the new-fangled cellular phones in her car, and she could hear the sing-song of the doorbell in the background. "And those damned trick-or-treaters!" Kaitlin continued to grumble in exasperation, "Are you close by and—"

Just then, the line crackled, fireworks of popping and sputtering. Bits of her daughter's conversation forced their way erratically through the line.

"Here … for …"

Mrs. Harrington sighed in frustration, " Your call is breaking up. Here, I'll pull over and stop. Maybe it's the cord on my end." There was no reply, but she swerved onto a small inlet off the road made for turn-arounds and moved the car out of traffic on to the crunchy gravel. The woods bordered her on three sides, and she could almost feel it breathing. From twelve to fifteen feet away, she could see the distant black ribbon of bike trail like an inky stripe of toothpaste. She got out of the car and stretched the cord for better reception. The phone salesman had told her this sometimes worked. "With these new phones, you know, some of the kinks haven't been worked out yet," he had advised. Not hearing anything right away but static, she pounded the receiver with her palm as if she could dislodge Kaitlin's voice that way.

"Is everything all right? Are you okay?" she said over and over.

The night, obsidian and foreboding swirled around her. Blackened shadows frightened her. Anything and anyone could be lurking around. She kept repeating, "Hello! Hello! Kaitlin, are you there? Damn technology!" Stretching the cord again in aggravation, she shook the receiver like a salt shaker, pounding it on the car door, showing herself to be a new cellular user who thought that brute force to the instrument would harness the voice of her daughter. Raising the receiver to her ear once again, she leaned on the car door and then she saw ... it.

Perched on a tree stump like a passenger waiting for a bus, was what appeared to be a massive black blob with needle-like tentacles which were weaving and bobbing about itself, from top to bottom, perhaps twenty or thirty of them, like the appendages of an octopus, only more sinister. It shifted the patent leather shininess of its form to and fro as well, and although she wasn't sure it had eyes, Mrs. Harrington felt like it was looking right through her.

Her high scream was the sound of a bomb whistling in the air. She dropped the phone, where it ricocheted on its short cord back into the car through the open window. Mrs. Harrington followed right after it.

One hand jimmied her keys, while the other rolled up the window, all the while watching the ghoul nervously through the windshield. At eighteen or so feet away, she could clearly see it stretch out in front of the car watching her, its ebony wings, now extending, glistened white in the moonlight's reflection. It was hideous and huge, its very presence seemed to beacon her, but its expression, if you could call that on its face, was unwavering as if caught in a trance. One by one, the wings reticulated and popped out even farther, moving rapidly back from their casings like the steps of an escalator. At their full span, the appendages extended into the forest nearly twenty feet across. From each of the fire-colored tips strung oily strands, which Mrs. Harrington would later describe as "strange string things, yards and yards of them."

Mrs. Harrington was now dumbfounded and frozen with fear. Was the thing now starting to smile? It was so ugly and inhuman, and no, this was no Halloween prank, she concluded. It was far too large, and yet there was no skin, no scales. Only pure blackness, and it stared at her with volcanic red eyes which now appeared to be opening automatically in conjunction with its moving wingspan. Its look was anticipatory, as if *she* were a toy or candy it wanted. The maw opened, revealing teeth curved backwards like knives. Without the frightening "dental" work, it almost looked to Mrs. Harrington like a curiously blackened angel, burnt in the oven.

The last thing she noticed before she regained her composure and shifted the car rapidly into gear was that the grotesque had some kind of a white tattoo. She thought she read the word "excuse." How was that possible to see with all the blackness of its body? Did it seem to glow?

❧❦❧

Skokie police arrived on the scene shortly afterwards. Someone in the neighborhood had reported a blood-curdling scream coming the woods and, Halloween or not, they responded. Besides that, minutes earlier, a young girl had called to say her mother was in the car, she was in Harms woods, and she had heard her scream through the car phone receiver. The caller had been frantic enough that the officers were obliged to check it out. The follow-up call from the mother, now safe at home, described an evil sort of monster as large as a helicopter in the woods.

The response team, however, found nothing, and even though they shined their lights northwards through the bare tree branches, they saw little out of the ordinary, not even the usual drunk high school students trying to celebrate Halloween in their own way in the woods. One thing the officers could not account for was the strange clicking noise they continually heard as they searched.

One officer, Ray Finn, tired to the bone with chasing Halloween pranks and vandals, noted he was ready for a drink. "Besides," he laughed, "something that big couldn't be missed if it had wings like the old lady described." During their search, they had heard through their radio from their police chief. He related that the woman's follow-up call describing what she saw, so they had something to go on all right. "Sounds like *she* hit the bars *before* the woods! Lucky she didn't end up with a DUI!" Finn sniffed. "Or maybe it took one look at her and just flew away with those wings! Ha! Ha! Ha!"

The fellow officers laughed uncomfortably. Two patrol cars had been sent out, normally manned with two officers each. But tonight, because his partner had called in sick, Finn rode alone. From their radios, they heard the crackle sound dispatching them to the nearby mall to see about vandalism now in progress.

"Let's go!" Finn ordered, and the two men headed to their cars, turning off their powerful flashlights. Meanwhile, Finn's car was parked a bit farther away from the other squad car, and consequently, he was the last to leave the woods. As he started the engine and got ready to hit the sirens, he heard the unmistakable and loud "Click! Click!" that they had heard all through their search, only louder this time, as if it were in his back seat.

Officer Finn, although polite when he needed to be away from work, concealed a horrendous gambling habit that had destroyed both his marriage and his current girlfriend's sanity and obliterated from existence any child support the divorced Mrs. Finn did or ever would have. The tangle of child-support cases laboring through the system in Chicago had only labeled Mr. Finn as "in arrears." And since it would be decades before the IRS would get subsequently involved, Finn was able to hide "his mistake of a wife," as he called her, and her simpering complaints away from anyone nosey enough to get involved. Timid and afraid, Mrs. Finn suffered in silence and tried make ends meet, mostly by praying.

Officer Finn never made it to the mall that Halloween, and his squad car, when discovered later by police, had to be thoroughly expunged of blood. Officials suspected foul play but did not know what to make of the unctuous residue surrounding the interior. "Like an oil slick opened," the investigating detective was quoted as saying.

CHAPTER 37

After the last visit, the old woman's words brought forth greater anxiety in Dina. However, the advice she received, as arcane and random as the dust motes dancing in the sunlight from the only window in the room, accompanied by Pramod's steely gaze, waxen and unwavering, kept Dina returning, and at times she did not know if she was running to or from the truths hashed out in their meetings. She sat simply accepting as necessity, the pull of the East Indian woman, her self-appointed therapy session in a kitchen smelling of spices and sometimes kitty litter, and in her presence, Dina became free momentarily from her ongoing heartbreak as Pramod prattled on about nothing—the weather, her cats' diets, or even the insalubrities of the city air.

"Feeling better?" Karen asked one day as she came into her office.

Dina looked up, unconcerned. "Yeah. And no."

"You seem better. Are you medicating with booze at nights?"

"I-I just found something out, but I am worried about what she—"

"She?" Karen dragged on the fish line of conversation.

"I-I've been to see Pramod, you know, the Indian women we saw on Devon that day."

"Son of a bitch! Why?" Karen almost whistled through her teeth. She leaned against the wall, one leg tucked under, not bothering to hide an obvious look of confusion.

Dina protested, "She seems helpful. I get a lot from talking to her."

"Oh, come on! That old lady? Look, she doesn't even know you! Hey, all kidding aside, I know a really good shrink if you think you need to talk to someone—other than me, of course," Karen reached out to touch Dina's arm, but Dina recoiled. Karen knew she had stepped on a land mine and backpedaled. "Ah, how *can* that old woman be helpful? She seemed crazy that day and talked mumbo jumbo, although I must admit, *you* seemed to know what she was saying. Why didn't you tell me before?"

"I I don't know. Maybe because I anticipated the reaction I'm getting now. She soothes. That is … sometimes." Dina recalled with irony how their last meeting was anything but soothing.

"Hallelujah!" Karen laughed.

Oh Christ, here it comes. Dina rolled her eyes. *The stand-up comic is loose.*

"If only every thrown-under-the-bus-lover could benefit from that old lady, she'd make a fortune! She could make a sign to read, 'Jilted Lovers' Retreat!'"

Dina scowled. "It's not all moping over Frank! The last visit, she told me such a fantastic story—"

"Well, tell me! Has it got any juicy parts or sex in it? Although I can't imagine that old bat ever had any."

"Stop it!" Dina snarled.

"Okay! I'm sorry!" Karen whined. "What's the old lady got to say?" She covered the embarrassment by reaching for a nail file on Dina's desk and began industriously filing her fingernails.

Pramod's words were still fresh. Dina could almost see the death, the blood before her eyes. "It was about her mother's life. How can I explain? As she retold her past as a little girl, I sensed it was not just melancholy meandering but significant—for me. About how she had gone through her own personal introduction to evil and all and how it becomes manifested in some and that I should beware. She almost hinted at something in *my* future—yet, how can that be?"

"What about her mother?"

"She died in this horrible pogrom. In India. In 1919 ..."

Dina drifted off.

"She told you all this?" Karen cocked an eyebrow and stopped smiling. "Why would *that* have anything to do with your future?"

"More like a fundamental learning process in the telling. Does that make sense?"

"Everybody learns something from wars and bad things from the past. Why should you or she be any different? And hey, why didn't she ask for me to be there?"

Dina ignored the question. "This Amritsar thing—that's the town where it took place—was showing me that everything surrounding her that day had the feel evil and un-holiness in light of the fact that she *knew* I saw that ghost thing and that it was, ah ..."

"And?"

"Inadvertently dispatched by me, but I *have* to or *will* do something about it all! No, I was not fully responsible for it, but her event, for lack of a better word, hangs somehow in the balance of *my* life. There was a reason she told me about all this evil. I guess she was implying me to be careful of danger of another kind?" Dina was shaking her head, staring into the distance, her thoughts still going over the inscrutable warning.

"Dina, she's just some nice old lady, and yeah, something bad did happen to her mom. But she just wants an ear—a warm body—to listen to her. A lot of old people are that way and—"

"No," Dina insisted, "there *is* significance. I just have to accept for now it is a mystery. She only doles out so much information, you see, because she can't know," Dina trailed off, "and those crazy words she used once, about running."

"Sounds like she's not even a good soothsayer if she can't even tell you this *future*!" Karen threw down the file, exasperated at her friend's childlike beliefs, as if Pramod were Santa Claus coming with good cheer, yet only given out in small doses once a year! "When *was* this last visit?"

"L-last night."

"That was Halloween."

"You went to this goofy woman's house on Halloween? How apt!" Dina became paler, her shoulders quivering like a shimmer of disturbed water.

"That's enough!" Karen ordered. "And look at you shaking now. What's it all for? A silly woman and her predictions! Between good-for-nothing Frank and this old lady, who's got you all mind-boggled and unable to work, haven't you had enough of these two people already? I think it's wrong you've visited her so many times. You've become a different person since I walked in here. Do you really think some magical advice is to come out as she tells you about her sorry past! That it's going to affect *your* future?"

"No, no! You see, I *can't* stop seeing her." Dina's voice was a squeak.

"Yes, you can! That silly old coot is probably filling your head with fantasies of Frank taking you back! I'm sorry, Dina, but nothing she is saying is true, and she may not hang out a sign, but she's a fortune-teller nonetheless. And I can see the *distress* that old dinosaur has placed on you! And—"

Dina's grasped the edge of her desk for support.

Karen stopped her lecture. "Honey, what's wrong? This can't be all because of Frank, the louse! Was it last night's visit?"

Dina broke through Karen's protest. Her eyes were searching as through an atmosphere of silt to find some suitable path to a place where she felt safe, all of her questions answered. "No … I mean, yes. You see, the story Pramod told wasn't a story. It *was* history, although you and I never read about it in our high school history books."

"And?"

"And this is odd. I feel totally crazy, an unanswered question on my part. I know she *had* been there, naturally, as a child, mourning beside her mother, but how does she account for everything she knows now? She made me think she *knew* about all that past slaughter, how imminent it was, laden with its evil and all, so she says. And yet, I can't quite piece together or relate it to *me* today. I think I need to see her … again."

CHAPTER 38

Hendricks stood before the group of four men and Dina in Sandoval's spacious office meeting room, which was sometimes used surreptitiously by employees as a lunchroom when the boss was away. The heavily paneled room was ornate with exquisite framed pictures, which Hendricks, with his simplistic taste, could not have picked out. At the finest restaurants among important clients, Dina had actually once witnessed Hendricks turning down the steak tartar or foie gras for his usual unadorned hamburger—no cheese.

Their boss stood at the head of the lengthy office desk, the kind one could imagine some more important CEO or the president of the United States standing behind. He tried to look pompous, but he just came off looking silly. He was weaving back and forth on his heels, hands in his pockets and nodding at his employees with a simpering smile. Frank was there, as well as Dina, Wyatt, Andy, and Benny.

Dina chose a spot far away from Frank, partly because she could not bear his grim look if she unwittingly took a seat next to him. From this vantage point, she could study him, fuel the longing of her eyes to take in unobserved, his nuances: how he held a pencil, flipped it unconsciously against his head while listening. Or when he felt the need to put on his reading glasses, a gesture she especially liked when they were dating. She remembered staring at him reading with spectacles while she, standing afar in another room, would sigh with heartbreaking emotion.

Hendricks began to flip over a text as he stood at a podium adjacent to a desk. He certainly did not need to use such a prop for such a small group, but he probably did so to stroke his puny ego. Everyone looked up from their small talk as he rattled some papers. Behind him, picture windows showcased the jaw-dropping view of the Chicago from their point in the sky. Sandoval's floors looked down through the gray sky, with wheeling birds and skyscrapers sharing it, the length of Michigan Avenue below in its glory, teeming with people, and now small trucks that trolled the avenue in the November rain preparing to drape naked trees with Christmas lights.

Hendricks coughed a few times and launched a stentorian voice totally unnatural for him. His head behind the great podium looked like a pumpkin on display propped on a ledge.

"We're going on a trip … er, rather you people are."

He broke off suddenly. Dina leaned forward anticipatorily.

Hendricks continued, "You five here, who have been working on the Boyko project, will give Sandoval's presentation to the company in New York City in December. This is what I feel we need to do."

Everyone gasped. A free trip to New York City! And during the holiday season!

"Don't get too excited, you have to travel over a weekend. Travel arrangements will be by Glenda St. James, of course. You will fly mid-December, Saturday morning. I want you all there fresh for presentation on Monday morning so you can take Sunday off to sightsee and shop, courtesy of Sandoval, since you will miss the Saturday Christmas party here. But I stress: the presentation must go well! We must win Boyko's bid!" He empathized this by pounding his fist on the podium like Khrushchev. "This is why I have drafted something for each of you to do to fuel the presentation, so to speak, and persuade Boyko. I need all five of you at the helm of this important project!"

Another gasp rocketed through the group at Sandoval's generosity, Dina watched Hendricks, thinking he looked like some faith healer rousing a crowd.

"Don't get too carried away now," Hendricks, sniffing and rubbing his nose, "as this trip is Sandoval's way of saying thanks. I've been elected by the CEO to tell you that because of this generosity, this *will* cut into your Christmas bonuses somewhat." There were audible sighs in the room at this. "But think of the Christmas shopping you can do in the greatest city in the world!" Hendricks was smiling broadly.

Leave it to Hendricks to give a positive albeit trifling spin on a business trip, Dina thought as she chewed her pen, although her mind was plotting how she might talk to Frank on the journey. But suddenly, she realized that for all her hopefulness, she couldn't doubt that he and Toni were rooted like a pair of potted plants in Sandoval's foyer. She put down her pen, crestfallen, barely aware when the texts and brochures of Boyko were being passed out.

"You have four and a half weeks to prepare," Hendricks continued urgently. "Glenda in HR and I will let each of you know the times and exact dates of the flights and your particular duties in New York. But plan on that second weekend in December."

The brochures before her, Dina barely looked at them, instead turning her attention out toward the murky November day, wool-gathering. Why was she not *over* him by now?

Hendricks, meanwhile, was droning on about page three of the text before them. Dina flipped the pages of the text half-heartedly. Hendricks concluded the meeting and asked for questions. A few hands were raised.

Could she get him back? Could there be a night in New York that could prove so wondrous? Perhaps if she spoke to him over drinks in some cute little after-hours bar? With a piano player on the side crooning romance and with the dark, murky interior, how could he not resist her?

She was one of Boyko's leaders and should have been paying attention. Then a question was posited by Frank, and she looked up sharply. "Will we be getting our own rooms? I mean, come on, I don't want to bunk like schoolboys, Mr. Hendricks." It was a rude and cynical inquiry and Frank was rolling his eyes.

At this, Hendricks shook his head. "No, sorry. We have to save a bit somewhere. You and Wyatt together, Andy and Benny. But it is at the Hyatt, a top-notch hotel. Only Dina will have her own room, obviously."

Dina surmised that Frank had asked because, down deep, she knew that he actually hoped there would be roommates, perhaps even counted on it, even though his question complained the opposite. For if he *had* been in a room alone, she could possibly pay a solitary visit. In her own room, she could not count on him coming to her.

There were a few more mundane and stupid questions. Then Hendricks announced, "I will be speaking with each of you over the coming days as to your individual duties." Then the meeting concluded, the male quartet almost joyous as they shuffled out, Frank leading the pack. Dina followed glumly after Hendricks. But while telling Karen about the trip later, she had renewed expectations. "Maybe there could be a chance—"

"I don't know, honey," Karen warned between gum cracks. "I wouldn't hang my hat on this one!" For she had seen Frank go immediately after the meeting to Toni's workstation, probably to carry the exciting news. Not exactly the behavior of a man plotting rendezvous on a trip with a woman he didn't want.

CHAPTER 39

Relics of color were still hoarding their beauty on the boughs of trees in early November. Another abstract idea to communicate to Frank surfaced within Dina. It came in the form of a small furtive package of renewed discovery. She settled upon the daring approach of directly contacting Frank's coworker friend.

Why hadn't she thought of this before?

Wyatt Little, the reedy young African American man who played wastebasket hoops incessantly with Frank and whose infectious personality scored everyone's affection, was Dina's mark. The two men occasionally lunched together, often with Benny along—that is, if Frank was unaccompanied that day by any female companions. Wyatt was looking forward to New York City.

She caught up with him right after work as he cruised down the sidewalk. The wind was blustery and icy and chopped Dina's hair about like a bad hairdresser.

"Do you mind if I walk with you?" she shouted over the gale to Wyatt's left side as he strode down Michigan Avenue. His pronounced and hurried gait made Dina whirl in the wind as she panted beside him.

"I'm just walking to Bloomingdales to check on a sale. Gotta get some new shirts for the trip. You can come if you want, although I think I know why you want to talk." He half-smiled and looked sideways at her, the accusatory gleam in his eye almost taking away Dina's nerve.

"Y-yes. I won't kid around," she blustered. The sharp gusts stiffened her words and hijacked them into the windy void. "I thought you could talk to me, or at least put in a kind word for me? To Frank. I know I sound desperate; you don't have to remind me."

"Last I checked, I wasn't in the *savior* business," he had inadvertently lapsed into his Southern drawl, a thing he seemed to do when there were women about. Dina felt he did it on purpose to make himself more charming and innocent. Despite that, he had rubbery legs and appeared almost Gumby-like. He had a voice that enchanted feminine company, tactile as a Persian cat and just as sultry.

"I-I know," she agreed. "Maybe it's more than I want to understand."

Wyatt interrupted, "There's one thing my mom back in Hattiesburg taught me. She would say, 'There's no meddlin' in other people's love affairs! Got to pay attention to your own! There's energy enough in that!'" The crooning voice and affectation of accent made Dina smile. Wyatt missed his early calling all right as an actor.

"Oh, so you can't give me advice or even tell me if he is serious with Toni?" Her rival's name was tossed from Dina's lips with its usual snarl.

"No," the black man said patiently, his own voice softening if that were possible in this high wind. He gazed at the curb as he walked a shy schoolboy. Maybe he was flirting. They had stopped at Huron Avenue, waiting for the light to change. "I said I don't want to get into it, but I will tell you something that may interest you." He turned to look at her, his deep brown eyes sympathetic but guarded.

"What?" Dina swiveled toward him, pivoting her whole body on her heels with eagerness. The wind leapt forward at her again, jarring her like a bowling pin on the curb. Wyatt reached his arm out to balance her slight figure and looked her straight in the eye.

"You want to catch him alone somewhere? Besides work? If you wanted to talk to him like—"

"Where? When?" Dina pleaded. Tell me! *Please!*"

"Once in a while, I noticed, on Wednesday nights, he would confide to me that he 'dawdles in the office' at day's end so he can slip out unnoticed. He stops at that church—oh, you know the one, that Presbyterian church right up there on Michigan Avenue." He pointed. "See, you can see it from here! Up ahead. He says it's just to have a tête-à-tête with God. I don't know exactly what about. I didn't make him out for a religious fella. Man, I called that wrong."

They started to walk now that the light had changed, and Dina listened, craning to catch up to him not to miss a word.

"And, woman," Wyatt became grave, his hardscrabble Mississippi entering his voice now, "you ought never to let him know I tol' you, 'cause it's one bad scene 'tween us if you do!" He reached over and grasped Dina's hand with force, then dropped it.

They continued to walk, Wyatt moving even faster now. Pedestrians going the opposite direction mashed into them bumped Dina to and fro, their wool coats raking her shoulders. She felt pummeled like a pinball.

"Go on," she urged "Any more?"

"He wouldn't tell me *exactly* why." Wyatt's timbre was once again lilting but sedate. He looked off into the dull twilight, his wiry frame silhouetted like a shiny piece of a toy erector set against a concrete gray sky. "He did say once, very mysteriously, that he feels 'angry and cheated' and that he'll 'meet heaven too early.' Those were his words. Whad'ya make of that? Maybe he's askin' for a change of venue? He's just a regular dude. How would he know the future like that?"

There was nothing. Dina was just as confused. They walked in silence for a minute. Bloomingdales was just a block ahead when Wyatt muttered grimly to her, "Well, I hope it helps." He turned away, hurrying his step, almost running. His rapid departure from her was as if to say that was all he was comfortable in confiding to her.

Dina stopped dead in her tracks, bemused. People moved irritably by her, thrown off by her sudden immobility. No one, least of all Wyatt, heard her weak "thanks," which was delivered with teary eyes.

CHAPTER 40

As she raced along the rain-spattered sidewalks that following Wednesday evening, through the twilight fog, she could barely discern the great cathedral up ahead on Michigan Avenue, stalwart, as if it had been standing there for centuries.

It was a church to quietly gather one's thoughts, Dina imagined as she quickened her pace. No wonder Frank came here, but why question his length of time on earth? He had a good job with promising upward mobility, as they say. And his health? Dina believed it to be sanguine, almost unfairly so. Were the strange premonitions concerning another family member who was ill, or a friend? But no, she would have remembered him mentioning something that serious; he, at *her* goading, had poured his heart out about his life in the short three and a half months they had dated. So why would he feel he deserved a self-imposed abbreviated life?

She slowed down her pace now and was just about to jetty up the few steps to the entrance. It was surrounded by a small courtyard that housed a bevy of leafless trees upon whose branches some organization had pinned hundreds of yellow ribbons—for the troops in Afghanistan. The courtyard trees were a monument to causes that the parent organization had decorated to amplify the public's concern, sometimes blue for child abuse, sometimes pink for breast cancer awareness, and such. Dina remembered seeing different colors all the time, a showcase that made people stop and think, ponder *more* attentively over these tiny fluttering flags than for any bling-y purchase on Michigan Avenue they coveted. A reminder of conscience.

What Dina did not see in the growing dusk that November, beyond the trees and ribbons, high upon the gables pinnacled to the sky, was a wraith. Seemingly gnawing at itself, the ghoul glared down on her, meaningfully and menacingly. It was uncomfortable where it was perched and seemed now to heave itself into the background behind a high gable, its oily string-like appendages holding grip upon the flying buttresses at the church roof. It sank slowly down but occasionally jerked its torso away suddenly while grasping a foothold with its prehensile digits, as if the cathedral roof would scorch its body.

Dina approached the door and was about to take the handle, but she stopped. What was that noisome smell? Was it coming from inside the church? No, it was in the air.

But by now, the creature, which had observed the woman as she hurried down Michigan Avenue, frustrated with its position and eager to get away, methodically reticulated its appendages in preparation to depart. Like some ugly black bird, it raised its wings high into the air, but not without one agonizing growl, which, had the traffic and bus stop noise not interfered, would have split the sky wide open as it tore through the human eardrum with the announcement of its anger. The claws came together, the strings yo-yoed back inside, and it flew upwards with an accelerated thrum of its wings. The monster had clearly despised the place where it had landed, but it had stayed ostensibly to watch particularly Dina. It *could* not and would not linger here.

Below, Dina, affixing her scarf to her nose and dismissing absently the smell that caused the gesture, hurried into the church. Her eyes adjusted to the gloom. She saw Frank sitting halfway down the aisle in a pew, his head bowed. The inside lights, dim and comforting with its garden square of votive candles to the left, made his sharp features all the more prominent. The chiaroscuro of the elongated shades cast along the pews was welcoming, so distant from the noisy, wrangling traffic just outside, with the people shoving along with the greedy excess of Michigan Avenue.

Dina held her breath as she ventured forward to sit in the last pew. She was not going to interrupt his musings. She would intercept him as he left. Many minutes went by. Dina sat staring fixedly at the back of Frank's head, not bothering to observe any of the pristine beauty of the walls, the stained glass windows, the beaconing, beautiful church altar.

Am I a stalker? she asked herself. *Following him like this?* Yet he *would* not *see her.* He sent others, Wyatt or Benny, to intercept or carry paperwork about Boyko while they were at work. Her calls still went unanswered. She *had to* see him.

Dina sat with her fingers crossing and uncrossing restlessly in her lap, arguing to herself. She pondered just *what* their relationship had amounted to. She could only come up with one answer: unfinished. Maybe more time? When he left the church, she would tell him—

But now he was rising! Frank crossed himself, and with a self-effacing shrug, walked slowly to the door. *He doesn't even see me,* Dina observed. *This is better!*

As he stepped through the double doors to exit out into the small vestibule, Dina sprang from her seat. "Wait, Frank!" she half-whispered in deference to where they were. Frank heard it and slowly turned around. Two visitors were dabbing their hands in the nearby holy water fountain and preparing to enter the sacristy. They looked up, curious as they passed by the beautiful woman who had suddenly bolted from her pew with her arms outstretched, a frantic look in her eyes.

Dina caught up to Frank's side, almost breathless and although she had only run a few feet, and guilty that she had intruded on his space. "I'm sorry I startled you. More sorry that I-I am bothering you—"

Whether from the complacent milieu, or from his immediate exit from a restful place in his meditation, Frank was unruffled and languidly asked "What are you doing here? How did you know—?"

But then he stopped short, already figuring out the answer.

"Wyatt, but don't blame him!" she blurted out. She grasped his arm, and her eyes were begging, her hair mussed from the wind. She looked like one of the homeless people she had seen leaning on the sidewalk. "It was me. I nearly forced him to tell me—"

"And so you found me." That being said, he quickly reached out for the handle of the vestibule door to the outside. She had found him out. So be it.

Dina quickly pulled his hand from the slatted handles and held it in her grip not letting go. "Wait, please!"

He pulled his arm away and stood staring at her. "What? Well, if you have something to say, we should at least get away from this front door. People will be coming through, and we don't want to knock them down as they enter." Here he gave a half-smirking smile that almost convinced Dina the old Frank was back.

He jostled her to one side of the dark vestibule, where it was eerily quiet. "Stand here," he commanded. "I know why you've come. It's useless. And for me? Well, yeah. I guess I'm a coward, like a lot of guys. I could have told you goodbye days before instead of letting you me see me with Toni and hear the gossip. It was wrong. I know it now. But all I can say is I'm sorry. Sorry I hurt you, let you go on believing we were still together."

"We are! "she corrected with plucky insistence. "I know that you think of Toni as some kind of accomplishment! Get rid of her! I'll forget about all that! Think of what we had and—"

"I don't want to get rid of her." He said it perfunctorily. Then his face relaxed, the harshness falling away. He turned back to Dina. "Even if everything a person believes in feels *right*, sometimes, well, it's just not. You have to think of the other person."

"Who? Toni?" Dina spat her words as if she had been a cat, her face constricting with rage foreign to this holy place.

"No. Me." Frank looked at her, emotionless. "I'm out. Nothing's changed."

"But! No!" Dina cried, and she was flabbergasted when he turned and exited the church so quickly that she heard his footsteps skipping down the concrete steps to the sidewalk before the door even shut.

Her hands fell to her sides, her head drooping like a decaying lily, sad but still beautiful. Her eyes searched the mosaic tile floor for answers. She remained this way for several minutes. When she finally raised her head, tears were flowing down her face in torrents.

A young couple was passing through the vestibule, and the woman, whose amorous and familiar grip on the man's arm Dina ruefully remembered, stopped her companion before exiting. Upon seeing Dina, she whispered, "Oh, is something wrong?" The stranger let go her companion's arm, who looked miffed that his girlfriend was interfering. She approached Dina as she dug in her purse for a tissue.

"Oh, did someone die?" she asked compassionately, for the church these days seemed to have almost more funerals than weddings.

"Yes, yes." Dina sniffed and let her eyes roam almost spastically around the vestibule as she dabbed them with the tissue. "Y-yes. My boyfriend."

CHAPTER 41

Mr. Hendricks was a puny man. Puny in stature, looks, spirit, and personality. In high school, he was just *dismissed*, one of those forgotten students who teachers overlook. Years later, his own classmates would say of him, "Yeah, I think I remember him, but wasn't he in the grade below?"

Nepotism enabled him to rise through the ranks of his father's company. With a paternal nod and a looking away from Ralph's foibles, the long-deceased Hendricks the elder insured that nothing should go wrong in the future by padding the workforce with talented people, including a handpicked CEO who actually ran the company. His son, Ralph, ran only one division, but by far the most important one. It was the largest in scale amassing sales, distribution, and presentation. Some decisions, however, the CEOs could not take on themselves, such as the final say in hiring, although no one new had been hired lately except Frank. Hendricks' greatest of errors would be overlooking Big Sandy's credentials when he was hired.

Hendricks (no one ever called him Mister, if some new employee did, snickering would ensue) had a high forehead and bald pate and seldom smiled, a characteristic that probably made an uninformed audience think he was contemplating grave thoughts, possibly worrying over the company's economic front. The staff knew otherwise. In truth, it was not the master at the helm of Dina and Frank's division that improved the company's profits but the industriousness of the workers beneath him as they chose to shelter and correct his mistakes. To their great pleasure, that they were running the company by themselves, an automaton that ran smoothly while a clown bumbled through the halls looking important.

The Daddy-made man floundered around, bypassing decisions, handing them discreetly to other managers. He would not take the credit if a suggestion by an employee succeeded, but he included himself as a partner to the idea if some extremely efficient plan worked. All his staff watched as the less than endearing *kindly old uncle* walked around, content in this puffery and fooling himself, but surely not anyone else, about his misappropriated credit.

Hendricks also talked with his hands frequently. When they weren't in motion, they were scraping at the remaining hairs on his head, trying to slick them back with his palms. Eyes set deep in his chubby face made him look a little bit like a chipmunk. His voice sometimes whispered with uncertainty. He quaked, and to an outsider, he no more seemed like he could be handling the reins of this mighty company than he could drive a fire engine down Michigan Avenue during rush hour!

Karen would often laugh and kid Dina, "He's got the sense to know the office isn't fooled! He doesn't have any hairs left to push back! I'll bet it's sympathy pain! And have you ever seen anyone walk like that? A turtle would win a race with him because his feet move no faster than his mind! I think the walk is a manifestation of his goofiness! He probably buys shoes in the wrong size too just because they are on sale when he can't get his regular size! That's why he walks like that!"

She peeked out Dina's door, checking for ears. Then she slap-waddled in an exaggerated manner across the office. "Have you ever!" She threw up her hands, flapping them the way Hendricks did when he spoke to someone. Dina begged her to stop, tears running down her cheeks.

So Hendricks ebbed and flowed amidst the cubicles like lost flotsam and jetsam, staying quiet on the things he sensed the staff needed to decide, innocuous and mute, and yet possibly ten to twenty men and women under him could've run the business with even more profit. During the workday, he was greatly taken advantage of, letting some employee go home early for a farfetched excuse or believing someone's five-day run of "sick days." Even with such miscreant behavior, the company thrived, but it could have seen even more incredible growth every year. Hendricks, in short, seemed more suited to the life of some shut-away accountant who delved in numbers and not human beings all day. "If it ain't broke" was his effete mantra, and if change was implemented, it moved forward so slowly that the exasperated employees challenged Hendricks and shouted, "Let's get the lead out! Let's do it!" And with a puny nod, he acquiesced, and the changes took place.

Coworkers wondered how his wife could stand him. It circled around the office, although no one was sure if it was rumor or not, that she was probably having affairs. He had no children. "Did he even know how to produce them?" the office would snidely giggle.

Karen, by contrast, was a powerhouse with her job, multilayered in personality so she could shock-absorb anything, especially Hendricks. Frank was confused by the man and was reluctant to rock the boat.

To Big Sandy, Hendricks present modus operandi was irrefutable. He wanted to go after Frank, and he knew all about the trip that sent him with Dina to New York. Although temporarily thwarted by the previous meeting with her in her office that night, he still desired Dina and was not at all discouraged.

While holding some papers, he approached Hendricks, who was meandering down the hall.

"Oh, hello, Sandy." Hendricks hands flew to his hairline, flitting like a hummingbird on a flower. His eyes shifted as if he wanted to duck down a corridor and avoid him altogether, but Sandy's massive bulk darted in front of the little man, the papers he held, just slightly higher than Hendricks' eyes, making the boss look like a little boy looking over a whitewashed fence.

"You see all this?" Big Sandy shoved the two-inch-high pile towards Hendricks' face. He ducked just in time to avoid a collision with his cheek.

"Y-yes?"

"Well, this is Dina's work! Four of her clients and deadlines before the end of the year! Why, she can't possibly go to New York!"

"I know. I gave her the assigned clients, Sandy."

Big Sandy seemed affronted, but knowing how he could dynamite his own personality into Hendricks' reasoning, he slapped emphatically at the pile. "Well, they're not done! Not even close to it!"

"H-how did you get them?" Now Hendricks' look was of a frightened doe.

Big Sandy smiled a rueful smile. "Well, Toni's working with Dina, and she let me have them to show you." It was a lie, but Sandy betted Hendricks couldn't care less at this moment.

"Ah, well ..." his dry voice rattled in his throat.

"Curo-Co Incorporated, for one, can't wait on this! Neither can Amrand! Do you really think the clients should be put on hold while she travels? You understand me, right? Dina was the one appointed by you to close these deals by the New Year!" Big Sandy's voice became cajoling, almost affectionate. "I really think *you* should rethink this and put Toni on that flight instead. She can do just as good of a presentation, and we can't afford *not* to have Dina knuckle down on these files here at home base! These clients represent a lot of money, you know."

"You're right." Hendricks nodded like a bobblehead. "I never really gave Toni a thought. Maybe she should go. Dina's too valuable to take her away at this time."

"Yes-s-s-s," the sibilant response slithered down the corridor. "Put Toni on that flight and let Dina stay. After all, Toni needs to learn the ropes."

Hendricks seemed to think things over for a minute or two. His eyes darted from the paper stack to Big Sandy's foreboding face, looming over him. Sandy lurched toward the little man momentarily, and

Hendricks had to grab his glasses to keep them from falling off. Myopic as Mr. Magoo, he clutched at the frames, startled at the suddenness of the maneuver.

The drawbridge then went down for the final convincing battle. "Why don't I just go and tell Toni now? Save you from facing Dina. Then you can just send out a memo to everyone. No sniveling or groveling on Dina's part." Sandy knew full well, however, that Hendricks was apt to turn coat and change his mind if Dina's fury encountered him face to face. He *had* to get to Toni and make it look like it was Hendrick's idea. He consoled the little man by saying, "Just in case anyone—say, Dina—asks, say it was decided 'at the top.' Out of your hands."

"Well, I guess you can tell Toni all right. I hope Dina won't be *too* disappointed." He was mincing around his fear of Dina's reprisal like a terrified mouse in the gaze of a looming cat.

"Yes-s-s, a memo, an important email. Make Dina look good now. Play up how important she is to be the only one solely trusted with these home fires—our biggest clients. Women like that, you know, the flattery. She'll take the compliment and run and not give a backward glance." Big Sandy kept smiling, knowing it was a severe understatement. Hendricks had little notion of how deep Dina's longing was for Frank.

"Y-yes, I …" Hendricks hesitated.

"Do it!" Sandy said. "For the company's sake!" Those last four words glistened in Hendricks' mind now, like an icicle dripping truths. How his father *would* have been proud of this move, if he were here! Toni was a newer employee, and this would help her without upstaging Dina. After all, it *was* best to keep the more viable employee at home!

"So, I can tell her now?" Sandy wasn't really asking.

Hendricks hadn't realized the *faux pas* of making the improper assignment on this trip, and it grated on him now. He was anxious to have it done. Out of sight, out of mind. His hands soared up to his hairline again. "Er … I suppose so. I'll release an email memo."

Sandy smiled like the Cheshire cat. How incensed Dina would be, for he knew she was adamantly counting on that cozy trip with Frank. What heartbroken woman wouldn't value face time like that? When the memo was a done deal, Dina would blow a gasket, if she didn't hear it beforehand, and Hendricks could quietly slip out of the office, shrouding his cowardice.

"Well, gotta go! Gotta return these documents to Toni and give her the exciting news!" Big Sandy practically skipped down the hall.

Hendricks stood there, knowing he had again been manipulated. He had no stomach for drama, so he was glad Big Sandy was walking away just now. He quietly searched his pockets for a Rolaids.

CHAPTER 42

Glenda St James should have been born with a beautiful face, given she had such a glorious Hollywood name. Fate is cruel. If people were insects with outward resemblance and characteristics, Big Sandy would be a cockroach, Dina a rare tropical butterfly, Toni an exquisite moth, but Glenda would be a stick bug. Her body would be of resilient material, an unfeminine straight rod, with bulging but not bulbous eyes, the color of which was an almost unnatural shade of blue, offsetting dishwater blond hair. Her skin was pale, and lightened half-moon circles under her eyes made her face appear as a wild lemur in Africa.

Glenda abhorred crowds. She hated her job and longed to be a librarian delving in research so she would not be forced to encounter too many individuals each day. Hair pulled in an airtight bun, she looked like one's storybook image of a librarian, the gesture surmised overall as deliberate.

She was rife for Big Sandy and his irrepressible plot of moving the plane flight schedule. In order to get the Boyko-bound employees onto the flight Big Sandy wanted, he would have to change the booked reservation, and Glenda was in charge of the transportation division. She *had* to be removed somehow for the day so Big Sandy could get his hands on the system.

Convincing Hendricks would be easy, he figured.

Big Sandy sidled into Glenda's office one afternoon, as treacherous

as a spider. The greeting he gave to the bespeckled and startled Glenda
would sugarcoat her down to her neatly tied shoes.

"Hello, Glenda" came the mellifluous greeting. "What's up?"

Glenda pushed back her glasses and stared at him as if he were a
Martian. "Big Sandy, I-I mean Sandy, what brings *you* here?"

"Well, you know." Sandy twirled his fingers together, hoping he appeared somewhat cute. To anyone else's opinion at Sandoval, this would
be an act, contrived for some personal gain. To Glenda, because of her
non-history with men, Big Sandy seemed almost charming.

"No. I don't know," she squeaked.

Big Sandy winced. Surely this mouse should go down in history as
the youngest-looking old maid he had ever encountered! He braved on.
"Well, just that I have been noticing you and wondered ..."

"What? Wondered what?" Now her voice was not squeaky but en-
meshed with curiosity. Was he flirting?

"Say," Sandy said, leaning absentmindedly against the wall and folded
his arms, "ya wanna get a drink tonight? I mean, right after work?"

"I don't drink!" The retort was scolding. The fluctuating duality of
her tones from one second to the next frustrated Big Sandy. He had not
counted on her being obdurate.

"Well, you drink Coca-Cola, don't you?"

"Yes, Diet Coke! Why?" The tense remark was like a nail gun to a
board.

"Why what?"

"Why ask *me* out to a ... a bar?" She spat the word out and reached
to scratch at her bare white leg. Big Sandy wondered just how repulsive
taverns must be to this homely little specimen to get such a reaction. *If
she could only see herself,* he thought. *She has to be the least sexy person alive.*
What foibles motivated such a drab person? He left his rambling thought
and cleared his throat, trying inwardly to push his opinions away. Usually
he was good at maneuvering *some* girls into his web. He stabbed for the
psychological reverse.

"Well, if you don't *want* to go …"

"I didn't say that!" the reply came back with what he perceived to be affront.

"Well, then, good! I think we'll have fun. You know where Eddie's bar is, don't you? It's not far from here, just down the street. East side. Say I meet you at six? I'd really like to talk to you. You know, you aren't all that different from me. We're both kind of pariahs in this company, don't you think? Uh … not the most popular and, well …" Sandy was rambling, and he knew it. Better to quit while he was ahead, but Glenda seized on the comment.

"*You*, maybe! What would you have to talk to *me* about?" It was more of a dare than a question.

"Yes, yes, Glenda. My God, we work here day after day. I see you in the lunchroom, the halls, when I need to book a flight. Why is this so strange? Can't a guy just get a drink with a lady?"

"But I'm probably much older than you."

"Not by much. What does it matter? We can just chitchat about the company, gossip about people who are probably gossiping about us!" Although he doubted that anyone even found anything about Glenda to talk about. "More to life than just work! Time you let your hair down!"

"Okay, I'll go." The mincing reply was hesitant.

"Super! Then I'll see you there!" As Big Sandy turned, his eyes rolled back in his head, a gesture of disgust that he felt translated into a familiar old saying—"like leading a lamb to the slaughter."

He shut the door to Glenda's office. No lamb here. A mule maybe, with her stubbornness and whininess.

Was the stubbornness a game? He couldn't tell. One thing he knew: she was definitely a mule; no thoroughbred here.

They sat down immediately. The old tavern was dark, with low ceilings, not for the fast-moving crowd. Here, people drank their cocktails slowly, and lots of them. No one gave up a seat too early. It was the kind of bar that was good for an affair, a one-night stand, or even to plot a murder or a robbery. The dark, heavy oak booths, one candle clinging desperately for air on each tabletop, called to mind a fifties dive. It smelled of danger and cigarettes. A few low-lifers resided here. It was a place where a nod implied the danger of money, lives, or reputations.

This joint was not unlike the joint my father spent his free hours in, and most of my mother's money, although not all of It, thank God, Big Sandy mused as he eased himself into the oblong booth, not an easy task for his bulk. He winced at the endeavor, but when he raised his eyes, smiling, Glenda was already seated, her purse before her like a prayer book, her eyes downcast as if she were about to hear Big Sandy's confession.

"Ya like it here? Been here before?" he inquired, already knowing the answer. He continued puffing as he adjusted his ample girth beneath the plane of wood, less like a booth and more like a plank erected for graffiti and self-absorbed personalization. So many cuts and gouges from patrons braced the surface that it was rippled, and the owner half-heartedly considered retaining the ambiance by serving carving knives with the customer's brew.

Glenda began running her hand along the tabletop feeling the texture, as if it gave her a thrill. Sandy sized up the gesture. *She is tactile—probably never been stroked in her life!* He wanted to laugh but coughed to stifle it. Glenda had not answered his question but remained looking down, fascinated by the slashes imbedded before her.

The waiter appeared, and she found her voice even before he had a chance to offer his hearty. "What'll you have?"

"I'll have a Diet Coke!" she blurted loudly, emphasizing the word "diet," making the couple in the next booth turn around and wonder why a beanpole like her would need anything diet. Bathrobes hung better on hooks than Glenda's clothes did on that frame.

The young waiter was probably new, Big Sandy thought. Sandy was a regular Eddie's customer, and he had never seen him.

"Oh, okay, got it," he said tepidly.

"You see, *I* don't drink," she continued, as if incriminating everyone in the place as bootleggers or criminal elements because of their refreshment choice. "I just want a *soft* drink!"

The waiter wanted to raise his eyes in astonishment, but he didn't. All this Olive Oyl needed was a prohibition sign! What kind of ruckus did she want to make, anachronistic abolitionist as she was? He was tired and saw this table as a low return on his investment of energy; he did not need to hear any more chastisements of his establishment and its industry. He sighed and turned to Sandy, who, surprisingly, was chuckling.

"She doesn't drink, and I'll have the usual beer—uh, a Bud." The waiter went to turn, but Big Sandy caught his arm. "Hey, say, can you make any of those 'lady' drinks—grasshopper? Pink lady? She may want to try one."

"No! I won't!" Glenda almost growled.

"Just to taste," he said hurriedly. "Bring a grasshopper anyway."

"Yes, sir. We can make those." The waiter turned away quickly.

"You're wasting your money—unless, of course, you're going to drink it with your beer. But then my mother told me once, if you don't mix drinks, you never worry."

These were more words than Sandy had heard from Glenda so far, and they left him wondering if her mother was a teetotaling zealot or the opposite—a swilling drunk. What inspiration *had* Glenda been raised under to appear so awkward, defensive, and afraid? He had never met anyone like her: one minute, a rabid dog, the next, a gerbil on a treadmill going a thousand miles an hour—in silence.

"Yes, that's true, but this ol' frame can handle it." He pointed to his ample stomach. "It's gotten a lot of practice."

"Re … ally?" she mocked, her voice cold. "That so? I wouldn't have guessed." Clearly the rabid dog was out.

Anxious to move the conversation into a friendlier arena, Big Sandy coughed again and asked self-deprecatingly, "Well, enough about my sorry drinking habits. Now, what do you do for laughs?"

"Laughs?" Glenda squeaked the question at him. "I laugh at my TV. Or my cat's antics. Who doesn't?"

How about laughing at yourself? Sandy wanted to say, but he didn't. He cleared his throat again and chuckled. This was not going well. His plan to get her woozy by slipping something into her grasshopper would not work if she continued to be so uptight and stubborn.

In Texas, no female alive who he had ever dated (*or raped*, he thought to himself) could resist the smooth ice cream taste of that lime-colored concoction. It would be so easy to slip in the drugs, as he had so many times before, and his victim would fall, half-sober, more drunk, into his arms, after which he would lead her to her home (never his), holding her head high so she would not vomit on him, and then, while offering soothing coffee laced with syrup of ipecac, the harrow would begin. The retching and embarrassment reaction would push the poor lady over the edge, and when the regurgitation finally ceased, she would lie down, with his help, almost catatonic, on her bed, and he would have his way with her. His own "Southern Texas manners," he called this to himself.

In the morning, he was lucky. The women were all too ashamed to report to the police. Peons! More than likely, they would not remember. He was good at *cleaning up* his crime site. Such was the cocktail of drugs he used in his ammunition, with all the women from different towns as well.

But there was one …

He pushed the niggling memory away. So he had a record! So what! The others hadn't come forth. He had moved quickly away from Texas, and besides, Hendricks hadn't checked anything out when he was hired. In Chicago, he had not yet used his modus operandi. Of the two Sandoval women he had been able to date, he simply broke up with them without explanation. That way, no problems. And no one was the wiser for all the exonerated rapes, only the victim's sadness, shame, and confusion left behind. They were nothing to him.

Animals don't fraternize where they do their business.

He stroked his arm with the tattoo unconscientiously pushing the already unbuttoned cuff upwards.

"You have a tattoo! I shouldn't wonder! Let's see it!"

"No!" He said it so firmly that Glenda jumped. "Uh, let's drink now." The waiter was easing the glasses onto the table.

"Why not?" she whined. She was persistent; he had to give her that.

"Well, let's see. Maybe if you drink a sip of this grasshopper—it's mostly ice cream—I'll show you the whole tattoo," he coaxed.

"Don't want to see it *that* badly."

"Oh, c'mon. It's … unusual! Just a sip. The inscription on my arm is something to tell your grandkids!" He was stretching his wheedle. As if she would ever have a husband even! Maybe forty-five and not a date on the horizon. Probably never had one either.

"One sip?" she countered. "I mean, not half the drink?"

One sip, but you'll want more, trust me." He slid the glass across the scarred surface.

Glenda picked it up, peering at it like a fascinating icicle she held in her hand. *God, this is easy*, he thought, but then, all of a sudden, he noticed she seemed to be chugging it all at once. His hand shot out.

"Hey, hold on—"

"Why? It's good! You were right! Like Mr. Softee ice cream from back home, when I was a little girl! And the mint flavor!"

She was an anomaly of womankind, smiling like a fourteen-year-old drinking champagne for the first time, babbling about Mr. Softee! He couldn't it!

To his surprise, she asked hesitatingly, "C-can I have another?" She was smiling giddily, and Sandy thought she was flirting.

"Sure!" One hand was in the air clicking his finger at the waiter, while the other pawed in his pocket for the pills. "One more of that green drink!"

Glenda continued to giggle, and he reached over. "Hey! Leave a little. Let me have a sip," he complained as he grabbed the stem of the glass. Turning ever so slightly to the left side so Glenda would not see, he quickly slipped the pill into the creamy mixture. Like a marble going into chartreuse quicksand, the pill fizzled slightly and disappeared. As he turned back to Glenda, he saw her eyes were shiny. She hadn't touched the Diet Coke, He relinquished the glass to her greedy hands and watched her imbibe the rest of the frosty mixture. This was too easy. *Won't take long now!* he calculated.

The waiter brought the next grasshopper, not concealing his astonishment very well at Glenda's rapid transformation. His second shock came when he heard Sandy request softly, "I'll take the check now, pal." The youth looked at him in semi-disguised alarm and then back at Glenda, who was almost slurping the drink, the tattoo long forgotten in her effort to satiate her sweet tooth.

"Mmmm …" Her eyes sparkled glassily, and Sandy studied them. He knew the pill's reaction time and had planned his operation well. There would be no seduction here. *Just get her outa commission, he figured, so I can get at those flights!*

When yet a third grasshopper came along with the check about ten minutes later, he was able to push two more pills inside the glass right in front of her. When Glenda began weaving in the booth, Big Sandy knew he was right on schedule.

"Think we oughta get you to your place," he muttered. He knew where she lived, as he had already snooped through the records. Five minutes later, he left thirty dollars on the table and went around to help the gangly, drunk Glenda to her feet. No, he would certainly not rape this skinny chicken. His work was done.

The thirty dollars was a generous tip for the waiter, who had added a double shot to the last grasshopper at Big Sandy's request. The waiter would wonder later if it was really a tip or hush money. In either case, since he was new, he said nothing, even though Glenda was clearly drunk, hair undone with a small clump of ice cream clinging to it, Sandy's Budweiser untouched on the table.

As she stumbled to her feet, Big Sandy's ample arms wriggled her into her coat. He half dragged, half supported Glenda as they exited into the freezing November night.

CHAPTER 43

The rumor mill fired up following Glenda's absence from work. It rocketed from cubicle to cubicle the day after her date. Glenda, who had barely been able to rustle up a lunch companion, unknowingly was sending all jaws flapping into overtime about what had happened to her. Glenda was the matriarch of human resources, which involved travel postings, sick day credits, or anything else pertaining to your job. And although she was, in a sense, invisible, she wasn't unnecessary.

The whispers in the corridors were growing louder.

"I heard she called 911 from some bar."

"Yeah, I heard she was in the hospital."

"That's true. Ya know anything?"

"Don't know."

"Someone said *she* had a date!"

"A date? Her?"

"But she's really in the hospital?"

"Yeah! You see that cop at the front desk?"

"No-o-o!"

"The admitting nurse is a friend of my brother's cousin, and she said she arrived in an ambulance! Something about a drug overdose! I didn't get the rest. She won't be back for a while."

"Her? I still can't believe it! She *never* misses work! No way!"

"Yeah, way! I heard she bought one of those new handheld telephones. What else is *she* going to spend her money on? Anyway, she dialed 911 herself from her home!"

"Wish I could afford one of those! Hey, Jeanie, love, would you buy me one? I'll do your taxes next year!"

"Hey, how do you know so much?"

"Like I said, I got it from—"

"No, she's not just *in* the hospital. She's critical. I called myself!"

"Yeah?"

"Yeah, and she may not recover."

"You mean she may not return?"

"For sure not anytime soon—if at all. You know, I wonder if she'll have to take a drug test to get her job back." There were snickers at this.

"No, seriously! I heard it from Hendricks."

"You did?"

"Yeah, he's all wound up wondering about the future scheduling, payroll, and now looking for a temp."

"Jeeez …"

"Wonder if that'll impact that December Boyko flight?"

"What do I care? I'm not going! But I did hear that Hendricks might be replacing Dina with Toni for the New York presentation."

This tidbit flew along the gossip chain, and Dina, seated in her office with Karen, who sat half-perched on her friend's desk like a mermaid preening on a rock, heard it and slammed her hand down. She had gotten Hendricks' sniveling email this morning and was about to burst.

"What! Me not go? This is my best chance to be with Frank! Maybe sit next to him! I *have* to talk to him to—"

"Win him back?" the mermaid questioned coldly.

Dina swiveled her chair to turn and face Karen better. She had almost forgot her friend was in her office.

"Well, what's wrong with that?" The claws came out. Dina's eyes narrowed.

"It's all wrong, babe," Karen said, fumbling in her purse for her compact. "Just because you started with him doesn't mean you'll be crossing the finish line."

"What's *that* supposed to mean? You *know* I love him! Every day here is madness, having to face him, let alone work with him!"

"That's just it." Karen swiped a lipstick to her mouth and sighed disgustedly, hardly looking at Dina. She had been at this argument for so many months, it had become rote. Time to try a new tactic. *"Desperation!* We've had this counseling session so many times before, sweetie." She glanced apologetically at her friend. "And you I know, I've said, he's very much a player. In fact, Hendricks waffled, and Frank's actually angry about the replacement!"

"Hendricks didn't do it," Dina interrupted, her eyes gleaming like a cat who has recognized that the mouse is cornered. "Big Sandy did! *I feel it!* He even had Hendricks appoint him temporarily in Glenda's place, I heard! What's he up to, anyway?"

"Poor Glenda! She—"

"We're talking about me!" Dina growled selfishly.

"You! You! You! You should be finding other men! What is it with you? Don't you have an ounce of sympathy for Glenda?"

"I don't know her that well. She's an old maid and—"

"And you want to make sure *you* don't become that?" Karen said snidely, snapping the lid of the compact for emphasis.

"*You* can talk! Look at you and your marriages!" Dina was on fire now.

"That ... wasn't nice and ..."

"Well, it's true and—and you're alone now. Is it so bad that I don't want to be alone?"

Karen slipped off the desk. Keeping her emotions in check, she said, "Sometimes being *alone* is better than being with the wrong fellow." She stepped to the door. "But with your looks, you could have—"

"It's my beauty that got him there, where I want him!"

"What? Sometimes people don't have to buy into the beauty, you know! Case in point: Toni doesn't have nearly your good looks, yet Frank's into *her*. You act like beauty is some kind of power tool you wield—"

"It is! Maybe I'm right! Now get out!" Shaking, Dina rose from her seat and pointed. "I know you're my friend, but I'm sick of the same old saw you come up with! I love Frank. I would die for him!"

"This will not go well, Dina. *Please*! I know that business with Big Sandy, how he humiliated you that night you told me about. You're still hurt, and you think—"

"Fuck Big Sandy! And I'm now sorry I told you about that!"

"You think he may pull some hijinks, probably nothing serious, so perhaps it's better you get over Frank! You gain control over Big Sandy that way—if you're worried about what he'll do! Say, I hear two other guys on the ninth floor are interested in you and—"

"Fuck them too!"

"Well, maybe I will! Young meat! Sounds good!" Karen said haughtily, her hand on the doorknob. "But one last piece of advice: go to a therapist, a priest, even Pramod! You've come unhinged! I don't deserve this abuse when I am trying to look out for your welfare—"

"My welfare is forever with Frank! And *only* Frank!"

"You owe me an apology. Don't you see yourself? Be careful! You've fallen too fast and too hard! This will all get you nothing but more and more pain!" she said softly.

"Yeah. Like you know." But the words were lost in the air, as Karen was already gone down the hall, where whispers were forming alongside of her path like hedgerows.

CHAPTER 44

Pramod examined Dina in the dim light of her kitchen and spoke with hesitation. "It is natural you feel upset about your encounter with Big Sandy. And that Frank has disappointed you. Frank is not an evil person, per se, but it seems that he ignores the good in people—on purpose. Unfortunately, it shows he is on the way to being a person who is worse than he is now."

"No!" Dina exclaimed. Learning about her expulsion from the New York City trip had made her even more peevish than despondent. She wondered why she had come to Pramod's at all. It had been snowing heavily when she left, so she took public transportation. Now she was tired and did not know if she could stomach another lecture on evil, which seemed to be navigating through her own world on its own recognizance.

Sensing the change, Pramod tried to soft-peddle what she had to say about Frank. Dina *needed* to know, so she said quietly, "I give you a warning that you are still trying to ignore and deny. You must realize that some things are evil's baby steps. We are all tempted. You see, the two opposites of goodness and evil must coexist in our civilized world. Fortunately, good usually wins."

"I don't feel like a winner," Dina snapped, not liking the path Pramod was going down. She somehow sensed it might take away a little of Frank's luster.

"You ignore the truth, but it is all there. Frank is seemingly taking a path toward his own kind of blackness. However, I must reassure you: he won't succumb to evil's side, even though he treated you badly. Don't doubt my words."

Here Dina stood up. "No, I don't believe it!"

"Do not be discouraged. I see hope for him, child."

"He's not diverting from some path! Besides, how can you analyze him without knowing him and say that about him? How do you *really* know?" Dina tried to squelch the anger she felt entitled to now, especially since Big Sandy's meddling had caused this last dirty trick to be played on her. She took out all her rage and doubt on Pramod. "Because I think he'll come back to me! So there!"

"He *will* be … overtaken, but not by you. It will be in evil's game. That is all I know … about him," Pramod said.

"But you're a forecaster of the beyond! A clairvoyant!" Dina's irritation was taking the form of worry now.

The Indian smiled again with understanding. "As are you, although not as skilled. I can only say what I know—that he will be the victim of evil, and yes, it will be unwarranted. "A cat, whose head Pramod had been lavishing strokes on jumped down and then up on Dina's lap, startling her. "What *comes* to me comes in little stages."

"No! You, you can't mean he'll be hurt or …"

"Do not alarm yourself." Pramod stood and leaned to pat Dina's hand, but she paused when she saw the sudden chill in Dina's eyes. "You *must* leave this subject at peace now. Things and predictions change, but you alone can be the one to change this … *history*. Be careful. This conjuration was brought up by *you*! Listen to me! You *must* keep yourself in an open and compassionate state of mind!" Pramod emphasized by grinding down her thumb along the table and steadily pounding it. Another cat, who moseyed by, looked up confusedly at its owner. "Surround yourself with good. This is how you will survive this … future! You have no control over some of the strange forms and forces! The universe has made their untimely spiritual presence known. You do have strength in your favor. Your choices should aim higher." Pramod sat back down. "Frank will work his way through you, in some way."

"What? How? In what way?" Pramod was starting to sound cryptic again, Dina thought.

"Again, I say I do not know, but your hysteria too attracts … unhealthy things."

"How can I possibly relax with those words—danger, keep evil away? I don't understand you. I thought you were a friend who could advise me! Now I'm just going to leave here frightened!" her voice rose in panic.

"Do not leave scared! Bravery is what evil fears! It impedes its progress! I cannot, after so many meetings with you, let you walk off into the darkness confused and angry. I *am* your friend, and you must just accept that my advice is necessary at this time!" Pramod looked away distractedly and loosened her cloying sari a little.

"So your main advice is only to … beware of danger?" Dina's face transitioned to a scowl. "This all seems all out of *my* control anyway."

"It is all deadly serious! I do not take evil lightly, and neither should you!"

"That's it! I'm to be brave, not worry about Frank, surround myself with good feelings, and avoid Big Sandy. And *this* is the answer? The only advice!" Dina felt screaming. This all seemed like rote prayers, ascending to heaven only to go unanswered. "What the—?" she began, but she was interrupted.

"Above all, I fear there is no turning back for this large man. He has totally given into the darker side, and he has been that way for a long time."

"Do you have visions all the time? Do you read other people's auras or what?"

Pramod laughed. "No, I wish it were that simple."

"What have I said that's funny?"

"Nothing. It's just I don't believe in oracle readers. I feel my mother passed this blessed trait along to me. It has no name, really. It's just a feeling that comes over me. I do not accept my small gift in any such haphazard way. You see, only *certain* individuals are allowed to hear and feel … certain outcomes."

"So, it isn't really what you do for a living?"

"No, not my job. I am retired," Pramod replied. "I do not read palms and tea leaves. Nor do I hang out a shingle that says 'horoscope' or anything else. But if I am near a person and have a feeling, and if they seem receptive and possess enough equanimity to handle my words, I will mention my feeling."

"And I was receptive?"

"You are Irish, right? The Irish have always had the advantage of feeling a bit of what the *other side* is like. Maybe one of your relatives had strong feelings like this and never told you? And where do you think the *scary season*, the darker side of us, the link between the living and the dead, the foretelling—what you Americans call Halloween—originated? It comes down from Ireland."

Suddenly, Pramod grew quiet. Dina sensed it was the older woman's signal that she should leave.

"Thank you."

She stood, turned, and grabbed her jacket. As she rounded the hallway, she heard Pramod's haunting voice call out, "Do not forget to surround yourself with light! That is the way! It will not touch you!"

This residual advice did not contain enough ammunition to kill the gnawing fear of what might happen—and to whom.

CHAPTER 45

Staying late at work one night, Sandy flushed out Compass American Airlines where he knew his buddy, Duffy worked. In just a few phone calls he had secured the flight changes. It was still somewhat warm out for November, and Sandy's open window rattled with the breezes, the lamp on the far side of his desk unsteady and knocking to and fro, dust blowing off its dirty shade.

Flights from Chicago to New York—like elementary school. He smiled, for he had found a flight with an unnecessary stopover. It took off out of Midway, not O'Hare, with a dismal layover in Philadelphia. It would save so much money; he could hear himself saying to Hendricks. Yes-s-s-s, the smaller airline for the employees going for Boyko's presentation? Hendricks would buy it. Perhaps Sandy could even see his way to somehow pocketing the few extra dollars he'd save his boss.

That's it.

He chuckled, typing, making his eyes squint like a weasel's. He pressed *send* on his word processor. Hendricks would find the new schedule in his email the next day. *Gotcha, Dina!*

He stretched out his arms to relax, and with that motion, his tattoo became visible, hellishly black in the tinted florescent lighted office. It was a crude bleeding crucifix, vile and sacrilegious, with the inscription

scrawled at its base and layered with grotesque, twisted goblin-like creatures of the underworld.

Sandy thought back, remembering his eavesdropping a few weeks
ago, when Dina and Karen talked about angels. He had stood loitering
in the hallway, pretending to tie his shoe. He laughed softly now as he
tickled a few more computer keys and bit into a sandwich. Ghouls and
angels? What had they been talking about? Foolish broads! It was 7:00
p.m., time to go home. He was finished.

What he couldn't see, just outside his window, and every window
from the city to the suburbs, was a black spirit pass by, leaving a gelatinous
trail, eel-like. Its exhaust was a vapor, fulsome, like ashes and death. With
the windows open, in the twilight in the November breeze, Big Sandy
suddenly smelled something terribly foul.

CHAPTER 46

"Naw, go on! We don't need any more coffee!" Big Sandy impatiently waved away the scruffy-looking waitress with the back of his hand. Sandy was churlish, and his mouth formed the shape of a "dangerous curves" road sign as he sat across the booth from Duffy Branson, eyeing him with scrutiny. "Now ya know what I'm sayin'? Your hands can work this miracle for me! You know what you're doing! You should! You're head mechanic there!"

"But do you know what you're suggesting?" Duffy whined. It was true; Duffy more than controlled the mechanic's hangars at Compass American Airlines, his position high enough not to pursue any kind of friendship with a creep like Sandy. Friend? The nomenclature that was a distant stretch. Pawn would be a better choice of words. But Duffy was malleable. Scorpions that associated with Sandy could be corrupted for a price and the scrawny mechanic. "You know what this means." Duffy looked around with guarded glances. "In terms of lives? I mean—"

"Look! I don't want any complications," Sandy whispered angrily. "Details! Details! You take care of it. You know as well as I do that you came here for a price. Since when did you take vows? You're no saint! I know about your history, about the drinking! And you *know* I know it!"

"But—" Duffy interrupted meekly. Sandy savagely cut him off.

"I just want this thing done quietly, ya hear! What d'ya think I picked this crummy dive for—to give you your money? We're not on swanky Michigan Avenue, ya know, ya fuck!"

"I dunno." Duffy looked doubtful and took a sip of his cold coffee. "You just don't know what you're askin'! Could be big trouble." He shook his head, and his eyes darted away in confusion.

"Damn straight I know what my money will buy and what I'm getting into!" His hand strayed to his jacket pocket, and he patted it slightly. "Thirty K. How does that sound?"

Duffy whistled low.

"Just for tinkering, like a toy." Sandy looked right and left. The gesture was a scant formality. In this neighborhood, they were used to violence and danger. Sandy whispered roughly now, grinding his point down with a balled fist. "Why, you could just take off somewhere when it's all over—fly somewhere! Quit! Retire! Hide somewhere forever! Hell, I don't know!"

"Oh, that'd rouse suspicion, wouldn't it? Me fleeing."

"Not right away. You could go later! You've got no family, no wife! Hey, I'll sweeten the pot with an increase after the job's done!" Sandy observed Duffy's fearful looks, worrying he was losing his prey. "All this for playing with a damn plane!"

"Ya mean playin' God, don't you? What makes you want this so badly? Or *who* do you want?"

"I just want to inconvenience a certain person, ruin his day, uh … vacation, that's all," Sandy said. "Kinda getting' back at someone for taking my … uh, girl. Look! You're just not allowed to know! It's better that way. Hey, it's only money. I just want the pilot pissed, make him land early, ya know, like he's frightened for his crew and passengers. His levers, dials gizmos, hell, whatever he reads to make him unsure. A little ways into the trip! Fuck, man, you know what you're doing! Make it look like that missile crack or whatever in that rocket that went up. It was some inconspicuous thing that played a part—"

"Shit, you're comparin' the Space Shuttle *Challenger* like this is a parallel! My God, you're offering up *possible* murder!" The old man felt a dampness on his brow now, and he swabbed it nervously with a handkerchief.

"Naw! You miss my drift. I don't want anybody killed—"

"But they could be! Likely would be!" Duffy's bleary-eyed stare arrested Sandy, but the younger man shook him off.

"Let's just say the pilot's annoyance at having to land in some God-awful and maybe inconvenient place before he hits Philly would give me pleasure I am willing to pay for."

"Oh yeah, I understand." Duffy studied his coffee, weighing in his mind the two years until he retired against the tax-free money. Why *did* Big Sandy want to buy his expertise? The enigma piqued his concern, but Sandy's money was slowly withering his scruples.

"You don't have to understand the motive. Just do the job! Jury-rig something in that engine to make the pilot land unexpectedly. Be careful though."

"But why do you want this someone so awful bad on the ground?"

"You ask too many questions. I've got a check for thirty now, and I'll have thirty more—"

"You mean forty more."

"Did I say seventy?"

"Eh, you didn't, but that's what it gonna take!" Duffy squinted at him, and the two men traded a stare reminiscent of a pistol duel.

"Fuck, seventy!" he snorted and handed over the small envelope. Duffy made the gesture to reach out for it, but Sandy pulled it back and grabbed the old man's wrist, giving it a cruel twist. "You know this goes nowhere now, don't you? And if it *does*, you'll end up … somewhere else, I swear! Somewhere you don't like, you know what I mean?" Duffy looked at Sandy solemnly as the younger man rode down his stare, an executioner's look, wearing down his victim with two choices—bribery or the noose.

"Yeah, leggo my arm."

By now, the affronted waitress was walking by them again, clutching the coffee pot. She sniffed at Sandy's grip on Duffy, raising an eyebrow, but continued walking. Sandy extended the envelope again, releasing the arm.

"It's a deal." Duffy squashed the check into his overalls. "I'll expect the other forty upon completion! *Or* I'll reverse my damage before the plane flies! You got that? Now when?"

"You must know when the planes get final inspection before they fly."

"Yeah. They go in rotation, but I know 'em. Check 'em myself last before they fly, even before they leave the hangar."

"Good. Here's the flight number. Looks like this plane originates in Chicago, as I can't have some willy-nilly plane that comes out of LA or something."

"Yeah, it'd have to for this to work."

"So, you'd know the exact plane to … tinker with?"

"'Course I would. What else! I'll make sure I'm on the job the night before it flies."

"Good." Sandy's tattoo was almost exposed as he withdrew his arm to his side. He licked his lips, an unconscious gesture of satisfaction, and then replaced his tongue. As it retracted back into his mouth, an impression formed in Duffy's mind of a nature show he'd seen on TV—a vile insect as retracting his proboscis from its withering victim. Duffy almost shivered. Just *who* was he aiming at?

But these thoughts were fleeting. Grabbing his coat, he hurried away. It was chilly and ugly out, pelting rain, and he shouldered on his parka, hoping that, after collecting the future forty, he never would see Sandy again. He had enough of the man, his dirty work and his secrets.

CHAPTER 47

Hutter Construction/Demolition was in charge of knocking down the decrepit building on Wabash Ave, in the Loop. The workmen huddled around the crane that chilly November morning, each clutching a steaming coffee and taking cautious sips as they listened to their manager, Ray Ogens, who was directing some men to the far side of the lot, while instructing others to work on the refuse pile.

Thomas Delavan was appointed driver for the wrecking ball crane that day. "Like handlin' a baby buggy!" he would brag to his friends about the maneuvering of the nine-thousand-pound ball. "Just goes where you damn well tell it to!"

Of course, the gear was formidable to the inexperienced. The hefting of that steel oversize bowling ball was jaw-dropingly scary, not only when standing below it but also just observing the massive demolition tool, swinging pendulum-style across the sky to smack into the side of brick wall and begin to shatter the edifice like a sledgehammer on ice. The sound alone was deafening, and Thomas had his earphones in place as he took a seat on the crane and slid a few knobby gears to the left and right while charging up the engine to let it warm up.

Ray now stepped up on to the side of the machine and made a few hand signals through the glass. "Hey, Tom, what d'ya say?" he barked. Tom lifted the earphones.

"Gonna go over to the other side. You ready?"

"Yeah, knock 'em dead! Take it forward then!"

Ray plopped off into the dirt and scudded behind the machine. The great behemoth crane inched forward, slowly, so the ball wouldn't revolve too much. He cornered the building, aimed the crane, and laid his coffee cup in the holder, preparing to get a cigarette. As he eyeballed his target, a grand old lady of a building, he whistled to himself, hating to see it struck down, but damn, the city had to move forward. Chicago on the move.

He reached for his safety glasses now and wiped them clean. The yard in front of him had cleared of workers. Most everyone was on the far side lot, going over whatever else had to be moved from this space. A few of the men held blueprints. Others he didn't recognize. His job was to smash, and what an energy release that was! Like when he came running as a kid and kicked apart his older sister's Lego creations, much to his mother's consternation. "Thomas, you're just bad always!" she would holler at him.

He surveyed the yard once more, making sure everyone was free and clear from the machinery, but the workers had now all moved onto the other side of the building out of Tom's sight. The heavy chain groaned as if it floated the ball in midair. He raised it a few feet. Taking his eyes off the ball momentarily to take a sip of coffee, he slowly gazed up and out the window of the crane.

What he saw suddenly perched on the ball caused him to drop the scalding cup to the floor of the machine, and the next instant, he was jumping from his seat, his eyes never leaving the orb, which was poised and quivering in the air.

"Jesus Christ!" Tom squinted his eyes and blinked. Post-Halloween jitters? He questioned himself, shouldn't had those two shots before I left for work! Am I seeing things?

A wrecking ball measures approximately fifty-five inches across. Curled around it now, like a mother bird guarding its nest egg, was a black winged creature, its prehensile claws grasping the smooth, shiny steel like an eagle on top of a flagpole. But this was no avian species. It appeared to have some kind of reddish eyes, which bored into Thomas's. Thick, long, snake-like wires extended from it, which it whirled and whipped around furiously like the tail of an angered cat. The monster was huge, sinister, and ugly, and Tom, not believing his eyes, felt lightheaded and fell back into his control seat, tearing off his headphones and quickly looking around to see if anyone else had spotted the creature, whose ebony surface was so scintillating and lacquer-like that it made the wrecking ball look like a tiny opaque marble beneath it.

But no other worker was even near the crane. Suddenly, there was a sibilant sound coming from within the monster, which grew louder every second. The frightened machine operator put his hands to his ears to block the din and watched in horror as the ghoul raised up one wing. With that motion, the ball started to sway—on its own! It teetered tormentingly, almost teasingly, while it worked its maw crazily to reveal a mouth full of yellow canine teeth.

Tom let out a scream, and his hand reached for the compartment door to escape from the small windowed box he was imprisoned in. But as his hand gripped the door handle, he looked up, as he heard a loud "swish," like the passing of rapid air, as if he were in a fast-moving car with the windows rolled down. The next thing he heard, as he breathed his last, was the bomb-like explosion as the wrecking ball, all on its own, came careening backward at the glass enclosure where he stood. The machine's drive cabin shattered, windows and all, as it blew apart.

Just before the impact, Ray was discussing payroll with the owner, Mr. Hutter, who was in the area to observe and supervise. "I thought you were all set with your crew," Hutter argued, looking quizzically at Ray.

"Yeah, I thought so too, but I heard Delavan's been fighting with other employees. Not just once but twice. Beer brawls in bars after work, enough so the bouncer had to throw him out. That stuff gets back to you, ya know. Gotta let him go. Just too much of a hothead. And he's operating the goddamn wrecking ball too! I gotta get me a new driver! Tom's a wastrel! Thought today I could smell the booze on his breath, even with

the coffee he's drinkin'! Jim, he's a danger to my men, and if he comes in
here semi-intoxicated, well, that crane's walking dynamite, and we don't
need OSHA down our necks with a serious accident—"

Their exchange was bitten off by the sound of the explosion, the force
of which sent shrapnel of the crane's mechanical parts both vertical and
horizontal. Ray and Hutter as well as the hard-hatted workmen were
too busy ducking and slamming their bodies to the ground to notice the
strange black bird (as someone from a nearby four story apartment window later reported it in yet another sighting) ascending casually into the
sky, dripping blood from its claws.

CHAPTER 48

"The *Chicago Tribune* newspaper was all over that weird death of that construction worker downtown. You know, the site with the wrecking ball? Near Randolph Street?" Dina ventured on a quiet evening as she sat across from Pramod. They had mostly exchanged small talk over the last half hour or so. Dina had surmised that the old woman rarely left her abode, if at all, and usually commented very little on the goings-on in everyday Chicago.

Pramod suddenly turned to face her and nodded.

"I knew this would happen."

Dina sat open-mouthed, wanting to ask how, but merely chalked it up to one of the old woman's mysteries and watched Pramods's eyes as they followed one of her cat's antics; the felines chased dustballs and each other, wrangling over a chew toy, rolling on the floor one minute, the next, leaping like Superman from the countertop to the high-topped glistening wood cabinets, where ledges provided perfect perches for their tiny paws. Pramod smiled as Dina remained watchful, trying to figure her out.

The old woman looked up and remarked grimly, "Evil—it had its excuse."

"What do you mean? Evil—it's all too vast! Too overwhelming, excuse or not!" Her words came off indignant. How could *she*, one meager individual, overtake the whole human iniquity? She longed to drop the disquieting subject altogether, feeling as Pramod was singling her out. Why? And these vague interpretations gave no straightforward answers!

The Indian interrupted her wild thoughts. "Small things bring great things and great understanding in the world! How one lives brings hope for good encourages others to seek out and *do* good by *example!* We will never have a utopia, I fear, but we can all start small. Like a good virus, it infects others, bringing change. And hope elicits change. Your small gesture will allow that."

Dina now, her hands in the fur of a bushy black cat that had strode up away from the roughhousing to claim a place on her lap, said, "Oh? How—"

"*You*. Your small deed, which I know *will* happen, will elevate the world a note or two, even as good people shiver in fear and purport their wishes for universal kindness and compassion, hoping that someday, it will be written into normalcy. It will be telecast, and others will know."

"Me? I'll do something that will … become known? I can hardly get out of bed in the morning because of my depression!" She was flabbergasted. She barely had room in her thoughts for a good deed, let alone struggling to keep abreast of work these days! Why, just last Saturday, she turned away a little girl who was at her door selling early Christmas wrapping for her school. And she had always been a sucker for little kids and their quiet gumption to get out and sell door-to-door in this angry world. She always bought something, from useless magazine subscriptions to Hanukah cards—and she wasn't Jewish! She had been at home, barely able to bring herself to answer the phone or the door, and when she did, she waved away the crestfallen youngster with a listless "No, thank you," shut the door, and returned to the couch to bury her head under an afghan and cry. And *now*, Pramod was saying she would give hope to the world? Maybe Karen was right. Pramod was dosing out a lot of baloney.

"You will run for yourself but stop for others!" Pramod's pronouncement came. Dina's eyes grew wide.

"What's *that* supposed to mean?"

"I cannot say."

"You *always* say that! And you leave these messages hanging in the air, confusing me! How do you expect—"

"I *really* cannot say what I do not know. I only know it will be up to *you*. When it happens, you *will* know."

Dina cocked her head and shook it. This time, a white cat approached her chair with its quiet "mew." Dina dropped her hand to pat its head.

"But …" she started protest, but realizing it was useless to badger the old woman to give up information that she seemingly was incapable of pulling forth, she sighed and said, "Well, I have been here awhile. Maybe it's time to go. But hey, I don't remember seeing this little fellow before." She pointed to the white cat that luxuriated under her caresses. "She seems to like me."

"She does indeed," Pramod said emphatically. "She should. She *must*. I wouldn't doubt it for a minute."

Dina rose to her feet after giving the animal one last loving stroke, and with her eyes slanted up curiously at Pramod, she smiled wanly but said nothing. She thought to herself, *Now, why did she say that?*

CHAPTER 49

Duffy Branson maneuvered though the aircraft repair hangars at O'Hare, observing wounded planes, stacked parking-lot style, end to end. Copious Hangar B, practically the old codger's residence, housed these overly-serviced Compass American Airlines planes—weathered trolleys, floundering with their last breath by the time they reached here, became Duffy's responsibility as well as his crew's; the mending of these particular giants just couldn't seem to outpace their poor reputation, despite aggressive ad campaigns.

Hangar B was an ugly brown structure, shaped like a lady's A-line skirt. Inside, mechanics took their job seriously, their bodies sometimes working twelve-hour shifts, boring in and out of the planes' "innards," as Duffy called them, like so many ants penetrating dark holes, then reappearing from chambers again, strutting along the narrow-platform scaffolding with the ease of trapeze artists. Duffy, the oldest worker and highest in command, a four-star general to his "army" would breeze by like a shopping cart, placing bits of his knowledge about, overseeing, complaining. He was a man not really liked by his team. The overly large poster on the wall set about 8 feet up said it all:

"Faulty Inspect, Lose All Respect!"

To every worker in "B," his aircraft's passenger might as well have been God Himself! Responsibility was answered to, on this shift, Duffy alone.

He was in crabby and jumpy mood tonight, impatient for his mischief to be done because he had spent the day tinkering, testing, and constantly questioning. A few tools clipped to his belt clanked the announcement of his arrival, and the mechanics, as always, weary of his constant presence, muttered remarks of "Here comes the Tin Man! Gimme a break!" Duffy was considered unlikeable mostly because he never inquired much about the people under him—details of his workers' personal lives, their events, much less their happiness. The title "Tin Man" was not far off the mark, for he had no heart. He was an icy, questioning, unsmiling commando with no bedside manner, and he liked it that way.

Now, nearly midnight, he was half-crouched along the platform scaffolding, 25 feet in the air, in front of the plane that would bring Big Sandy's plan to fruition. He plunged his hands into the engine door opening, like a doctor extracting a miscreant tumor, but not before his eyes shifted warily to the floor, searching for witnesses. Seeing no one around, he turned back to the 747, picked up a needle-nose pliers, and explored inside the plane's guts for the dial he wanted. Toying with the motor's frame, he sought out and loosened but did not yet unwind a "failsafe" mechanism that would compromise this next plane's flight—a hot button of sorts to alert and override minor and perhaps temporary damage when the pilot would notice its warning. It was this trouble button that Duffy wanted—damage enough to make the pilot overestimate and possibly want to …

"Evenin', Duffy! Workin' a little late, aren't you?"

Duffy almost fell onto the engine floor. He cranked his face around to the jowly man perched below the scaffolding.

"You about done?" the visitor offered pleasantly. "I'm quitting for the night. You're lockin' down tonight, right?"

"Almost done, Dave. Jesus! You scared me!" Duffy growled. "Sure. Sure. Me or Harry will take the lock down."

"Well, c'mon then!" Dave ventured, although he knew the negative answer already. "Let Harry do it and come have a brew with the guys!"

"Naw, don't want to!"

"Can still catch the West Coast game at Shakey's, ya know!" Dave coaxed, but Duffy bit down on his impatience sullenly. He looked away. The money riding on his final twist of gears made him anxious, and he longed to descend the ladder and push Dave out the door.

"Well, let Harry know I've gone then."

"Yeah, right. See ya." Duffy's eyes darted back to the gear, a pretense of tightening while actually he loosened. Dave shuffled away, shaking his head at the old dotard, his lunchbox at his side, rattling with a metal thermos inside, sounding like a small animal clawing to escape.

Hearing the door slam behind Dave, Duffy sighed and stretched further into the eye of the engine, where the computer was kept. It stored a vast amount of dials and displays, including the autopilot. He lifted his body and leaned higher with his arm, opening another smaller door inside. More overriding mechanisms peeked out at him.

Suddenly more men's voices could be heard, laughing and coming closer. Three more men. This time Harry was in the group. He called out, "Christ! It's about midnight! That plane had its baby by now, knucklehead?"

Duffy's shoulders slumped as he moved away from the engine, almost a little too nervously, and he sat down on his haunches, disgustedly eyeing the mechanics below, who jostled one another's shoulders good-naturedly, guffaws echoing along the colossal structure until the sound pierced and pricked Duffy's impatience enough that he snarled dangerously, "Get outa here now! Dave left, Harry. I'll finish and lock up. Go on! And no, I'm not interested in going to Shakey's for a beer with you, either!"

"Jesus, who asked you?" The men turned to leave.

Harry's voice sailed up to him. "You're in fine form, I see. Christ! The personality contests you could win, Duffy."

"Probably just needs to get laid," the next man said, laughing.

"Who'd have him? His own mother doesn't want any part of him."

The raspy voices became distant, a scratchy vinyl record winding down.

"If he had a sister, she'd give ya the clap just lookin' at her!"

"Is that who you was in the bar last week? Did ya get the vaccine yet? Ha ha ha ha!" The derision continued until the ceilings no longer carried the sound, although the men's foul comments recycled over and over in Duffy's mind until he grimaced, his hand crushing the needle nose a bit tighter than needed. Just a few more turns and he'd have it. Just enough to disable. That's what Big Sandy said.

His hand poked into the opening again and patted the aberrant nut. *Loose enough to cause trouble*, he thought, *enough for, yeah, a pilot to think about the next possible airport runway he might want to slide into—just as a precaution.*

Job's almost complete, Big Sandy, Duffy thought to himself, and he smiled giddily. *Can't go too far, just got one more little thing to do before …*

Duffy turned around for another tool. He had pretty much completed his jockeying of various nuts and cranks to make an annoying but semiserious mess and could see the autopilot out of the corner of his eye. *Better not monkey with that*, he noted grimly. Something like that could be noticed in the light of day, and that *would* be bad. Computer-regulated too. He smirked to himself. The great Duffy's labor went unquestioned, sacrosanct after all these years with the airlines.

He removed his hands from the machine's guts, knowing he had compromised the 747's next flight out, and he leaned back against the scaffold rail, satisfied, the needle nose still dangling from his hand.

The hangar went completely dark.

"What the …"

He heard his own voice quaver a little. The lights then went back on, but they were lower and lambent. The plane in front of him was barely discernable, although he could see the large white compass drawn on the side of the aircraft, a trademark of Compass American Airlines. A heavy sound, like the creaking of compressor, could be heard, an ominous, low hum.

The hangar was obscure except for a spot of small light on the far left below him and about twelve yards away.

Funny, the other generators didn't catch on, he reasoned to himself. They always did in bad weather. Why only this small unit and not the main one? Was it storming outside? What the hell! His eyes raced along the floor. Little by little, he could discern things, but his gaze kept coming back to that small forlorn humming spot of light. Why would there be light *there* in particular?

The hum grew louder.

"Who's there?" Duffy shouted with impatient fear, because what he now saw was truly repellant. A most repulsive face seemed to be literally escaping from the building's floor, in that lighted square of space, rising up slowly like steam from a kettle, a visage of total blackness.

"D-d-do ya know you have to have authorization to get in here?" Duffy blustered, hoping it was an intruder he was addressing, maybe someone pulling a prank. The thing expanded now, rising, climbing higher and higher, its body enormous and dappled with gray but mostly black. Its arms were spangled with several tattoos. The ghoul dragged its *threads* forward and upward, like Marley, the ghost who visited Ebenezer Scrooge, without the clanging but with the steady foghorn hum. The bulk of its body was so capacious, it seemed the height of the hangar wouldn't hold it; the head of the colossus had to duck forward to make room for itself. It towered over the 747, spreading out wider from side to side its *wings*, assuredly trying to accommodate itself. Fat, noxious-smelling clouds, black ooze, and inky smoke were everywhere. Droplets of grease dripped from the smoke.

The monster gave the impression of a smile as it ominously raised its wing/arms, which depended the long, slinky twines, threads the color of dried blood. Grinning with hideous yellow teeth, the thing opened wider its eyes and its jaw. It was as if the giant wraith was gaining volume and strength from something the expansion triggered, as if it desired to outsize the plane. As it hovered, he was sure this thing was from hell. Its description in the daylight surely spat in the face of anything earthly, let alone good. If this was the *other side* unleashed, and Duffy was praying now, the violence in its putrid face could have caused a heart attack. And Duffy was not strong.

The mechanic never felt his foot moving or anything after that. The needle-nose pliers still in his hand, he attempted to turn away from the sight of the ghoul to get to the scaffold ladder.

He was not fast enough. The tattooed monstrosity peered down on him, wildly grinning. Duffy's jaw dropped, and he turned away again, moving forward, but the monster was too fast. A large "ooooohhhmmm," followed by the sound of a hiss and whips, moved through the air. This was accompanied by a flash of blackened ropes streaking along the hangar, like the loud acceleration of hundreds of black birds across the sky. All at once, the threads flipped down, curling around Duffy's fingers, tightening like a constrictor snake. They encircled the knuckles two or three tines in such rapid precision that Duffy never knew when the digits left his hand. They snapped off wildly, like bloated yellow blobs of Play-doh, shot up in the air, flung from his palms as neatly as a person would break off a piece of string cheese.

The two fingers that held the needle nose, however, for some reason, flew forward into the guts of the plane, the tool bumping loudly against something, possibly a switch, the pliers lost forever inside the plane guts. Duffy heard that "clink" sound of the pliers before his own screech of terror-filled compromise. The thing had him in control.

Duffy, in mid-scream, gaped in shock at his fingerless hands. There was no blood! Only stumps, immediately healed and not sutured, as if he had been born with a deformity. He hoisted his hands up higher, still screaming while inspecting the marvel. The ugly face came closer. Finally, it relinquished its malevolent grin and this time hissed, "Evil's excusssssseeeee!"

Duffy screamed again as he fainted. His heart was collapsing, and he fell into a heap on the scaffold while the monster's face, astride the mechanic now, wove its threads around his neck tightly. The "twine" was not the same greasy stems from its body. It was more like an everyday clothesline, albeit black, and the wraith tightened this noose so much that a mark was made on Duffy's throat.

The old man gasped a death rattle one last time, eyes opened in surprised expiration while the end of the rope was threading around the scaffold. The ghoul's noisome breath as it exhaled, like an unearthly wind, blew the body upwards and tossed it over the edge of the scaffold, where it suspended eerily in the air. The 747's mechanical door slammed shut, appearing as a "finished" inspection, ready to fly. Meanwhile, Duffy's body jiggled with an unnatural force for a while, the corpse slamming from side to side like a bell. The gargantuan creature, if it had emotion, seemed to take pleasure from this, and its grin returned. Then, like a vacuum, there was a strange sucking noise, and the monster floated upward, Duffy with it, and vanished. The lights in the building came back on.

❧〰〽〰☙

Two days later, the detectives on the scene, unable to explain the ablated digits scattered on the hangar floor and fearing the bad press associated with Compass American Airlines—out of sympathy, payola, or for whatever reason—were hesitant to suggest suicide, since no body had been found. Desertion was the offer. Duffy's thirty-thousand-dollar check, hidden too well in his apartment, was never discovered

It was rainy the day Big Sandy found all this out. Reading the timeframe later in the papers, he noted quizzically the absence of body and presence of a removed finger. He knew the job had been done. He also felt no compunction to attend any injunction meeting by the police of those who knew Duffy. Nor did Sandy feel any sympathy at all for the hapless mechanic, only greedy delight when he discovered, days later, that his check to Duffy had gone un-cashed.

CHAPTER 50

Dina's continued to feed everyone dry crumbs of herself, scrupulously play-acting out little slices of time, like a daily prison sentence, until five o'clock, when she could retreat to her home. During the day, the women clustered around her, thinking her so "adjusted" and "cool." Since Frank had shifted his allegiance to Toni, most thought him as callous, a below-standard gigolo who helped himself to female attention for his own private diversion. Most were only too happy to point out their own past and present heartbreak: Sharon from Accounting described her horrors with a married man; Brenda in Advertising hissed her own lover's foibles, (without mentioning her own, of course). Females all, recounting, usually ended their diatribe by calling Frank a bastard. Dina wasn't sure she liked this particular take on Frank's character, but it put a temporary Band-Aid on her heart.

The unfortunate fact was, Frank was doing well at Sandoval, especially with the Boyko project, grabbing the spirit of all its technical procedures and running with it successfully, like some golden boy on the football field, while Hendricks pretended to ignore the gossip of broken hearts that had now risen up to him, whether through the grapevine or otherwise. But as Frank's work became more stellar, he did notice the subtle but sluggish pace at which Dina was again working, this time on Amrand and Curo-Co. He came to her desk one day.

"After all," he cajoled, "these two projects will be in your own pocket, your very *own* babies! Toni couldn't do them!"

When Hendricks brought up her name, the hair on the back of Dina's neck stood up. She could see her, that twenty-two-year-old vixen, whose nose was too long but who had pretty eyes, bushy Sophia Loren hair, and a small mouth. She was petite in stature, but that body! With its overhang cliff of breast, small waist, and long legs, no wonder Frank wanted her. But her rival *did* have a flaw: Toni wasn't really comfortable in her own skin! Queer that this lack of confidence existed in so lovely a picture.

Mr. Hendricks seemed to parallel her thoughts just then. He tried to smooth things in referring to the forfeited Boyko upheaval. He reasoned "Of course, Toni doesn't have your style or years of experience. But you seem so out of sorts, and I need you badly to focus on Curo-Co and Amrand here at home base! I *know* Boyko is more your style. Besides, you could be available to her if she needed advice, and ..."

He trailed off, sensing he was in alligator-infested waters.

All Dina heard was the word "advice." She would soon tear out her own liver! What was Hendricks driving at? She said nothing, only looked at him angrily.

Hendricks straightened his tie, coughed embarrassedly, and patted his bald head nervously, feeling as if he were a principal and had to fire a teacher.

"If you want to know, Toni is anxious to fill in for you and hopes she can follow in your footsteps with half of your finesse—those were her exact words." His eyes roved around the room so he didn't have to note Dina's expression. "And that she'd love to work on the New York presentation, and she said she hoped Frank was a good enough sport about switching horses in midstream."

Dina could think of a more fitting equine word for both Frank and Toni, but she kept her mouth closed.

Lacking any more to say, Hendricks cleared his throat with difficulty, as if hoping to dislodge this egregious task from it, and with a meek voice, he said, "What do you say?"

"Fine, but I already *heard* the rumors—and of course the email! So *this* is what it comes to!" Dina said arrogantly. "Well, where are the newer files on Amrand? Curo-Co?"

"I'll have them sent over to your computer. They have a year-end deadline, not so pressing as the Boyko. By the way, you can bring your notes, files, and any unfinished work on Boyko around to Toni—"

"Ah, how about I just bring them to *your* office later today?" Dina interrupted.

Hendricks nodded and quickly left her office.

CHAPTER 51

Early in December, after receiving the New York City flight details, Frank stormed into Big Sandy's office without knocking, a paper grasped tightly in his hand. He had heard from Hendricks that Sandy had made the trip's changes after Glenda was taken to the hospital and was said to be still in guarded condition. He had long since believed Big Sandy had something to do with Glenda's condition but could not prove it. He could not go over the simpering Hendricks' head, since his boss was now satisfied with Sandy's choice of flights. It was all so ugly and disturbing, and now he had to contend with the big man's purported screwing of perhaps something else beyond the awkward schedule? The displacing of Dina? What more?

"What the hell is this, and why have you got us on a layover in Philadelphia, for Christ's sake for a Chicago–to–New York flight? There must be hundreds of non-stops! And what is this Compass Airlines? What hamster-cage, puddle-jumping airlines have you booked us on? What about United or American? And what about my miles!"

"Compass of America is a good although small airline," Big Sandy breathed out easily, looking up slowly and menacingly from his work, like a satisfied rattlesnake rolling out of a prairie dog burrow. "Hey, the boss pays me to save him money on flights I book! And I did. I am flying five of you out there, for God's sake! We save at least a thousand dollars this way. Haven't you noticed, it's mid-December, and half the world is

225

booking holiday flights? I did what I could in the interest of saving the
company money. Besides, you're going back on United Airlines; I got that
for you all."

"Yeah, and I see you got Dina bumped off the flight and instead put
Toni in! Is this some sort of revenge tactic? You got Hendricks to keep
Dina here? She's practically given birth to Boyko! I know you twisted
Hendricks' arm, didn't you, you ass!" Frank felt some odd sort of em-
ployee loyalty toward his beautiful coworker, even if he didn't love her.

Big Sandy ground his teeth silently, anger forcing down the heavy
lines in his face as if it were in a vice. Why should that chisel-jawed
schmuck get all the fucking merry-go-round rings in life? He thought
but he put down the pen he was holding, making his voice obsequious as
it practically slithered forward.

"Sooo, you're upset the pussy you dumped can't sit by you on the
plane? And your *stand-in* will? I find that odd. By the way, how is ol' Toni
Stand-in these days?"

"Her name is Spaulding, and you know it. My affairs are none of your
business!" Frank shouted.

"Hmmm … affairs …" Sandy twirled the pen now, picking it back
up and examining it like a hypodermic needle. "Interesting choice of
words."

Frank now moved forward and began to flap the schedule in Big
Sandy's face. "Get this changed, you jerk! You think because you peddled
this favor like Girl Scout cookies to Hendricks that no one knows your
exterior is showing? You brown-nosing, sick, greedy bastard! You are so
full of misguided hate that—"

"It's common knowledge that Dina dumped you!" Big Sandy blurted,
testing the lie. "Get over it, pal!" His voice was lower now, hoping to quiet
down Frank's loud accusation. The office might hear, and questions might
be raised. He was not completely comfortable that he was out of the clear
with the Glenda investigation. "The schedule is set," he said evenly and
calmly. And there's no sense whining about changing it. It is so late, and

with the holidays coming, we'd be lucky to get a flight to Joliet, Illinois, for five without paying more than $800 each! There's nothing I can do!"

"There's nothing you *want* to do, you mean, you loser! I know you did it on purpose!"

"Dina's got plenty of work here," Sandy mumbled, beginning now to type at his computer, his chin raised in a hoity-toity manner, making Frank even more irritated. "She doesn't need to go. Shouldn't go!"

"You're so full of crap!" Frank tore the schedule into pieces and flung it in the air like confetti. They flurried to the carpet by Sandy's desk. He shoved a finger accusingly at the big man. "You like disturbing people, messing with them, don't you? Irritating them, humiliating them. Better yet, maneuvering them to you *own* God-forsaken purposes! What *is* your angle? Is that what *does it* for you? Huh?" A sneer widened on Frank's face.

"You better watch what you say—and lower your voice!"

"Why should I watch what I say? *You* just want to insure your own self-preservation so it doesn't get back to Hendricks. You're such a *bag man*, Hendricks' whore, and you know it! No! Wait! That's not it!" Frank balled his fists, and with controlled breaths, leaned forward and whispered in Big Sandy's ear, "You're just evil! Most men evolve, grow more human. But others, like you, remain cold-blooded like the reptile you are, all the way down to your soul! Really, you actually come from a class *lower* than reptiles! Lower than slime!"

Big Sandy kept on typing, as if he had not even heard him, even though Frank's words were like blue ice cracking as they escaped his lips, and he continued to hover, his posture crouched over the corpulent man for almost fifteen seconds. At last, Sandy gave a dismissive, uninterested wave of his hand, saying nothing. Frank straightened up and rushed out of the office, slamming the door.

Big Sandy stopped typing for a moment, thinking, a smirk smeared across his face like the makeup on the face of a clown. He picked up his coffee cup, tasted it, decided it was no longer hot, and put it down.

Listening tentatively for noises in the hall and deciding there were no questioning voices of workers nearby who might walk in and ask what all the yelling was about, Sandy slowly rolled up shirt sleeve partway and began to admire the skeletal masterpiece on his chubby arm—the skull face, the inverted crucifix, the socket-less eyes, the various entangled limbs twisted like thicket. Perhaps the limbs reached for unanswered solace. All encircled the letters printed indelibly on the tattoo.

"Yes, maybe you're right, Frank," he muttered to himself with satisfaction. He slid up his shirt sleeve, and his fingers moved gently along the outside of the tattoo, like a child deliberately outlining a picture in a coloring book. He traced over with his index finger the two familiar words within the frightening image: Evil's Excuse.

CHAPTER 52

The Friday night before the Sandoval group was to fly out, Dina was suddenly assaulted with a fear that seemed to elevate into feeling of doom, nearly supplanting her angst over losing Frank. This time, she did not resist the telling hand that seemed to reach into her soul, and so, in pounding the badly stained door, the knob itself jiggled so violently that it threatened the already weak hinges. Some cloying harbinger had lingered far too many weeks now, whose meaning she did not understand. But Pramod would!

"Please! Please! Pramod, answer!" The cold December wind pinpricked her skin. She wasn't dressed warmly enough, and yet sensed little discomfort beyond that strange but familiar *sensation*, climbing steadily within her, around her.

Her life. What was it now? Unanswerable mysteries, ghosts, deaths, loss, pain, fear, now danger? Did all these events mean something? Were they merely a stage for events to transpire, be acted upon, either to throw her off course or reveal something sinister? It had to be explained. The last visit of obscure forecasts from Pramod had managed to heighten to uncontrolled panic by now.

"Pramod!"

The howling wind spitting sharp snowflakes dug pocks into Dina's cheeks, plowed upward to the underside of her short skirt. Coming directly

from work, she knew her blouse was as askew, her tights baggy from running, and her legs felt cold and unprotected from the frigid blasts. Her
fingers grew icier as she stood wildly rapping. Running through the streets
in the north side, she passed house after house in Pramod's neighborhood,
looking into brightly lit windows, people sitting inside in front of TV
screens, oblivious. She had sailed along the sidewalks like a specter, yet
they sat in complacency! These uninformed viewers, whose faces were lit
up from the electronic information in front of them. They had no doubt
heard reports of a ghoul loose in the city. Did they care that this *thing* had
been scurrying around Chicago for several months? Had the mysterious
deaths been attributed to her ghoul from the condo pool? She was sure
they were one and the same now! Yet who would believe her? Karen barely
did. She had seen the reports—the policeman in Skokie, the construction
worker—bodies never found yet so much blood, but no monster!

She shivered. *Please, Pramod, be home!* She clutched at her muffler
and yanked it tighter, fingernails scraping the door again. Frank shouldn't
go! What if something should happen! He shouldn't leave Chicago! She
banged the veneer harder. Why did she think such things? Her suspicion
had been let loose the minute she had heard of all the airline changes, but
now she just needed reassurance from the only one she felt could grant
her that: Pramod.

Slowly the door opened, and the wizened woman looked out. Her
hair was no longer in the bright turbans she usually wore but must hanging like long vines from the center of her head, trailing her breasts and
combing over a yellow cat who sat in the crook of her left arm. "Ah, Dina!
I expected you."

"Y-you did?" she gasped, more from cold than surprise. "I'm so sorry
to bother you. This is important, although you may think it ridiculous—"

"Child, the world of clairvoyance has little time for ridicule. It only
makes those who don't believe in it ridiculous, in its telling aftermath.
You've had a sign." She knew! Of course she would! "Come in out of the
cold."

"T-thanks you. I know it's late, but I must talk with you.

"Come, sit in the kitchen."

She followed the old woman down the hallway. As they neared the kitchen, the warm, inviting coffee-bean smell arose, the dining area steeped in chiaroscuro, a dimness from a tiny night light pasted in a socket and many candles providing the only brightness. Pramod did not turn on the lights but stood and lit two more candles on the table, contributing to the nebulous but spooky feeling.

Unlike before, Pramod offered no refreshment but stood solemnly, looking at Dina, who hastily grabbed a seat without being offered one. Three or four cats nuzzled one another, standing and blinking their curiosity in the doorframe, waiting for an invitation. But a look from Pramod, and they lay down on command, like obedient servants, not venturing as much as a paw forward. This eerie gesture was lost on Dina. She was lost in wild thoughts and had trouble focusing. She flung the knitted beret from her head and tossed it so violently that it flew across the room and bumped into one of the gray tabbies sitting at attention. He bent to sniff it.

The air became pungent now with the smell of candles. Still, Pramod did not sit. She remained standing behind a kitchen chair, clutching it and all the while peering at Dina as if to inspect her.

"I'm so glad you answered the door." Dina's speech rattled in her throat and seemed to reach out beseechingly. "It's Frank I am worried about! I still love him, but that's not why I came. He's traveling, and I *sense* something—like he shouldn't go! Does that have any meaning for you?"

No expression appeared on the Indian's face, but her calm black pupils were as implacable as the thin drawn lips. Dina stared, until Pramod commanded, "I know you still love him. Give me your hands."

Dina dutifully extended her hands, which were still icy from the weather outside. The touch of Pramod's hands arrested her, like plunging freezing fingers into a creamy warm liquid. Equally disturbing was the unwavering and electrified stare, which dropped its usual amicability and pulled Dina forward, pressing her into her own internal world.

"I will not hesitate to tell you that a large tree will fall, and when it goes down, as is nature's way, many things under it will be disturbed, hurt—"

"W-wha-what? Tree? What? Riddles again! Please, Pramod! Not now!"

"The world of my unknown provides many clues. Each clue is a fruit from this fallen tree, and there will be danger. Yes." Pramod shut her eyes.

"But what does it mean? Be more specific!" Frightened, Dina tried to pull her hands away, but Pramod gripped them tighter, as if trying to impart the seriousness of her worlds through touch. Her squeeze was painful—perhaps it was meant to be so—but Dina plunged on urgently, "What tree? Is it a person? Frank?"

Pramod continued, monotone and expressionless, as if reading text from behind her eyelids. If Dina had not been so worried, she would have been giggling uncomfortably at the lunacy of this scene: the cats in the doorjamb, the dim lighting—like something out of Steven King, or a séance from a Hitchcock movie.

"The tree, it falls hard, but it is not the red rust color of oak bark or even the white birch." She squinted far into another worldly dimension. "The things below, it must be aware. *You*, as well, must be very aware."

"What are you talking about?" Dina almost shouted now, pulling her hands free. Pramod's eyes half opened now. "Stop dancing around with these clues! I need you to help me! To tell me something other than trees and clues!" She fingered the collar of her thin coat frantically with her free hand, dazed and unnerved by the blind alley of all this mumbo jumbo. "Please, please, Pramod! You're my friend! Tell me! What more? What can you see? Or sense? I need to know, for Frank! Is he in trouble? What *will* happen. You know so much—"

But her pleading speech was abruptly broken when Pramod leaned ominously toward her, causing Dina to shudder at the eerie move.

Suddenly, the trancelike demeanor evaporated from the old woman's face, and she saddened a little.

She spoke softly now. "As I have said when we've spoken many times before, people who have the capacity to explore what is *beyond* do not get a testimony of the things soon to occur! My signals are only gates to things, places, and clues to describe a future. The future is danger. I do not know what or who. You yourself came here based on somewhat of the same hunch. You have that power. And a fallen tree, perhaps, not a man? I do not know. But I do see a color ... almost. The bark is hard, and the soul of this tree is old and bitter. It is an unusual color. Perhaps an unusual person. Not like any other. The tree *reclined* is not at all powerful. It *will* fall. Danger waits beneath."

Pramod shut her eyes now and gyrated a little, as if a whisper were calling her back into that world of clues and secrets. Dina waited breathlessly, watching the transformation.

"It's bark is beige or taupe." Her words came out almost mellifluously. "Maybe, ah, the color of sea shells. No, not shells ... *sand!*"

With horror, Dina touched her hands suddenly to her lips and shrieked, "Big Sandy!" and she flew from the room.

CHAPTER 53

After leaving Pramod's, Dina flew carelessly along the slippery sidewalks in the dark, clutching her coat closer against the harsh weather. It was sleeting badly as she deftly zigzagged through various umbrellas, underneath which housed homeward-bound pedestrians. If only *she* could be going home also, curling up on her sofa, forgetting the madness that *drove* her to tear through these streets in search of—her chance—to save Frank?

If Big Sandy was involved … oh, God! She knew there was trouble, a probable catastrophe ahead! The slimy bastard had caught Frank at the apex of his distorted revenge. What could he be planning? Why Frank? Or was it the best way to get to her, using the most diabolical means at his disposal? Had he summoned his revenge in the past, against other women who had spurned him? Pramod hinted at as much. And Glenda? Was Big Sandy at the root of her hospitalization? Glenda had never returned to work. No one really knew.

Dear God, she prayed, *let it not be Frank!* She could not afford to lose him! Better it be her. She had resilience. She could bounce back from whatever Big Sandy planned to dole out. She could again *feel* the danger. Big Sandy and his tattoo as if he had *meant* to show it to her alone! She had a thread of hope that the plan she was hatching might work!

The rain pummeled her arm, drumming down on her unsheltered

head. "Just go!" it seemed to chant. Could she get to Karen? But Karen *had* promised her, many months before, in her office, that she would always help her. Was that, in fact, a premonition? That she would likely put Karen assurances to the test? Would she really agree to the far-fetched plan? In the days up until now, Frank had never returned her answering-machine messages. Nor did he have one of those new portable "cell phones," and neither did she. They were expensive, and Hendricks, of course, wouldn't spring for them, as cheap as he was. And now that she wasn't on the Boyko project any longer, there was no reason to consult or contact him at work. So grave was Frank's warning on her last visit to him at the church, to leave him alone, that she would not even think of bothering him at his apartment now.

It was this or nothing! She and Karen would start out right away, early enough to catch up to the plane, so to speak, in Philadelphia. There she could meet him unexpectedly at the airport. Oh, God! If he *made it* through that leg of the journey (she didn't put anything past Big Sandy). At the airport, she could get him away from his coworkers and talk to him! The ridiculous two-hour layover planned by Sandy would buy just enough time. She and Karen could intercede when the plane landed. He'd come away convinced, wouldn't he? He *had* to!

Besides, she could back up her serious warning by describing her friend Pramod's feeling of imminent danger and the recent warnings tonight of what Sandy was capable of! Maybe the group could schedule a different flight to New York on some other plane? Would he believe her? Believe an old woman's notion? Or would he laugh at her concern? She could only hope the first rung of the journey would render the plane harmless. If only she could get all the Sandoval employees to believe her! Perhaps the very act of her driving so far to secure their safety would reinforce the critical nature of her warning!

The flight was not until morning, and yes, it was farfetched, overly dramatic, she thought, but Frank would never see her tonight at his place, let alone believe her! Besides, Toni might be there, and …

If she and Karen could only make it to Philly.

An ominous gloom settled all around. Warnings screamed at her from all sides. Suddenly, a street-corner Santa Claus, standing like a sentinel by a large kettle, caught her arm. "Merry Christmas! Can ya help?" he greeted loudly.

She stopped abruptly, almost regurgitating with fright and surprise. Jesus, even small incidents were unending her! "N-no, let me go!" she ordered.

"Wasn't detaining you, miss. Really, just brushed your arm. Sorry!" But Dina was already running again, his words floating back in the wind, distorted. By now, she was wheezing a little with the shock of cold air filling up her lungs.

Can I convince Karen? Will she go? I can't trust myself to drive alone!

It was asking a lot, but she couldn't deny her! Was this rash behavior how people acted when they truly loved someone? Rain was changing to snow now, billowing with the fury of all its natural strength, what this city was known for.

Dina swiped snow from her eyes one last time. She saw her car and bounded in. As she fumbled for her keys, Pramod's words floated back to her: "You will run for yourself but stop for others." Now what did that all mean? And why was it coming back to her now? As she ground the car into gear, a strange sibilant sound, like a cat's hiss, changing quickly to an higher octave, came to her ears. It rose almost physically and ominously, like smoke from lava, cascaded along the car hood, in through the interior, the seats, and ended up in the trunk, where it exited through the tailpipe, a warbling sound that had the physicality of waffled air, much like that which surrounds a mirage on a torrid highway.

Dina screamed and stopped her ears with her mittened hands. Was she going crazy at last? Recent bad occurrences that paraded before her closed eyes now—the conjuration, the apparition in the pool, Big Sandy's thwarted advances, the sight of his tattoo, and most of all, Pramod's urging of caution tonight. Did it all contribute to some diabolical and unforgivable scheme?

Stay focused! she scolded herself. *It's probably just the wind and snow hitting the windshield.* Placing her hands on the wheel, and with the wipers swishing the snow away into oblivion, she screeched, unaware of the horns honking angrily behind her.

She had been to Karen's place any number of times, but tonight, as she approached from the north, her sense of direction seemed off. Where was her apartment? What was happening? She crunched her knuckles tighter on the steering wheel, and the car skidded a bit. She could feel the sweat on her forehead underneath her wool cap. Possibly rousing Karen out of her quiet evening now would not inure their friendship much, but when her friend saw how distraught she was …

Karen knows Big Sandy. Knows what he may be capable of! But would he stoop to hurting Frank, along with many other innocents?

She saw a phone booth up ahead and swung the car into a stop. She barely entered the booth when she began punching numbers. "C'mon, Frank! C'mon, answer!" she yelled, but only got Frank's goofy message in response: "Hi, you! How ya doin'? Leave a—"

Dina blew out an exaggerated puff of air. Damn! He was still screening all his calls! Perhaps he was out to dinner with Toni, talking about their flight in the morning.

She returned to her car, her heart hammering. The roads were getting slicker, but she barely noticed. Going to Midway airport in the morning wasn't an option. The men—Wyatt, Benny, and Andy—wouldn't believe her. They laugh and board the plane anyway. And she could just imagine Toni's mocking smile! No! She had to create just enough urgency. She and Karen *could* get ahead of the plane tonight!

She felt nauseated now. Would Karen really go willy-nilly into the night on the harebrained journey? Race to Philly? Why did she believe Pramod's warning? *Because the warning in your own head is greater!* She almost veered off the road with that realization—that she had sometimes doubted her most poignant intuitions, but now it was making itself heard, loud and clear. The task seemed beyond impossible, and although Karen *was* quirky and usually up for anything … but this? In this weather, their own lives were also in jeopardy!

Would Big Sandy show himself at the airport, disappearing into the crowds like a noxious vapor? He wouldn't dare, would he? If this sleet didn't clear away in the morning, maybe the plane wouldn't go! She argued and prayed back and forth. Drive perhaps 800 miles! Jesus Christ! The plan regrouped in Dina's mind: They would take Dina's car. It was over the weekend, so no one would miss them at work. She could almost feel Pramod's eyes on her. Her breath produced high little squeaks, as if she were having trouble in a high mountain altitude.

Suddenly she found herself there in front of Karen's building. She pulled forward, searching for a parking space. She calmed herself, thinking of a convincing argument to Karen, stepped up to her friend's house, and began knocking. An insufferable, cloying vapor now cloaked her shoulders, heavy and gyrating, like those old-fashion mink stoles her grandmother wore on her shoulders, where one animal's teeth seemed to gripping the other's tail. She reached up to her neck as if to tear off the invisible fur with both hands and almost screamed. The urgent hiss "Big S-s-s-sandy!" reverberated again.

The door opened. "What in God's name is wrong with you?" Karen asked, standing arms akimbo in the freezing air, clad only in a light robe, her face more angry than worried.

"We've got to drive to Philadelphia tonight to intercept Frank's plane where it's laying over!" Dina said hurriedly. "He and the others are in mortal danger!"

CHAPTER 54

"Get in here! What have you been doing? You look like you've been running through the streets! And in this weather!" Karen motioned Dina in, the backdraft from the door's closing throwing an icy blast to Karen's body. She could feel it through her robe, down to her pajamas. "Why are you here on such a foul night?"

"I've been running through the streets! It's important!"

"Oh now, that's real normal. Christ, I need a cigarette. C'mon, sit down in the living room. Something tells me it can't wait until tomorrow, right?" Karen oozed into an easy chair, grumbling and grabbing up her lighter and pack of cigarettes while Dina bounded onto the sofa, eyes and hair wild.

Oddly, for a moment, no one said anything, so Karen plunged in. "You say we have to go to Philly? Are you out of your mind? I wouldn't go even if the weather were better! It's too far!" She blew out a billow of smoke.

"But we've *got* to go to intercept Frank! He *is* in danger! They all could be! I also have to tell him something! We'll go to the airport where big Sandy made the flight for that stupid layover—"

"Something?" Karen's interrupted "What something? So call him!"

"You *know* he won't take my calls, ever! Not even at work! And besides, I just tried him fifteen minutes ago on a pay phone! I told you how long I've tried—for weeks!"

"And this is *my* business? You know I love you, hon, but it's been over! Nothing more you can tell him—"

"I'm pregnant!" Dina blurted loudly. There was a pause, tension hanging, a loosened chandelier about to drop and crash.

"Oh. Well, now that's something. When was I going to know? Your best friend—"

"I wasn't really sure until I saw a doctor recently. Look, I know Frank would want to know—"

"Yeah, hey, they *all* do, honey!" This time Karen blew out another puff of smoke almost indignantly "But why *this* way?"

Dina ignored the sarcasm and carried on, seemingly stricken with anxiety. Karen had never seen her friend this upset. She looked anything but pretty right now, with makeup smearing from wet snowflakes landing on her face. "Karen, I could be saving his life and everyone else's too! Pramod said tonight in so many words that Big Sandy, well, he may make something go wrong. That's what I gather."

"Pramod? You're *still* making visits to that exploiter? And believing what she says? Oh! Hon, I know it is tough, but get a grip on things! What will you do? Will you keep the baby?" Here Karen replaced her cigarette in the ashtray and moved over to sit next to her friend on the sofa.

She gave her a hug. Dina was crying, shaking, and blubbering. "You don't believe me. I knew you wouldn't—"

"Shh, calm down!"

"I've got to go! I've got to try! Yes, I want this baby with all my being. Maybe with this news—"

"Hon! Some men just can't be *had*." Karen patted Dina's dripping hair. "With or without a baby! I think he's made up his mind. Frank's a dead end!"

"No, I can't let that be true! I've never been rejected like this!"

"Obviously," Karen muttered to herself, low enough that Dina's crying masked the comment. "Although," and she said aloud, "I wouldn't put it past Bluto to have mucked something up with his sick, jealous brain!"

"See! That is also true, and more importantly, why we need to leave! I believed Pramod's hints—I don't know why. She thinks I had a gift of foresight too! Big Sandy attacked me, you know! He'd stop at nothing! We've just gotta go!" Dina continued to plead, "I'll pay for it all! We'll drive straight! You *must* come with me! Please! We'll start tonight. I'm so jittery now that I feel like I could drive all night!"

"Yes, I see that." Karen reached to retrieve the forgotten cigarette and inhaled deeply "But *should* you, in your condition?"

"I'll never ask for another thing! I promise! Not even babysitting! I promise, I'll clean your place for free the next year."

"Now how you gonna do that with a baby, huh? Listen to yourself!" Dina cracked a smile.

"See, I got you to smile." Karen studied her, contemplating. "Have you packed?"

"Yes, er, no, but it won't take me long, really. And besides, weeks ago, you promised me you'd always help me! Remember? And no matter how crazy it seemed! I can't go without you, Karen. I need moral support! I don't trust myself!"

"For Christ's sake!"

"Please, please! It's over the weekend, and I—"

Karen cracked through Dina's whining with the blast of a shotgun. "On *one* condition, I'll go!"

"Y-yes?" Dina sniffled, her eyes hopeful.

"Don't give me that Bambi eye! If I go and the response to you and your *news* is anything but welcoming, you will *really* forget him! Totally! I mean this! He's dead to you, baby or no! *And* refrain from seeing him by transferring to another division of Sandoval! Even better, another department! Or get a new job altogether, although I don't want you to leave."

"I-I ..."

"Don't take too long now to agree! This whole thing is nuts, and those are my terms. I don't think it's too much to ask, considering. Yes or no? Right now!"

Dina looked around Karen's apartment thoughtfully, as if looking for the guidance on her friend's various possessions—her dining room table, her grandfather clock, the luxurious and expensive Oriental rug purchased by Karen's last husband, which she got in the settlement. Her eyes returned to her friend.

"Deal!" she said firmly. Karen threw off her robe and went to pack.

CHAPTER 55

On the early-morning flight, Frank settled into his airline seat next to the window, quickly fastening his seatbelt. The low hum of the jet engine growled beneath his body. His seat companion, Andy Grafton, leaned across the aisle, laughing loudly at something Wyatt had said. Frank's face set, brooding. Some foreboding, which had established itself along his nerves the moment he set foot on the aircraft, now made his fingers drum impatiently on the seat divider.

Andy continued to laugh, although quieter now, the noise of the men's guffaws making Frank more disquieted. He finally jabbed Andy with his elbow, annoyed that Andy didn't sense any threat.

"Hey, man!" Andy turned his shiny face to Frank, his blond hair a bit too long, old fashioned for the style, which was clearly shorter these days. He looked like one of the Beach Boys in their heyday. "What's up?" Andy smiled broadly, a man whose natural disposition was to be overly friendly.

"Do you feel … something wrong … out of place?" Frank looked around.

"Naw, man! You're just jumpy. Not to worry! Pilot's got it all under control."

His reassurances did not sit well with Frank, and he whined, "But that doggone layover in Philly! What was Hendricks thinking?"

"Thinking of saving moolah, the old tightwad!" Andy rubbed his fingers together in demonstration and laughed again.

"No, it was Big Sandy's doing—I know it for a fact! So don't you feel … uneasy?"

"I don't feel nothin'! Now, c'mon! So Big Sandy changed the routing. Yeah, with a little twisting of Hendricks around his finger, so I hear. Otherwise, we would have gone straight to New York City! Whoever heard of a layover for so short a trip! Ha ha! Money talks, my man. It's all about saving the green! But yeah, it was Big Sandy, all right! The kiss-ass! Wanting to show off to Hendricks that he had it under control in Glenda's absence!"

"No, no, it's more than that. I don't like it at all. And what about the Philly airport? Is it big? You think we'll make the connecting flight?"

"Yeah, it's way later, but I'm sure Sandoval has the bases covered. I tell you, you're just too spooked! You act like you never flew before!" Here Andy whispered in jest, "Hey! You want me to check out the passengers? See if anybody looks suspicious? Like a hijacker? Could be that little old lady over there!"

"No! Cut it out!" Frank jabbed him again.

"No, *you* cut it out!" The smirk vanished from Andy's face. "You're spooking everyone within earshot! Have a drink! Hendricks will pay for it!"

"Hmmm, good idea," Frank muttered, even though it was morning. Not convinced, he wanted to bolt out of his seat and warn the pilot, the flight attendants, anyone! But he stayed where he was, clearly miserable.

The plane was taxiing out, and his mind wavered back to Toni. He looked around at her. She was three rows back, but she caught his eye and winked. They were not seated together. That was probably Sandy's doing too, picking the seats ahead of time so the lovers would be separated.

He settled back down in his seat, trying to be comfortable, although uneasiness still raced along his pulse. The smiling flight attendant was rushing down the aisle, glancing in everyone's lap, checking for seatbelt compliance. She stopped at Andy, who was still leaning over, laughing at Wyatt.

"Sir, your seatbelt," she ordered.

Frank heard the accompanying click and closed his eyes. This December day was too dreary to bother looking out the window, so Frank's thoughts ruminated back to ... *Dina!*

Now why had he thought of her just then? Some part of him felt badly about how he had treated her, especially when they had met that time weeks ago at his apartment. Would it have been right to lead her down some path to nowhere, with her following blindly along? These damned misgiving thoughts—now? He opened his eyes and sought the window anyway, despite the pewter skies and falling rain.

When he thought back on his life sometimes, he could hardly remember the bits and pieces about his past. Where did it all go? Had he done anything wrong? Was it all just nature's way of putting human beings together, a steady stream (maybe more of a mishmash) of idle personality traits poured into a man's soul, like pouring ingredients into a blender and hoping for the best outcome? And what *was* in him that he had the inclination to push relationships with women to the breaking point?

He was thinking of Dina again and the subsequent silent treatment he had given her, ignoring her phone calls over the last few weeks. How had he sunk so low? Were his bus-stop romances just a means of feeding his ego? Other men were able to select that *special one* and settle down at his age. Why not him?

He sighed in compromise to the beguiling questions. Perhaps it had been the influence of his mother—or the lack of her interest in him? His father? Why the urgent desire to keep moving on? Suddenly he didn't even want Toni anymore. Maybe he wanted more of ... himself. It was either going to be a conundrum or a cover-up, hard to face the latter. Maybe it *would* take decades to figure out. Maybe just a single second.

The plane took off ascending, and Frank, disquieted in his seat, rocked a bit momentarily and then squeezed his right arm with his left hand, a calming gesture he had done since childhood. If only he could sit by Toni, she would've made him relax. But her seat mate, an old woman hugging the window, wouldn't budge. If only they would bring the drinks around soon! And would they this early, no less? He hoped so.

If only … what? He hadn't gotten on the plane? Worked at Sandoval? Looked for another job? Started up with Dina? Allowed it to continue as soon as he noticed reluctantly that she had fallen in love with him?

The plane was aloft.

CHAPTER 56

"Where are we?" Karen lifted her head groggily from the front seat of Dina's car, eyeing the sky and landscape. The sun had come out briefly over the barren farm fields, painting the last frozen tips of long dead corn stalks a brilliant yellow, as if they were lit matchsticks, scattered irregularly along a hand-hewn fence.

"We're at the Ohio–Pennsylvania border," remarked Dina, eyes shifting to Karen momentarily.

"You've been driving a lot!" Karen straightened up and looked sleepily around. "You okay?"

"Yes."

"Should I take over? I haven't driven since east of Indianapolis!"

"No, no, you did your part. Besides, we're almost to Pittsburg. We'll take a break around there."

"But that would mean," Karen grasped a map and shuffled through it as she leaned against the passenger-side window, perusing it, "that we're three hundred miles from the Philly airport!"

"Uh huh." Dina squinted, her eyes behind sunglasses, where Karen couldn't see her expression of extreme concentration.

"Won't we be late? I mean, the flight is due at about one o'clock p.m., or so you say."

"No, there's a stupid long layover, and they don't re-plane until later in the day. We can thank Big Sandy for that!" At speaking the enemy's name, Dina gripped the steering wheel tightly. "We'll catch them," she reassured Karen.

"But I think I *should* drive now! You look pale, and it's been—what? Seven or more hours behind the wheel! We should eat. *You*, for sure, in your condition, and—"

"We'll stop just outside Pittsburg. I promise you, we will!" Dina snapped, interrupting her. "I-I ate some chips last hour, when we stopped for gas."

Karen looked unconvinced but refused to go back to sleep. "What city are we near, anyway?" Her fingers traced along the maps, which were divided into two parts on her lap, one Ohio, one Pennsylvania.

"I saw a sign that said 'Danesburg, PA—4 miles.'"

"You know, I still can't believe you talked me into going on this wild goose chase—"

"Let's not get into that now," Dina argued. "You've got to trust me. Do you?" She jerked her head sideways, pulled down her sunglasses with a finger, and glanced quickly at Karen, who could now see black circles under Dina's eyes. "*Do you?*" she repeated.

"Well, I guess if I'm here, it goes without saying, and there's little I can do about it. I think you must've lived in the time of the Crusades, honey, for you are the savior of lost causes! Okay, okay, I know you say catching up to Frank is worth it—for the baby."

Dina finally smiled, but it was faint, almost nonexistent, as all her energy was riveted on the spinning tires below going as fast as they could to reach Frank. For a few moments, the women were silent, and then Karen spoke quietly.

"You know, I wasn't going to tell you this, but awhile back, Frank asked to come see me in my office."

"He did? Why?"

"It was weeks ago, before you guys—as a couple—were officially off the radar. He wanted to ask me, since I was closest to you, how to let you down easily, you know, break up. He told me to promise not to ever tell you. Well, I guess all bets are off now. Right?"

"What did you tell him?" Dina was shocked at this news. "And why—"

"Nothing," Karen filled in. "Basically, I didn't give him any advice. Just ripped the fucker apart and pretty much insulted him for what he was—a cheating conniver and a coward for his actions."

Dina was quiet.

"And why didn't I spill the beans to you sooner? Because, before he left ..." Karen paused and wiped sleep from her eyes. "I asked him to reconsider ... going back to you. I had hoped that he would, and after all, I did make a promise to him to keep quiet. And I *do* keep promises. Within limits, of course. No matter how bad, even though this wasn't life and death." She slapped her hand against the road map perfunctorily. "Anyway, that's it!" Sheepishly she added, "And, I'm sorry ..."

Dina listened without comment, gazing occasionally out the driver's side window at the empty cornfields. She had earlier found a quick little state route that took her to the west of Pittsburg, which would skirt the city, hence avoiding traffic and even lopping off a couple of miles. The close-up views of houses, silos, and farm animals grazing added a halcyon element to their trip, a welcome relief from the burgeoning tollways that had screamed across Indiana and Ohio. The rustic little road, empty of cars, soothed her, like Pramod's voice.

Pramod?

I believe you, Pramod! She shook her head and smiled resolutely. Her eyes met another green mileage sign: Danesburg—2 miles.

"Well?" Karen's voice broke the monotonous hum of the engine as well as Dina's musings.

"Well what?"

"You're shaking your head. You angry at me?"

"No. Besides, you came with me, believed in me enough to do something this wacky. You are really a true friend, Karen, you know. You had your reasons to stay silent and not tell me. I found out about Frank's duplicity probably *before* your talk with him, and—" Her voice trailed off, then, suddenly: "Oh my God!"

"What!" Karen shrieked.

"L-look there! Tha—that plane! It's diving, and I mean it's going down!" Dina was hardly able to speak as she pointed at the sky. The sun, which had been there earlier, had now taken refuge behind darker, serious-looking clouds. From their gray apex, a small black object was hurtling down, and then securing horizontal levelness on a sheet of air while shooting peculiarly back upwards, only to dive again, its nose pointing south.

"Shit! It's coming this way!" Karen cried, staring in shock. Dina veered the car and slammed on the brakes, the momentum of this gesture rocketing Karen forward and straining her seatbelt so that her head bumped the windshield with a force that made her dizzy. Yet the redhead's gaze never left the scene. As the plane dove closer and closer to the adjacent field, she remained mesmerized by the sight, not registering Dina's frantic words as her friend unhooked her own seatbelt and opened the car door, screaming.

"Oh, God! Look at that logo! I can see it! It's a Compass Airlines plane! I think it's Frank's! It might be! I don't know how I know but—*it is!*" And then Dina was gone, running up the field, her words flying up into the air, her coat flapping crazily over her small rounded belly in the indignant and bristling wind.

CHAPTER 57

Dina ran on, her arms flailing in the air like unstrung puppet limbs, as if the plane she now saw up ahead, partially nosediving in the sky, were a toy she could reach up to and simply catch. Meanwhile, Karen, in the car, watched astonished as her friend catapulted out into the cold, car door left ajar. A pathetic little wind blowing like a warning whisper whistled through the car's orifice.

From the appaloosa sky and gray fog and murkiness of morning, the aircraft was sizzling through the clouds like a baseball thrown through a paper bag. The dark blackboard square of smoke on the aircraft's nose was rapidly being consumed by a small, bright fire.

"Oh my God. She knew!" Karen mouthed without voice, and her lips became slack as she watched. Her hands moved in slow motion now, nails digging into the dashboard, her face twisted forward, meeting the glass windshield as she craned for a better look.

The descending structure bumped surreally through its own gray inchoate clouds of smoke, a broken-winged dove. Hurtling and shivering, it spiraled down in slow arcs. Along with the roaring complaint of the DC-10s' sickened engine was a siren-like sound, moaning with inchoative reaction; it was announcing its pain.

The plane again jerked upward again, miraculously. Apparently, the pilot was trying to wrangle a landing in this cold, deserted field.

Karen continued to watch stupefied as Dina ran like a pursued antelope across the vacant stretch between herself and where she imagined the plane might land, screaming, "Frank! Frank! No! No! No!" In another moment, Karen heard another phrase come choking from her own lips: "Oh, no, no! Please, God! No!"

She could both see and feel within herself her friend's unbearable anguish, as she waited tensely for the meeting of aircraft and earth. It appeared that the pilot's leveling off was too unsteady. The plane was askew, the ground poised to embrace it like a pop fly, shivering and wobbling, peripatetic on its way to try and land in the open field.

One more time, the heavy plane jerked sideways, streaming black smoke into a furl. It rose slightly. But then, there was another unmistakable plunge, whining a plaintive cry, as if begging the atmosphere to sustain it. It choked a little, forcing a black mass of fumes out its nose, clouds obscuring it momentarily.

Dina tripped on a rock and fell down, but she quickly recovered, stood up, and, panting and grasping her leg in pain, continued to run on anyway in the plane's direction. Uncannily, Pramod's face flashed by in her mind in a flurry. Why hallucinations now?

"Oh, God! Stay up! Somehow! Or land softly! Please, God!"

She kept on running, taking her hand from her achy wounded knee and stretching it out skyward to wave in tandem with her other hand.

"Fraaaank!"

The name cracked across the barren field, but Karen barely heard it now as she sat spellbound in the car, still unable to move. She had once read that in a crisis, one moves either toward or away from danger, or one simply freezes, incapacitated. She knew now she was one of the latter group. The motor's groan grew louder still, the craft still falling, heading decidedly for impact, the engine screaming as Dina screamed back, even as Karen still remained glued to the passenger side.

She kept pumping her injured, bleeding leg, the plane now little more than a thousand feet above the field. It beveled sideways, a rolling-over motion like a wounded animal who, on its last breath, rolls on its side to die. Dina wasn't close enough to see the windows. Luckily she was too far. If not, she would have been burnt alive by the whoosh of fire and fuel backdraft that accompanied the plane and its explosive thud as it hit land. It cleaved asunder in three places.

The first third of the plane, the nose, which sustained the terrible fire, hit and slid eerily along the icy field in a repercussive spring-like latitude, not twirling, simply broken off and shooting forward like a wayward hockey puck at about fifty-five miles an hour. Suitcases, trays, and papers were sucked out of the gaping back hole, the torn, open fuselage vacuuming the air around and flinging the pieces into the December sky. Dina, unable to stop running, knew in her mind it was the first-class section. The break had taken this seat section as well as the cockpit, all burnt now and nearly invisible with the putrid, choking ebony smoke.

Seconds later, Dina, whether from disbelief, panic, or despair, simply stopped running and dropped to her knees, waiting. Frank would have been in first class!

The motion of the second section, which happened simultaneously—Dina could much later barely recall—now slowed and pivoted narrowly in another direction, the physics of the impetus twirling the aircraft section like a winding-down merry-go-round. At the rear of the torn machine, the plane had vomited a trail of chaotic debris from its hulk onto the flat-leveled field to the west of Dina. But as far as she could see in these brief seconds, nothing human could have escaped or was flung from the wreckage alive. The residual rocket fuel now burst the broken appendage into high flames. Dina's hand involuntarily tore up to her face, in her mouth, more piteous screams, and in that semi-genuflected position, she saw the colossal metal frame, once a flying wonder, slowly close its chapter of flight. Fine smoke sprouted almost condescendingly out a few windows, the nauseating and noxious smell of burning fuel wreaking in the air.

Dina knew it was over, but her voice squeaked out anyway, "Frank?" It was more a question, and she sprang forward now, limping, although she could not get close to the conflagration, both pieces immolating a telling funeral pyre. Those seated near the wing, like the first-class passengers, most assuredly had not survived.

CHAPTER 58

The third section of the plane had broken off somewhat forward, beyond the other two parts, skidding like a deft ice skater for a while only to thunder into a grove of heavy naked trees, stopping abruptly at a crazy angle. This was the tail portion and held only a few rows of passengers, the very last split of the plane which, along with the seats, held the bathrooms and area where refreshments were kept. The loud *bang* from the jolt reverberated in the air and caused Dina's head to jerk around while she was still observing the first parts of the plane disintegrate. She saw this part fly backward as if ricocheting, smaller than the other two. It had lost the tail before the crash, bouncing into a somersault, leaving it partially upside down. This section, not yet on fire, was closest to Dina.

From that distance, Dina saw a small movement by one of the windows. Had the skidding motion on the ground kept anyone alive in there? Surely the velocity would've killed—

But then she saw it again. One of the windows of the smoking plane distinctly showed movement, red and yellow, to be exact. And was that? A face? Dina inched forward, crouching like a cat unsure of its surroundings, taking her time. The movement was maybe thirty or more yards away, but from Dina's viewpoint, she was sure she saw two small hands embrace the window frame and then knock on it, one, twice then frantically, a steady staccato beat.

The plane was smoking dangerously. Making up her mind, she sprinted to the entrance at the best run she could and was now at the sheered-off back end, both ends being open, with the tail gone. The metal was twisted, its edges in saw-toothed formations, but she made herself climb onto its frame anyway and look inside. A small face peered back from the murkiness, and there was an equally small voice.

"Help me!"

Coughing constantly, she could discern only two passengers. The other surrounding seats, thank God, were empty. Perhaps those victims had been ejected? Dina forced herself not to think about that. She could see the child clearly now, a little blond-haired girl and perhaps her mother, although the woman seated in front of the child was either unconscious or dead.

The child's voice was weakening.

"Help!"

She was pinned under two large suitcases, which had probably fallen from the upper baggage storage. What looked like part of the bathroom or kitchen door—Dina couldn't tell—was also on the child. The girl was about eight or so and had possibly a broken arm. Her mouth was bloody, her face smeared with soot. She was starting to cry now, "Mommy!" as tears formed a wet canal along the dirt of her cheeks.

Dina instinctively clambered back along the ripped seats, scattered suitcases, and other detritus until she got closer to the girl. It was amazing. This piece of plane was not on fire, so heavy was the scent of fuel! How could this little person have made it through, and worse yet, her mother dead?

This absence of fire didn't mean much to Dina, as she knew she had to work quickly. It could conflagrate at any moment. She tried to ignore an obscure, ominous crackling she thought she heard further back behind the girl. Half-falling over numerous pieces of wreckage, she didn't even stop when some jagged metal seared the flesh and cut a jagged rut into her leg.

She flung one hand out, encouraging the child with her other. She lifted the two suitcases and door partly off, which involved pushing her body and using her shoulder as a wedge. Although the plane had righted itself from its previous somersault, it was still not level, and the child was on a forty-five-degree angle to the window. She was wailing frantically now and intermittently screaming, "Mommy! Help me. I can't get out!"

"Shh," Dina consoled, and she extended her hand even further. The girl looked at it quizzically, grew eerily quiet, and just stared, her eyes not moving from Dina's outstretched hand.

"Can you reach to unfasten your seat belt?" The girl only stared at the stranger.

"Can you? Little girl!" Dina pressed on, her voice louder. What was she running on anyway, adrenaline? Here she was, pregnant and wounded, and she probably should have been waiting for help herself! But the sight of her mother caught the little girl's eye, and she screamed as if waking up finally into a nightmare of reality.

Dina became terse now, commanding, "Unfasten the seat belt! Now! You know how!" Finally, all the while watching her mother's immobile face, the child placed her hand around the belt. Dina heard the click and caught her just in time as she crumbled into her arms, her oxygen mask still askew on her head. Dina's hand was forcing the suitcases further away to make room when the child screamed so loudly in Dina's ear that it tingled. Footstep by footstep, she started to back off the wreckage, her arm around the girl at her hip. Suddenly, her passenger attempted to wriggle free and stretched out her arms, which Dina was glad to see wasn't broken, just very bloody.

"No, don't move! I'm hurt too, and we've got to get out of here!"

"I won't leave without Momma!" she screamed back at her. Suddenly the girl was now out of Dina's grasp, and she fell upon her mother, taking her tiny hands and putting them either side of the lady's face. "Oh, oh! Wake up, Mommy!"

Meanwhile, Dina, fighting against the perception that the plane might blow up at any minute, quickly made up her mind. "Okay! We'll pull her out! But get off of her first!" The child obeyed and scrambled onto the top of a nearby suitcase.

Dina found the woman's seatbelt easily. Surprisingly, there was no debris on top of her. The woman had a big gash on her head, and blood was oozing out. Seeing this, Dina felt that they might be moving a dead woman out of the wreck. But for the child's sake, she complied. "Now! Come down!"

The child, like a monkey, scrambled down and, standing on another wayward bag, followed Dina's direction. "You grab one leg and I'll grab another! We'll have to drag her, but slowly! Mind her head!"

The little girl cleverly pulled off her yellow and red sweater, and in an instant, she wrapped it around the woman's head to muffle the impact. They heaved until the frail body bounced along the wreck to the broken exit. A passing lurid thought came to Dina: this might be how the seventeenth-century charnel house workers moved expired plague victims into their death carts, by dragging them feet first. She shuddered but kept moving.

When they had bumped off the plane and into the frozen grass, the little girl stopped and let go of the leg. "Mommy?"

"No! Keep pulling! We've got to get her further into the field. The plane could blow!" Dina commanded harshly, the smell of burning fuel in her nostrils. The girl returned to her mother's ankles and, together with grunting effort, hauled the victim about fifty yards from the plane, where they finally stopped. Dina dropped to her knees, exhausted, but not before she saw the trail of bright red blood behind her, either hers or the woman's. Smoky air spun around them. It was like some weird movie scene, and Dina could barely focus.

The girl bunched down to her mother's face. Picking up some ice from the field, she applied it to the woman's bleeding head. Now, where had she learned that?

Dina's chest was heaving for at least three minutes. She had all but forgotten Frank's demise. Through the mist, she saw Karen running up.

"What happened? Who's this?"

"Mommy!" the girl whined. Karen shrewdly knelt down and touched the side of the woman's neck.

"She's not dead," she announced. "Probably in acute shock. Did you do this? Pull her out?" Karen was not altogether sure, for she had seen two indistinct blobs moving across the field with something in tow, and that's when she started out of the car, jolted to reality.

"Y-yes. F-frank was … *huff* … first class … *huff* … and—"

"Yes, let it go for now. Save your strength. Dina! Look at your leg! You're hurt badly!" Karen hollered, the gore and the flames putting her in the mind of a warzone. She reached over and hugged her friend tightly. "Dina, I'm so sorry. And I am so sorry I didn't believe you! But we need to get you to a hospital!" She cradled her friend's filthy face with her hands and looked into her eyes.

At that instant, the plane's third section blew up, and the whoosh of propelled air and fumes forced the three of them instinctively to duck. The fire rose high, eerily, as if they were arms praying to the skies.

"You're safe now."

Dina extracted herself from Karen and patted the child's arm. "Your mom's alive," she said, although Dina didn't know for how long. The three of them sat staring at the mother without speaking for a moment. Karen threw her long jacket over the shivering child, and as she glanced back to the burning plane, she caught a movement to the side, twenty or thirty feet to the east of the wreckage.

What she saw was not burning. It was moving slightly, seemingly unaffected by the fire. It stood or crouched perfectly still but for forks of shiny black whips, which both rotated and spun around manically. Its eyes were red and angry as it observed them. The thing was huge, and Dina recognized it. "Oh!" she breathed out. "The thing from the swimming pool!" Her hand flew to her mouth. "No, it can't be!"

She was interrupted by the child. "What? What is it?" The little girl glanced sideways over her shoulder. She stared at the colossus but appeared unafraid, even though the bulk of the ghoul's body was menacing. It could likely snatch them systematically, at random, with its whips. Perhaps the child was too much in shock to be afraid now.

A malevolent hiss rang out loudly, above crackle of the flames. The little girl turned to Dina and asked more urgently again, "What *is* that?"

"What?" Karen dragged her eyes from the unconscious mother to where the two of them stared, like frozen antelopes on a tundra, waiting out a lion's move. "Where? I don't see anything!"

"It's really evil. And ugly!" The girl curled her lip, and suddenly, as if it occurred to her that it might attack, she got to her feet while keeping her eyes focused on the wraith. All of a sudden, the colossus seemed to inflate too many times its original size, and with a loud hiss, it simply vanished.

"It disappeared," the child said matter-of-factly.

"Where? Where are you looking? I don't see anything!" Karen was frustrated and angry, swiveling her head back and forth through the burning smoke.

A small twisted smile formed on Dina's face. "Doesn't matter. It's gone now."

"There's nothing there but the plane burning!" Karen craned her head further and stood up. "I don't see it!" Was her friend delusional? "You're crazy! Nothing there but the plane!" This time, tears were running down Karen's face too. "You're only seeing things, Dina, that you want to imagine are there. We should really try to take her mom back to our car and keep her warm until help arrives, or maybe we shouldn't move her. They say you shouldn't move an injured person—"

In the background, faint sirens could be heard far down a nearby country road.

"It *was* there," Dina said quietly.

The little girl looked right at Karen with the conviction of one far older than her years. "It disappeared. It's gone. Gone forever."

Dina's smile now continued, this time serene with knowledge. She finally understood. Having ignored her leg injury just long enough to accomplish the rescue, she now fainted. The last thoughts assembled before she fainted were Pramod's words: "You will run for yourself but stop for others."

CHAPTER 59

Some time later, paramedics had revived and put Dina in an ambulance, but she insisted on sitting rather than lying down. She needed to see out the window and did not want to be reclining in order to gaze out of the back windows at the smoldering wreck that was Frank's funeral pyre. She grew quiet then, less distressed. A sudden equanimity emanated from her soul, crowding out the adrenaline and sorrow. The little girl and her mother had long since been taken by ambulance. What was the child's name? She would have to find out later. Her eyes squinted now to adjust to her view, as she had lost one of her contact lenses in the melee of the paramedics moving her to the gurney and trying to stop her bleeding.

Leaning back now against the wall of the ambulance (Karen would be following later in her car), Dina let the hold of her eyes feel the magnetic grip of the catastrophic panorama before her, a sight as chaotic perhaps, as the pogrom Pramod described at Amritsar, both the result of some evil, horrific and bloody. She hoped she would never live long enough to see anything nearly resembling what was before her now.

A shiver ran through her, and she felt her body spasm and jolt, although it was not really caused by the aftermath of the wreck. *The ghoul!* she thought. The disappearance of that ghoul! Why had it shown itself again? Why now?

The scene from the small ambulance window was gradually disappearing, effervescing into the smoky clouds. She could no longer see the fiery split of the plane or the people running to and fro and would not know until much later how many passengers had been lost. Yet the vision remained in her head and rocked her with despair. She must be in shock. Had she perhaps imagined the phantasmagoric creature?

She remembered visiting a zoo with her parents when she was seven years old, standing before the aviary cage, which held all sorts of predatory birds—eagles, hawks, condors, and vultures. Yes! Vultures especially! They had all been gazing anxiously down at her, as if she were to be eaten! The sight loomed larger and larger before her now, and she could almost *feel* their prehensile claws holding the barren trees, the evil anticipation in their eyes! She had then urged her parents away from the birdcage in terror while they laughed good-naturedly.

But the ghoul was nothing natural like a bird, was it?

"Akkk!" she cried aloud. *What was it doing here? Why did I and not Karen have to even witness this Halloween-type thing!* No wonder she fainted.

"Something wrong?" the ambulance driver had heard her cry out and craned around to investigate. With his arm along the back of his seat as he drove, he asked nervously, "You okay? Need some help?" His eyes darted from her to the road and back. They were miles away from the wreckage now. Yet the air retained the eerie, ominous atmosphere. And the creature? Was it signaling something else it wanted her to know? And the little girl had repeated, "Gone forever?" Was it?

〰〰

The ghoul smashed itself against Chicago's low-lying skies, a runaway pinball, unable to stop. The light was dim, almost darkening too early in that December dusk, although no one discerned the creature swooping through clouds, which seemed to promise snow. After jetting along the skyline, it hovered low along the lake, an elongated piece of charcoal, never once ceasing its sibilant cry. Rapidly it spun snakelike through trees in Lincoln Park, whirled along fences in front of houses then back to cascade through the underground "El" trains. Like a lightning rod, the subway cars absorbed the flash of an odd brightness, and metro passengers felt the uncanny rush of wind inside the cars but saw nothing, only traded quizzical and weary looks with one another and then went back to their own nonchalant worlds within themselves.

It then appeared, as if picking out an appropriate place or person to hone in on. It searched with its scarlet eyes, evil seeking evil. It sought *the one that got away!*

From the dirty miasma of the uglier human species, the phantom refined its search, its target based on a collection of horrific acts committed against so many. The creature spread like ooze, speeding wildly. Like a stone dropped into water, it rippling outward. Evil will never become smaller, its circles inexorably becoming larger, only to encompass more, a cornerstone of how evil nestles in, becomes established as a cancer, which shows first on the inside, then ruins its outside and many others around it. This distorted value left behind Amritsar innocents, straying inadvertently into the path of its locomotive power without explanation. Was it revenge the ghoul sought or merely one of its own kind? Its finger could lift a woman's skirt as easily as it could tear down a hundred-story edifice.

The monster now returned to its original place beneath the Chicago River. Happy holiday shoppers stomped over the bridge on Michigan Avenue, ready to make their many purchases. Far below, the ghoul's noxious and disconcerting breath blew out, and the mob above suddenly walked a little quicker, wrapping their scarves in front of their nostrils, some uttering profanities, questioning why the river smelled like a cesspool tonight.

The phantom waited, twirling its many threads like a weaving loom gone haywire. No barges were out at this time of night. It could, perhaps, have rested there for many hours, but it shot suddenly upward, a black missile that tested the air for a scent, like a bloodhound. It had no plans for the petty pickpockets, adulterers, or thieves below, or for serial killers or hostage-takers either.

Only one. Big Sandy. And off it flew.

CHAPTER 60

Big Sandy hoisted himself into his La-Z-Boy, popped open a beer can with one meaty hand, and slugged it down. He clutched the remote in his other hand, a sniggering chuckle escaping him as the Chicago Channel 9 announcer materialized on the screen, describing the downing of Compass American Flight 552, bound for Philadelphia. The newscaster couldn't handle his emotions very well, his hands shaking slightly as the smoke billowed from the burning plane shown on the split-screen frame. In a blink, the frame fully enlarged, showing the ominous cloud of fiery black, regurgitated from the plane's open carcass, made all the more eerie by the frantic dashing about of rescuers sprinting helplessly alongside yards away from the flames like revelers in front of a seasonal bonfire.

"Freakin' farmers trying to help! Go on! Get outa the way!" Sandy snarled as he leaned closer to the set.

The announcer returned again with the split-screen. "Few survivors, it appears. We will keep you posted. It seems that the plane snapped into three parts upon impact, and," his voice droned on, "this tiny community of Danesburg has sprung to help in this Pennsylvania cornfield, where we share a heavy loss of life."

"Stuffy-headed toad! Don't look so sad, ya moron!" Big Sandy threw the beer can at the set, yelling loudly, "Bastard Frank and all the rest got what's coming to them! That ol' Duffy did a good job. Worth the money. Downed the whole damned plane, did ya? Duffy, you shit!"

The plan worked! Duffy's sticky fingers had sealed that loser Frank's fate. Hell, Duffy went beyond what I wanted! Even better! He snorted at the workers on the screen, who were scurrying across the blackened snow to help.

"Don't bother, assholes! Can't you see they're probably all dead?" A malevolent guffaw emanated now from his corpulent frame and rose up in a great booming noise that rocked off the high-vaulted ceiling of his condo in the sky. "Ya can't touch *me* here!" He glanced around his place, full of inlaid marble, Italian tile, plush carpet, and a magnificent wraparound view of Lake Shore Drive, with speeding cars headed north, while the southbound lane, heading toward to Hyde Park, touted just as many vehicles.

Outside, the snow had started to fall heavily. Luckily, the flight had taken off earlier with no weather concerns. And as for Dina? He was sure she would be friendlier toward him now. He could visualize her, tears on her face, crying about Frank (the schmuck!), telling her coworkers how miserable she felt over the deaths of the other employees on the flight. Yeah, that would be like her, trying to downplay her own anguish over her old flame. But then he, Big Sandy, would be there to assuage her, pat her back or offer a shoulder to cry on, agreeing that it was a terrible thing to have happened. Yeah, it wouldn't be long now.

So a few more Sandoval folks had to give up the ghost, so to speak. Well, it was necessary so his intended victim could be out of the way!

Hey, what do I care! Just a few more peons whose wives will probably cash in life insurances, probably sue Sandoval for the benefits to themselves and their brats! Hell, they'll get a hefty sum!

Sandy stretched his neck and shoved a finger in his collar and loosened it. *Well, sayonara to those unfortunate four who were on the plane with that sap Frank! Wrong place, wrong time! That's how I look at it!*

Lumbering to the fridge, he grabbed two more beers. He glanced out the window—3:45 p.m. and already dark. He returned to his easy chair and re-parked his bulk, eyeing the TV with a smile. He was almost queasy with delight that the plan was going so well. Okay, maybe it was the beer, gulped too quickly. *What the hell?* he thought. *It's a celebration.*

The handsome announcer, identified beneath by the name Henry Adams, was still focusing on the crash. This was a big story here in Chicago, since the flight list carried five Sandoval employees.

"Ho! I don't get any credit for all you news people and media scrambling for a story? Jerk announcers! All of them!" Sandy continued ranting loudly to himself.

Adams was now repeating the Red Cross info line for news about loved ones. "Please do not contact local Danesburg Police at this time!" The screen went split again. Adams' eyes were slightly glistening.

"Big wus! Channel 9 will can his ass for sure!" Sandy mocked loudly, and he jolted back another gulp. "Fuck you and fuck any survivors!"

It was as if someone were mopping up roadkill in Sandy's mind, the lives lost no more valuable than dead moths on a window screen. Big Sandy would never question his own staggering apathy, where or why it originated, although the media, if he were made culpable to the deed, to his chagrin, would certainly be inquisitive of its nature.

Suddenly, something on the set caught Sandy's eye. The announcer was addressing a local Pennsylvania newscaster, and the name "Glen Harms" was printed below the screen with the city: Danesburg, Pennsylvania. The scene was in a hospital room. A little girl was smiling broadly.

"I was rescued!" she told the microphone proudly. "Momma too!"

"More fuckin' jerks! So you're alive and well. So what!" Big Sandy groaned. He was about to switch channels out of boredom, yet some ghoulish arcane pleasure kept his eyes riveted on the fallout and havoc he had caused. He sat very still, totally absorbed, yet stony and cold but for the glow of pride that emerging on his face repeated in his smug, half-curled lips. "Yeah, folks. That's me," he called aloud to the set. "Me and ol' Duff! So, Frank—you're toast!"

Glen Harms and the scene flickered back now to Adams on 9, who touched his earbud and said, "We are still waiting on word from our announcer at WTCI. Wait! I think … Brenda, is that you?"

"Yes, Henry, it is. This is Brenda Cantell, on site now from the crash scene. It appears the fire *is* under control now, Henry. This pantheon of destruction has so far been incredible, with fire trucks arriving earlier out here from four different counties. It seems we won't know until much later what *caused* the wreck. We must wait until the black box is discovered." Brenda was ducking and bobbing. Behind her, the scene was snarled with fire pumps being dragged, making the audience wonder if she was ducking smoke with her nervous movements or just trying to get out of the way of the flailing hoses. "The fire now seems quite under control, and yet so many local townspeople have come out not only to witness but to help in any way they can. It is truly amazing, Glen. More on this update. I'm Brenda Cantrell at WTCI. Back to you, Henry."

Henry Adams popped back on the screen again. "Thank you, Brenda. We will cut in for further updates. Now, we're going back to Glen Harms in the hospital. It appears we have the two survivors there …"

Glen appeared, and was smiling. He touched his earpiece with one hand. In the other, he held the microphone he spoke into. "Yes, that's right, Henry. We're here at Mercy Hospital now, and it appears we have a hero in this horrible tragedy responsible for the lives of the little girl you just saw and her mother, who I understand has been upgraded to stable condition. Nevertheless, it was two young women, we're told, who happened to be driving in the area, one of whom pulled the two people to safety." Behind him, crew men hurried back and forth, some ambling by a little slower, perhaps to be caught on purpose in the eyes of the television camera.

"I have not been able to interview our hero, as she too has been hospitalized and is going to be here overnight for observation. It appears she sustained a few burns and a major gash on her leg, but all in all, in very good condition. I'm told the governor of Pennsylvania is talking about some kind of a medal, although I have her companion here, and she seems to think her friend doesn't want it, that she simply wants to go back to Chicago, her hometown. Apparently, the two women, who were driving by, encountered this scene in the farm field." Glen moved his mike out as if he were passing a baton to a red-haired woman on his left and continued "So, you were with the young hero who rescued the little girl and her mother?"

"Yes."

Underneath the face, Karen's name flashed in white letters. Seeing this, Big Sandy dropped his grip on the beer can and it slammed to the floor, spilling it everywhere.

"Her name is Dina Kinnit, and yes, we are both from Chicago. I did not take part in the rescue. *She* was the hero ..."

Karen paused, wisely not mentioning the reason *why* they were in the area, nor why she herself was not involved in the rescue. To tell an audience of millions that she was frozen in fear, mesmerized by the flames and the implausible crash, did not seem like anything she ever wanted to admit. Furthermore, it would be ludicrous to paint Dina in a bad light by mentioning her friend had practically abducted her to chase a plane from Chicago to Philadelphia so that Dina could make amends with one of the passengers.

"She truly is a hero." Karen smiled shyly. "And I am proud to be her friend. You know, it all happened so fast! It's incredible! But I expect Dina to recover quickly."

Glen gave a dazzling smile now and looked from Karen to his audience. "Well, we wish her all the best and can hardly wait to hear from her. What brought you two to the area?"

Karen brushed her hand vaguely. "Well, we were on a business trip, and we chose to drive." She said nothing else. When and if it were ever discovered that she was from the same company as the five deceased passengers, she would simply say Hendricks sent them at the last minute and they opted to drive. Anything to save face, no matter *how* harebrained it seemed. Karen, usually one to absorb limelight like a sponge, felt awkward now, pushed into a staggering event that had far greater ramifications than she had ever planned when they started their frantic journey. She, like Dina, just wanted to go home to Chicago. This was all too much by now.

Meanwhile, back from in front of the television, Big Sandy, his bulk extended over the La-Z-Boy, his shirt stained with rivulets of beer, sat frozen in shock. His mind was oblivious to the scenes in front of him now, and his jaw was slack over his triple chins. The same thought ran over and over through his head: *Dina was there! She chased after Frank!*

CHAPTER 61

Sandy sat fixated on the announcer and his plaintive report, when suddenly, as if a flash of bright light had hit the screen, the newscaster's face disappeared, and for a split second, a grim and gruesome image of a monster showed up momentarily, then went away. It happened again ten seconds later, then over and over, flickering so fast that the two faces meshed indistinguishable, like the picture tube of an older TV set where the vertical hold has long ceased to work.

"What the hell's wrong with this set? Christ, you pay more than three grand for it and *this* is what I have to put up with?" Sandy leaned forward, exasperatedly punching the remote, trying to recover the screen or change the channel. The screen remained unaffected by Sandy's control buttons, so he pushed them harder, more furiously. Setting his drink down now, he gripped the remote with both hands, like a dying man clutching a prayer Bible. But the set only went back and forth from monster to announcer, with Sandy sitting, dumbfounded, gaping at the phantasmagoric color wheel before him.

Suddenly, only the monster's face came to rest on the screen. It stared alertly into Sandy's eyes, its focus unwavering, as if it knew Big Sandy was the only one in the audience. A low growl came forth from the TV speakers, followed by a slight cackle and a loud clicking noise.

"What the fuck!" Sandy leapt rapidly to his feet and slammed the remote to the floor. So rapidly did he move from his quasi-supine state that the syncopated process of bringing his body to an erect status without toppling over caused him to wobble and his stomach jiggle crazily. He was irate, until, staring at the vast screen, he was arrested by the sight of the ghoul first placing one appendage *outside* the picture, then another. Next, it disengaged one of its crackling wings, sailing it up to the vaulted ceilings of Sandy's penthouse, eleven feet in the air. This was followed by the second wing, distending out from the screen as well, but in the opposite direction, this time horizontally. The ghoul reticulated slowly and scuffed along the carpet with a ghastly sound, until, bit by bit, the two wings were perpendicular to each other. Next, the body slithered along the floor, its unctuous ooze leaving large oily blotches in its wake. Its head rose now, free of the confines of the TV screen, up to its full height and as in Duffy's case, the high ceiling could not contain the behemoth's body, so it had to hunch forward, cramped awkwardly, glaring at Big Sandy with red swollen eyes full of blame and retribution. The monster had an ugly mouth and from it emerged sound from somewhere inside of its capacious depth, a screeching projectile of four words:

"Evil's excuse … is you!"

Big Sandy now buckled to his knees, glancing away from the beast, clutching his heart. When he turned his eyes back, he could not see, as though in a fog of fear—or was it from the creature? The pounding blood in his brain seemed to smear his eyesight in red transparency. What little he could discern, his last look on earth was of an ugly grinning colossus encircling him like a spider poised crazily over a nervous fly.

The lights in his place and in his eyes seemed to wane quickly and now he had no vision. Blood no longer flowed to his extremities, and pain bolted through him. Life was ebbing away sharply like a derailed train suddenly torn off its tracks, tumbling down and then resting in silence.

His nose and mouth were bleeding, but he did not know it as he slumped to the floor, resting on the carpet, which was disgraced with copious ooze. His right hand stretched toward the end table next to the La-Z-Boy, uselessly grasping for the pistol housed there in the drawer. There was a loud unnatural sound all at once. His hand never made it.

CHAPTER 62

The office was sepulchral in the days that followed the Sandoval deaths. The Boyko project was put on hold by the purchasing firm, whether out of deference to the demise of its key coordinators or simply due to the exigencies of business's ebb and flow, forcing Boyko to look elsewhere for their needs. No one knew for sure. There was also plenty of speculation about Big Sandy's disappearance. Since the apartment bore no trace of forced entry or even of possible remains of the giant man, though left on the apartment floor was a mysterious and unexplained oily ooze, the police shut the place up with yellow tape pending further investigation.

Authorities' called his relatives, but given Big Sandy's nomadic life and his attitude toward them, their concern bordered between disgust and profound indifference. Because Sandy never spoke of anyone even remotely close, the office assumed his iconoclastic and bombastic *raison d'etre* probably drove the hapless bunch rapidly back into their own lives, peevishly admitting to police that they really didn't care about their relative's body should it surface, which it hadn't. They offered that, given his peripatetic lust, he had probably vanished on purpose. So be it.

But in Dina's soul, she knew Big Sandy was dead, and feeling Pramod's last words so strongly, she knew that his demise had occurred because of something paranormal, not of this world. Perhaps the hideous pool monster? Evil had shut the door on Big Sandy. She always sensed Frank and the others were victims of his insidious plot, but how could she prove all that to the police without sounding like a nutcase? She didn't need the further aggravation to her pain, so she quietly let it go. Others might call it karma; she would admit to herself that Pramod knew about things far beyond the realm of this world. And she may have danced around naming the exact prediction. This was how Dina somehow knew she had to *learn* to pull the truths and mysteries from her *own* surmising.

Because she could not work, her mood balanced between total collapse and catatonia; she'd been given two weeks' paid empathy leave, since she had witnessed the catastrophic event firsthand. The company could hardly be flippant to her trauma. She wanted no part of media intervention because of her heroism, giving only a brief statement to *TIME* magazine after the television eyewitness report. Never had such an individual shunned the public eye more. She was only glad her baby was not harmed by the trauma, but at that moment, she was not thinking about she would handle things in the future. In the minds of her coworkers, she was mourning him as if he really *were* her husband; it almost felt as if she had done this for years. Something Pramod once said to her came back to Dina: "A new love can feel like a very old love, and you, Dina, have love as old as centuries." She thought maybe the new little life inside her to be the new love, all part of a chain of attenuated feeling, a bond that withstood rocky centuries—mother and child.

But the awe-inspiring mood that came to her that she was soon to be twinned in the world also put her on a roller-coaster of moods: anger and despair. Rocking on her knees in her apartment, she felt the duality of these emotions one early-January morning. Her blinds were drawn funereally, and the light ambergris sky without much sun could barely peek through the slats with their puny light. The room and the day outside matched her mourning.

How does one function? Frank gone. Not just to another woman, but missing from her entire future! She would will him alive and in Toni's arms just to have him walking on this earth! Dead. This was an altogether different feeling than when she was only jealously pining for him. The finality of death seemed obscure, painful beyond anything felt physically. When her father had died, it had felt altogether different.

Maybe if I go to work for one day ... no!

This "getting on with life" would only bring greater hurdles in her mind, for every pencil she picked up would weigh one hundred pounds, every key typed would hit like a sledgehammer, every call coming in would be a wall of cacophonous sound that would stop her ears and have her screaming at the top of her lungs. She *couldn't* talk to people, answer calls; she might as well be hearing their conversations as if from underwater.

So this is what mourning feels like.

Pramod was right. Not only love, but pain is centuries old.

The wake, the funeral, and flowers are gone, the memorial services completed—but how can I wipe away what is still in my mind, like he never left? It will take a thousand years! No, I can't do this! I can't wait that long! And what do they say about time mitigating the agonizing pressure of mourning? No, it doesn't! It won't!

Defiantly she let her health go, eating and sleeping little.

And so this morning, almost two days after the service (having been released from the hospital after her wound was treated, and the city, grateful for all the heroism, having sprung for her flight home), Dina was now rocking on her bed, her hands clasped around her knees and staring at the dust motes floating in the sliver of occasional sun. This is how Karen found her when she finally dragged the property manager, who lived in the building (the original concierge having quit shortly after the swimming pool incident), out of her morning sleep with her ruckus.

"You gotta open this door! My friend is in there!"

"It's against the law! You're not the police, are you?" the old woman whined argumentatively. She was in her late sixties, standing nightgown clad in her doorway.

"Yeah, well, we'll see whose neck it will be if you don't open it! She could be hurt in there or worse! Nobody's heard from her in three days.

I've been calling, and she doesn't answer! And she's just come from her ex-boyfriend's funeral too! That plane crash that involved all those office workers from Sandoval? Well, my friend was that hero! Think the police will buy your story of against the law?" Karen edged closer to the lady's open doorway, eyeing her with a surly stance, arms akimbo, intimidating the matron.

Karen was sickened that Dina might do something to hurt herself, or, God forbid, the baby. After the tragedy, Karen had spent her own days as on a carnival ride. She had to endure driving back alone to Chicago, and she did so in a daze, assuming Dina's mother would come from Chicago. But at the last minute, Dina reassured her mother everything was all right and she need not come. "Your health is not that good," she lectured to her, "and besides, we can make plans later. I'll come out on the train in a few days! Promise!"

Mrs. Kinnit agreed and never learned that she was to be a grand-mother. It was as if Dina couldn't handle pride and misery all at once. She would inform her mother later. Had Karen known this, she may have stayed in Danesburg. But because she was fooled, she went home.

Dina had been listless at the memorial, brushing off solicitous ges-tures. Later, when her mother had tried to call, as Karen had, the phone rang a busy signal, knocked off or put off, Karen supposed, by Dina. Finally in desperation. Mrs. Kinnit phoned Karen at the office, but Karen was way ahead of her, investigating who owned the property where Dina resided.

Now she stood in front of the nervous-looking woman, demanding an answer.

"Well?"

The old woman bustled down the hallway, muttering, "Yes, I read about that plane accident in the papers. How was I to know she was the same girl? I don't get into the lives of the people who live here."

"Yeah, well, hurry up! I was there too, you know," she snarled. "No newspaper asked *me* for a statement!"

Karen *had* avoided media, dodging behind firemen and policemen after she saw to it that Dina was safely handed off to an ambulance. After visiting at the hospital, she pushed cameramen away. Avoiding the limelight, she ducked back in Dina's car and drove back to Chicago the next day. Dina was kept only another day and a half for observation. The memorial was shortly after her return.

As the door clicked open under the matron's shaky hands, Karen raced into Dina's bedroom. Holding her hand to her mouth, shocked, she uttered, "Holy Christ!"

Dina looked like a corpse with a belly. At that point, Karen made up her mind to stay with her the rest of the week, handling Hendricks' excuses for them both not to return to work. Exasperated, he compromised every demand.

CHAPTER 63

Dina felt heavy after the death of Frank. It was more than just the outward heaviness of her pregnancy; it was a spiritual weight that could not be lifted. She believed she would eventually heal—in fact, she *needed* to heal to be more than just a despondent mother for her child. And she wanted her baby's life to be a pronouncement of joy and not of endless yearning and unanswered questions. She needed closure.

In the weeks that followed, many coworkers had taken off vacation days, partly for the Christmas holidays but mostly a necessary break from the agony of those five deaths—six, if one counted Big Sandy. So many people were reeling from the disaster that Hendricks had finally ordered his remaining staff to go home for an undisclosed length of time, a first in Sandoval history. They could resume after the holidays.

It was early January, and the office was back to normal, although nothing would ever be normal again for anyone. Corridors were eerily silent, except for occasional click of computer keys, the laughter and hijinks noticeable absent. Dina's body was showing now. She had grown used to the stares and whispers as she walked the Sandoval's corridors slowly and carefully. Mostly she had been grateful for the rebel spirit in Karen, which roused her back into the human race that December day in her condo. The return to work was made more endurable for Dina because of the loyalty, friendship, and, above all, caring, which stretched tightly between

them like telephone wire. And like wire, the women were resilient, ready
to weather further storms. She would pick Karen to be godmother. There
was no better soul on earth.

At the funeral and memorial service, Dina had been pensive, and she
came away with many thoughts and conclusions, one being that death
wrote the final chapter that she herself had refused to read or couldn't face
while he was alive, which was that this debonair young man would never
have made a good husband, possibly not a good father either. Secondly,
while the circus act of her looks and charm were enough to inveigle and
attract him, it would never have been enough to make him stay and not
stray. It was a great blow to Dina's ego, to this woman who had centered
her life on her luck in beauty and all it could and had achieved. This was
especially true now, as she, ponderous with her pregnancy, was not the
same kind of woman who could dash away hearts at any moment the
way she used to. She was single, she had a large responsibility, and she
was alone.

So, she became strong in ways only mothers and mothers-to-be know:
she said goodbye to Frank in her heart, only wishing now that she could
have seen him one last time, even though she could never have stopped
Big Sandy's treacherous plan. When she went back over all those months
in her mind, she sometimes questioned herself in darker moments. If she
had perhaps handled the breakup better, stood on her feet, un-tormented
by her own obsession, would he be alive now? Was she as responsible
somehow as Big Sandy? But with Karen's wise advice and almost ritual-
istic chastisements, she stopped playing the *what if?* game and forged her
focus to better outcomes for her child.

And what of Pramod? She missed her elderly friend as she looked
wistfully out the Sandoval windows at the lightly falling snow. The
thought occurred to her to visit her, for everything she had predicted
was right, even down to demise of Big Sandy, who never had a funeral and
who, according to police, had been rendered merely *missing*. His palatial
splendor in the sky was ruined, like the man, by spilled liquor and slime

over the lovely hardwood floors and a TV with a broken screen, impossibly still on and playing the night he disappeared.

When the weekend came, it began to snow heavily. Still Dina made up her mind to go and thank Pramod personally and to ask that she remain in her baby's future. Of course, Pramod probably would have known all about the baby—things from the old woman's tongue certainly achieved fruition. Airline investigators sought the head mechanic of Compass, Duffy Branson, but had a hard time pinning it on someone who had *also* mysteriously disappeared.

And what of all those other passengers? She had recently been in contact by phone with the little girl and mother she had rescued. She felt somehow close to them, paired together, the one thing Pramod hadn't predicted. Only indirectly, in that ghostly way, she had mentioned Dina "would run." The cryptic phrase alleged the death of her endless running, on her dependence upon those artificial things, such as her appearance, her good luck, or her equanimity over her own philosophy of living. And it was an end to the thoughtless way she imagined she could control another's feelings. These traits could not possibly establish any real meaning in life. It had all blown apart as surely as the plane had. She had stopped for others.

On Saturday in blinding snow, Dina hailed a cab and went down to Devon Avenue. She had not seen Pramod for weeks. The tragedy had not only discombobulated her life, but the Sandoval office was reeling from the lack of key people and was scurrying to find temps and replacement. Hendricks was on twenty-four-hour Tums.

Dina's mind was feeling good about things, accepting Frank's death and passing the first trimester of her pregnancy with ease. She was healthy and more attractive than ever, her coworkers had said.

"Ya sure ya want *this* address?" the cab driver eyed the building they had paused before, a dingy looking door with most of the windows boarded up. The door looked older than Dina remembered. The address number on the door was right: 31, although the metal 3 was hanging on its side by a nail.

"Wait here," Dina said dubiously.

"Okay, watch your step."

Dina moved carefully along the sidewalk. She tested the door, and surprisingly, it gave way. "Pramod?" she called out. Stepping inside, she felt a wave of dust and a musty smell assault her nostrils. The long hall did not look the same, the pictures were gone, and there were no cats to greet her. All cheeriness seemed as if it had gone south for Christmas vacation.

"Tell you what," the old cabbie called out, seeing her look of concern and worrying a little about Dina in her condition. "Being as you're pregnant and all, I'll check back here in a half hour! You're going to need a ride back home, right?"

"Yes, that would be wonderful! Thank you," she said as she paid the fare (and they said that big city people weren't kind).

"I'm just worried 'bout you, young mother to be and all, and this place don't look none too safe! You sure 'bout all this?"

"I-it's something I *have* to do, but thanks. I'll be all right. And I'll look for you in about a half hour."

Though her voice was shaky, her determination, as well as something unknown, unseen, propelled her forward.

"Okay!"

The cab spun out onto Devon Avenue, the wheels noisily throwing off ice and snow into the air like a live volcano.

Dina, now advancing forward in the dim light, saw that this was not the clean, welcoming abode of Pramod that she remembered. What had happened? Where was she? And her cats? Had she moved so quickly? Uneasily, she noted the discarded syringes on the dirty floor of the hall amidst the mouse droppings. Were there squatters here? Most likely not now. Too cold. Although there had been. It was freezing in here and she shivered when she finally reached the kitchen and had to dust away numerous cobwebs from the doorframe to get through.

What the ...?

Cobwebs were littered all over the once-cozy kitchen. And more mouse droppings! No cat had been here in a very long time! *Am I in the right place?* she asked herself. *Am I crazy?* Gone was the clean Mylar table, and an old wooden one, badly needing repair, replaced it. The counters were filthy, and the cabinets hung open, displaying nothing but more dust and spider webs.

Dina was so startled by this transformation that she moved extremely slowly, as if she were wading into cold water, step by cautious step. Looking around at the vacuous and pitiful surroundings, she could not make herself believe that she had come here barely five weeks ago, but this building hadn't been occupied in years!

I should have brought Karen, she angrily told herself. *It's like I've lost my marbles!*

She now sat down wearily on the one vacant chair that was as old and decrepit as the table, thanking God it supported her baby weight. She shivered in the unheated ruin of a room and grasped the black shawl that she had thrown over her coat. "Oh, Frank . . ." Her eyes grew misty as she imagined him, buried inside the plane's inferno, ebony smoke swirling into the air, thick and waxy around her shoulders as well as she had knelt in the frozen field. *Black smoke like my shawl, as if he's protecting me,* she thought with melancholy.

Dina wanted to stay a little longer and leaned forward in her chair. Then, standing again, she called uselessly, "Pramod?" It was a question. Gripping the chair, mouth agape, she twisted her head around to stare at the emptiness of the once clean kitchen. "Where *are* you?" Her voice was wobbly, frightened.

The snow had stopped—she could tell by the sun trying to peek out as she gazed at the view from the tiny kitchen window which was situated above a bank of cabinets. A shaft of sunlight dove down now, seeking a landing place. The bright ray settled on the table, upon a book that Dina had not noticed before. There, on top of the book, was one of Sonja's bracelets, the bracelet Dina herself had lost that day in the office!

She picked it up and examined it. "Oh my God," she whispered. "How could it be?" She brought her hand to her mouth. Her eyes watered a bit for Sonja's poor life, lost forever. There was something Sonja had been trying to tell us all, Dina contemplated now. Was it the very real evil that existed under their noses at Sandoval? Had Big Sandy and his thug-like ways hurt Sonja too somehow? Or was it that she merely could not forgive herself enough for not be able to bring her mother out of the horror she had escaped from in Bosnia?

The bracelet was oddly warm, not cold, as it should be in this chilly place. Dina's shoulders slumped forward in perplexity. This was preposterous. *It can't be true! My eyes are deceiving me!* But as she set the bracelet on the table, she saw the open book that the bracelet rested on, as if it had been left that way on purpose! She turned it around. Odd, there was no dust on the pages.

It was a Bible, and it was open to a page in the book of Hebrews. On that page, circled in pen, was a piece of Scripture meant to draw attention to the reader. It read:

"Be not forgetful to entertain strangers, for thereby some have entertained angels unawares" (Hebrews 13:2).

Dina leaned back, realizing it all at last. But who would believe her? Karen, maybe, but nothing mattered anymore now. As she stared out the window at the fading sunlight, she knew then that she was a stronger person and could go on facing a life more genuinely than she had ever lived it. She wasn't a particularly religious person, but Pramod? Yes, Dina knew it all now, or did she?

Maybe that was what this whole mystery of life was about. Was Pramod some kind of angel, another force, albeit opposite, raised from the book along with the conjuration, let in to fight whatever horrible evil that Dina's monster had shown was indeed present? That manifested in the form of certain people and needed to be stopped? Only measureless time would give up this answer, but Dina was glad Pramod had been her shield. The Indian knew evil had a form but could never be given an excuse, had known it all along, if only the world did.

All the answers were not and probably could not be given to her, maybe not now or ever, but in this moment, it did not matter, and she continued to stare out the small window, watching the sun bleed in, streaking the tabletop with its brightness. The riddles, her visits, were all part of a consuming answer one never gets when the universe and its ways are questioned. For Dina, in this moment, had conjured *her* strength from personal weakness, a weakness descrying what the power of beauty had wrought her. Being was not always beauty; living was not always beauty, but love, especially the desire to give it—now, *that* was the real beauty. The only force to live by.

She felt spiritual, not alone in the world, for she had the piquancy of her own stamina and a belief of things real, and perhaps, as Pramod was trying to urge her to see, things not so tangible. From people lost forever, she would derive that strength. And mystical or not, credible or not, angel or not, Pramod had been her advisor for a life she needed to live differently. To her, Pramod was real.

The End

Special thanks to my editor, David Bernardi for all his hard work. Lastly much thanks to my cover designer, Kim Leonard. My sincere appreciation to everyone who supported me in my long journey to my dream. You know who you are. I can be reached at: AngelDictionary8@gmail.com